LIFE *after* TRUTH

ALSO BY CERIDWEN DOVEY

Blood Kin
Only the Animals
In the Garden of the Fugitives
Writers on Writers: On J.M. Coetzee
Inner Worlds Outer Spaces: The working lives of others

LIFE
after
TRUTH

Ceridwen Dovey

SWIFT PRESS

First published by Audible 2019
First published in Australia by Penguin Random House 2020
First published in Great Britain by Swift Press 2021

1 3 5 7 9 10 8 6 4 2

Offset by Tetragon, London

Printed in England by CPI Group (UK) Ltd, Croydon, CR0 4YY

A CIP catalogue record for this book is available from the British Library

ISBN: 978-1-80075-013-5
eISBN: 978-1-80075-014-2

This is a work of fiction.

While certain events and longstanding institutions are mentioned, the novel's story and characters are the product of the author's imagination.

. . . the Love-god, golden-haired, stretches his charmed bow
with twin arrows, and one is aimed at happiness,
the other at life's confusion.

— Euripides, *Iphigenia in Aulis*

Harvard Class of 2003 – Fifteenth Anniversary Report

JOMO GÜNTER-RIEHL. *Address*: 200 Church Street, Apartment 7A, Tribeca, New York, New York 10013. *Occupation*: Founder & Director of Gem Acquisitions, House of Riehl Luxury Jewelers. *Graduate Degrees*: MBA, University of California, Berkeley '13.

Last time I wrote one of these updates it was to brag about my life. I'd just finished my MBA and launched a lucrative jewelry start-up, creating bespoke pieces showcasing gemstones with weird names like jeremejevite and wulfenite. I was flying around the world on private jets, partying hard, barely sleeping.

Then my business partner bailed on me, my company almost went under, and my mom was diagnosed with cancer. The going got tough for a while.

Five years later, I'm through the worst. I'm back to living the good life but not the high life. My mom's cancer is in remission. My company is doing great but not so great that I lose perspective or get too comfortable with success. I finally made the trip back to Dad's homeland, Tanzania, where I swam in the clear seas off the island of Zanzibar and camped with my best friend at the rim of the Ngorongoro Crater.

The learning curve has been steep, and I'm not immune to falling back into bad habits – one of which is that I don't always make as much time as I should for the people I care about. So I'm eager to catch up at the reunion with my blockmates and also my Spee Club brothers and, now, *sisters*. We were the first final club to admit African-Americans, and I couldn't be more proud that we are now also the first to welcome women members.

JULIET HARTLEY. *Address*: c/o Jackson Greene Entertainment Associates, 4400 Wilshire Boulevard, Beverly Hills, California 90211.

ELOISE ABIGAIL McPHEE. *Address*: Kirkland House, 95 Dunster Street, Cambridge, Massachusetts 02138. *Occupation*: Academic. *Graduate Degrees*: PhD, Harvard, '08. *Spouse/Partner*: Binx Lazardi (AB, Harvard '13), December 31, 2015.

It feels like just yesterday I was proposing to my wife, Binx, on the dance floor at our tenth reunion. On that mild spring evening, we were honored to have so many of you witness – and celebrate – our decision to commit ourselves to each other for life. (Thanks, also, to the kind soul who anonymously sent a magnum of champagne to our hotel room later that same night.)

In my professional life, after grueling years sprinting around the tenure track, I've been appointed as Professor of Hedonics, which is the science of happiness and pleasure, if you're wondering. The epiphany that led me to where I am now took place in the basement laundry of Weld Hall in my freshman year. I was filled with a positive emotion I realized I had no proper vocabulary for – something to do with the smell of the fabric softener and the sense that my future was wide open. At every freshman orientation event, we had been educated in how to recognize the first symptoms of depression, and all the varieties of misery and anxiety we might expect to feel in the coming year as students. Nobody had prepared me for those early symptoms of great joy at being young, bright, and bursting with hope. Nothing had been said about the human capacity for happiness. Then I'd paged through the course catalog during Shopping Week and discovered – cue angels singing and sunlight piercing the gloom – an obscure class on positive psychology. And the rest, as they say, is history.

People generally ask me, when they learn what I study, if I can share with them the secret to being happy. I usually respond by quoting my wise colleague Daniel Gilbert: 'Happiness is a noun, so we think it's something we can own. But happiness is a place to visit, not a place to live.' The thing to remember is that very little of anybody's day is spent feeling *happy*. It's an emotion designed to be fleeting. And you cannot pursue it directly, which is why the things that we think will make us happier – a promotion, a windfall, a new car – have little lasting effect. This is called the hedonic treadmill, which is like a personal-happiness metabolism. Even after a big change in our lives, whether positive or negative, in time most of us return to the same baseline.

Binx and I waited until all our compatriots could legally marry nationwide before we officially tied the knot, and we're now fortunate enough to be residing on campus again . . . as House Masters (Mistresses!) of Kirkland House, though the official title is now Faculty Dean. I miss the top-floor garret I lived in my senior year, though I don't miss the weak water pressure of those ancient showers (Jules and Mariam, you know what I'm talking about). Our current quarters are rather roomy, and, Kirkland alums, you'll be glad to know that every Sunday evening at the Open House we still make sure to serve the giant wheels of baked brie that are responsible for many a sophomore fifteen . . . but in my opinion are worth every extra pound of flesh around my middle.

We will be hosting drinks at our place from five to seven pm on Thursday evening of the reunion long weekend, all classmates and partners welcome (though no young children, please). Donations at the door will go to the non-profit organization Binx recently founded, Who-Min-Beans, which advocates for posthumanists suffering discrimination for their beliefs.

MARIAM WEBSTER. *Address*: 1609 Bushwick Avenue, Brooklyn, New York 11207. *Occupation*: Mom, pastry chef, and educator. *Spouse/Partner*: Rowan Anthony Webster (AB, Harvard '03), May 25, 2003. *Children*: Alexis, 2013; Eva, 2017.

Greetings, friends!

Rowan and I are still renting in Bushwick. From our decrepit brownstone we look out onto the Evergreens Cemetery. We almost named our second daughter Bojangles in honor of Bill 'Bojangles' Robinson, the legendary tap dancer who is buried there and near whose grave we picnicked frequently while I was pregnant with her. Luckily childbirth brought me back to my senses, and we called her Eva.

We love the area, though we're conscious we are part of the first wave (second wave maybe?) of gentrification that is destroying the community around us. We placate our consciences by being active supporters of the Do-Not-Go-Gentry network. I contribute muffins to meetings; Rowan contributes much more useful community-organizing skills. In September, our older daughter will start kindergarten at the local public elementary school where Rowan is the impassioned and tireless principal.

On the one day a week I'm not home with our girls, I put my chef-school skills to work as an educator at the nearby Rising Dough Collective, teaching at-risk teens how to bake really amazing bread so that they can get jobs at up-market bakeries beloved by gentrifiers everywhere. There's an irony in this I'm not yet sure I want to unpack.

Since my father passed away two years ago, and with everything that Syria has suffered in recent times, I have felt a resurgent interest in exploring my family's Syrian Christian roots. This past winter, I took Rowan and the kids along on a memorable visit to the Syriac Orthodox Church of Antioch in Paramus, New Jersey. I also recently learned that my name is the Syrian Christian version of Mary, mother of Jesus, or something like that, though I assure you nothing about our children's conceptions was immaculate.

To stay sane, Rowan and I like to invent haikus to record our experiences of full-contact, 24/7 parenting, which many of you are no doubt also reeling from. I will share our most recent – scatological, of course – composition:

'I'm ready to wipe!'
The summons most dreaded by
parents everywhere.

ROWAN ANTHONY WEBSTER. *Address*: 1609 Bushwick Avenue, Brooklyn, New York 11207. *Occupation*: School Principal. *Spouse/Partner*: Mariam Webster (AB, Harvard '03), May 25, 2003. *Children*: Alexis, 2013; Eva, 2017.

I should start by saying I have no idea what Mariam – my soul mate and fellow Class of 2003er – has submitted to this class report.

Next confession: I discovered my first cluster of gray hairs today. The horror, the horror! They decided to sprout all at once, clinging to each other as if they're afraid of being alone. I'll probably regret writing that, just as I now semi-regret sharing, in my tenth-anniversary report entry, the gory, wondrous account of the birth of our first child, Alexis. I will spare you the details of the birth of our second daughter, Eva, though let me be a proud birth partner and tell you that Mariam got through this birth, too, without any drugs except the concoction her own brain was making. I'm not supposed to weigh in on these things, and I know all births are beautiful however they happen, so I mention it here only because seeing what women are capable of, I keep thinking, *why are they not already running the world?*

Which leads me to the calamitous state of our country.

Since the election of the fascist Gerald Reese as president, I have felt an unyielding anxiety most midnights, as I lie awake looking out into the dark. Often on those nights my thoughts turn to our classmate Frederick P. Reese II, who is not only the spoiled son of this abominable man but his most trusted political adviser, the one whispering in his ear, guiding his every morally bankrupt move.

Our college's motto, *Veritas*, had never been his creed, and now, thanks to him and his father, we have all been forced to live in a post-*Veritas* world. Who knows if Frederick will brazenly choose to show his face among us on reunion weekend. If he does, I vow that I shall say to his shiny, boyish face what I write here:

Shame on you, Frederick Reese.

Prologue: Mariam

Dawn on Sunday morning of Reunion Weekend

(May 27, 2018)

Her daughter had just fallen back asleep in the crook of her elbow when Mariam noticed the man on the bench in the courtyard below.

It was very early morning. She'd been up for over an hour, rocking her toddler as if she were a baby, mumbling snippets of lullabies, her eyes slowly growing accustomed to the dark outside. Her arm had gone numb from the weight of Eva's head.

From the attic room in Kirkland House, she had a view of the enclosed garden quadrangle, which all the windows of the elegant redbrick undergraduate residence faced.

Mariam smiled to herself when she saw the awkwardly angled silhouette of the man's upper body. He was going to have a very sore back later today, when he awoke from his drunken stupor on that bench. They were almost too old for these antics. Behind her, in the narrow single bed they were sharing, just as they had through their years of dating in college, Rowan was passed out with the same oblivion, clutching a pillow to his chest as if it were a life raft, his hot rum-and-Coke breath making the air in the small room smell tropical.

In the other single bed, her older daughter slept the enviably deep sleep of a 5-year-old. Ah, to sleep like a child, or a drunk!

Mariam was dying of thirst – the post-alcohol kind, which no amount of water can satisfy. Normally Rowan would be the one settling Eva; with both girls he had taken on the diaper changes, the soothing, the settling. They'd made a commitment to divide the night load straight down the middle, but he had always tried to do more than his share, aware that during the day, as the stay-at-home parent, Mariam carried the full burden.

But for now she wanted to let him sleep, after what had happened at the reunion dinner-dance at Winthrop House the night before.

She'd been astonished to see him like that, breaking loose, letting his appetites surface. It had been a shock, at first. Then it had been thrilling to be reminded that he, too, had other selves he sometimes kept secret from her. That there were still mysteries for her to solve, after all their years together.

If they'd been at home she would have let Eva cry for a bit longer, but as soon as Mariam had heard her whimpering she'd leapt out of bed to pick her up from the crib. For Jomo's sake, and Jules's, too. Jomo was in the room just down the corridor, within the same senior suite, and Jules was in the room closest to the door out to the landing. If either of them needed the bathroom, they had to tiptoe across the room in which her whole family was sleeping (or not sleeping), but that night she hadn't heard them come through once.

It had been a long time since Mariam had shared a bathroom with people who weren't family. The evening they'd all arrived,

Thursday, it had been a fun game to negotiate the use of the shower and toilet, just as she and Jules had done back at college as roommates. It was easy to romanticize communal living when it was no longer your daily reality. But the novelty had worn off fast. On Friday morning, she'd been busting for a pee and had to hold it in with her sub-par pelvic floor while Jomo shaved, shat, and took a long shower. How selfish the childless could be!

While she rocked Eva back to sleep after her night terror – which was so much worse than a nightmare, her eyes wide open, not awake but not asleep; why had nobody warned her about these before she was a parent? – Mariam was trying to figure out how she felt about the fact that Jomo was not sleeping in his room alone.

His door was closed, but Mariam knew someone was in there with him. She'd heard scuffling sounds a bit earlier, familiar from those long-ago years of close living, when it had been normal to listen to other people having sex and think it was no big deal. Once, in their junior year, Eloise had brought back a guy who had kept going at it for *three hours*. Mariam had sometimes wondered if that's what had turned Eloise off dicks forever.

It wasn't exactly surprising that there was a woman in Jomo's room. This had been his standard behavior at college, a new woman every weekend after some party at the Spee. He was a good person, so this wasn't as sleazy as it sounded. He was just so very attractive to women. It was almost like a public service he provided to the opposite sex, to be that hot, that charismatic, that talented at playing singalong tunes on the piano, that creative, and also so respectful, someone who genuinely enjoyed the company of women . . . it was too much for most girls to bear.

Plus there was the fact that he was best friends with Juliet Hartley, the most famous person in their class. They all wanted to get closer to Jules through him, perhaps, though they couldn't have known that he was in fact the barrier denying them access to her. Mariam suspected that Jomo had charmed the room on all those social occasions in order to give Jules a break from the spotlight that shone on her relentlessly. Jomo had been the insulating force, absorbing every bit of negative energy he could before it affected Jules. Those other girls must have known how it would end, that they wouldn't be *the one*. Yet they'd all greedily taken whatever he'd offered them of himself.

It wasn't that Mariam felt bad for Jomo's current girlfriend, Giselle, either. They'd only met her a few times, though Jomo and Giselle had been together for a year and a half. She got the impression Giselle didn't exactly love hanging out with Jomo's old college friends.

But she and Rowan had tried to make an effort to get to know Giselle better, and persuaded Jomo to bring her to their place in Bushwick for Thanksgiving dinner the year before, when they'd stayed in the city for the holidays.

Jules had come too. She was about to go overseas for a shoot, she'd said, though there had been nothing in the celebrity magazines about upcoming films she was starring in (Mariam checked them regularly because she still didn't like to ask Jules too many direct questions about her work life). Jules had brought gifts for the girls that were beyond their wildest imaginings: tiaras from the set of *Sleeping Beauty*, and a life-size toy Olaf, the snowman from *Frozen*, whom Jules had pretended was her date.

When she wasn't entertaining the girls, Jules had seemed tired, maybe from the effort of preparing for the new film. Mariam had felt glad to be doing something to cheer Jules up, feeding her a home-cooked meal in an environment where she could let her guard down.

Like all of Jomo's past girlfriends, Giselle was gorgeous, and she'd made every effort with her appearance that night, while Jules had made none. Sitting on opposite sides of the dinner table, they had looked like Rose Red and Snow White (and Olaf their idiot brother): Giselle with her red lips, and glossy dark hair matched to her shaped eyebrows; Jules with her alabaster skin, her white-blonde hair sticking up at the roots – she'd put no product on it – and her lips slightly dry from the late-fall weather.

Jomo had made a joke while he was carving the turkey, and Jules had guffawed in response (it had been the thing Mariam immediately liked about Jules when they'd first met on move-in day as freshmen: such an ungainly laugh from such an exquisite being!). Giselle had seemed puzzled – she was Italian, and, though her English was good, she'd missed the context of Jomo's joke. Seeing him laugh with Jules, she'd looked threatened, which was another common trait of Jomo's girlfriends. They could never get their heads around his being best friends with a woman like Juliet. Over the previous summer, Giselle had done everything in her power to prevent Jomo and Jules from making the trip to Tanzania that they'd planned to do together since college. She'd failed to stop them, but Mariam presumed Jomo had paid a price for it for months afterward.

No, she couldn't care less about Jomo cheating on Giselle.

But she was jealous of Jomo's return to a carefree, careless existence. His mother had lived. He got to sleep with sweet-smelling strangers without any guilt. All was right in his world.

She and Jomo, at first, had bonded over their parents' cancer diagnoses. But when it became clear that Jomo's mother would recover and Mariam's father would not, she had felt betrayed by providence. She didn't need any more lessons in humility or a deeper awareness of how precious time was. That was the daily stuff of her life as a mother, a wife, an educator, a daughter. All she did was care for others, count her blessings, check her privileges, give more of herself away.

Her father should have survived. What reward was there for her dutiful behavior if not that? What was the point of being good every moment of her life if things went wrong for her when it really mattered?

Outside, the light was changing. Mariam could just make out the Kirkland tower's white wedding-cake tiers topped with a green dome and gold cross. The sky had turned a shade of lemon. She felt her spirits sink. It was already dawn, and she had slept for what – two hours?

It was going to be a long day. Soon she'd have to drag herself and Rowan and the girls to the final reunion event, the farewell brunch at Quincy House.

At least there would be waffles, the crispy ones with the Harvard crest imprinted on them. In spite of their bland flavor, these had been Mariam's treat every Sunday morning at college. It had always felt as if she were ingesting the spirit of Harvard itself as she chewed on the crest, as if, with every bite, she became a teeny bit smarter.

And there would be bacon. Lots of bacon.

After last night's shenanigans, though, perhaps it was better that she and Rowan go straight to South Station for the Acela back to New York.

She wasn't sure who had seen what, and by then people had probably been boozed up enough to not notice anything, but still. Some part of her relished making a dramatic final impression on their classmates and then disappearing into thin air, not to be seen for another five years. For anybody who had noticed her and Rowan's small but passionate marital drama, it would be a let-down to see them standing in line in the dining hall the next morning, wrangling their kids, looking haggard.

Yes, they should skip the brunch, she decided. No more chitchat with people she only half-remembered, no more asking and answering the same things over and over. She and Rowan would vanish, leaving a frisson, a question mark, hanging over their names.

She looked down at her daughter's face, which had gone very pale – a sign she was in a deep sleep. Eva's black curls, identical to Mariam's own, were matted with something sticky, probably the lollipops she'd used to bribe the girls to go to bed before the babysitter arrived (the trick had not worked).

By force of habit, she began to compose a haiku about watching her daughter sleep:

A tiny blue vein
pulses at her right temple

She paused and looked out the window again, searching for the right words for the last line.

The man on the bench had not moved.

In the yellow dawn, she could see his face clearly for the first time. It was Frederick Reese. There was foamy vomit all down his tuxedo shirt. His eyes were wide open – just as Eva's had been in the grip of her night terror.

Much later that morning, the proper emotions would swell in her, the shock that a person had died under her gaze, perhaps at the very same moment that her daughter had descended into a dreamless phase of sleep. But in that first moment of recognition Mariam felt only relief. The president's son was dead. Somebody had finally taken a stand.

Chapter 1: Jomo

Thursday morning of Reunion Weekend

(May 24, 2018)

The turbulence was worse than any Jomo had experienced. In London, the plane had soared up into blue skies, but soon after, through his window, he'd seen the electric storm approaching, the lightning soundlessly stabbing the clouds beneath. He had never seen lightning from above the cloud layer before – down on earth, it felt as if it came *from* the clouds.

When the ride got really bumpy, he took a few photos, hoping to tame the sight by snapping it for future upload to one of his three social media feeds (recently pruned down from five). Morsels of life, packaged and presented at a safe distance. If only he could post them online now, nothing bad would happen to him; his plane would not go down.

He clung to his armrests. The rush he'd felt when called to board first – taking a left to the front of the plane instead of back to its rear where the masses huddled elbow-to-elbow – had long faded.

He wished he hadn't felt that rush. At least he wasn't upstairs, as he used to be on most flights. One of his resolutions made during the bad times in recent years – now over, thank God – had been to never fly first class again, no matter how well his company was doing, because of the feeling it fostered of being at the top of the human pyramid, like a pharaoh, looking down on everybody else. It had definitely affected his ability to empathize.

That false sense of being able to cordon yourself off from life's hardships was what made wealth so appealing, and so disorienting. The first time he'd flown first class, for instance, he'd been surprised to find he was as jetlagged as usual upon arriving in Europe: as if spending that much money on a ticket should have insulated him from the physiological effects of jumping time zones.

The tin can in which they were all hurtling through the sky lurched sideways, down, and sideways again. The man in the adjacent seat had pressed the button that raised the partition between their pods as soon as he sat down, which normally Jomo didn't mind; it was the point of traveling business class to be undisturbed by anybody's needs but your own. Yet if the plane spun to the ground in a ball of flames, it would be impossible for Jomo to see over the partition to make eye contact with another human as they approached death. He began to wish he were sitting in economy, so that he could huddle together with the other people in his row, holding hands, screaming their lungs out together.

Jomo pushed the button to lower the partition a fraction. The man next to him was fast asleep.

He considered trying to call Jules from the satellite phone. A single call would cost more than his airplane ticket, probably. She would be flying into Boston too, from LA. She wouldn't answer. It would go to her voicemail, set up as an automated voice reciting the phone's number as safety from stalkers, and also because she couldn't be bothered recording a new message every time she had to change numbers – he wouldn't even hear her voice one last time.

Maybe she already had a new number, and had forgotten to tell him. It had happened before. Those awful few months at the start of last year when she'd been out of reach, when she'd failed to give him her new number, her new email address, and her new, snarky agent had refused to pass on any of his messages. He had tried his best to understand that she needed to take a short break from him, from their friendship. Yet he was still healing from the hurt of those lost months.

Their trip to Tanzania the previous summer had helped him feel less bruised – as had thinking they were going to die in that tent at Ngorongoro. He smiled, remembering the murderous bushpigs. And the feel of Jules's entire body pressed up against his in their mindless fear. They had lain so still at the center of the tent, their racing heartbeats had become synchronized.

The plane dipped.

To distract himself, he considered the weekend ahead. It had been Rowan's idea that they all stay in Kirkland House, always an option for returning alumni who wanted to slum it in undergraduate housing for their reunions, pretending they were back at college. Eloise had used her influence as Faculty Dean of Kirkland to arrange for them to stay in the same suite that she, Jules, and Mariam had lived in during their senior year. There would be alumni staying on other floors of the same entryway, but nobody else on the top floor, to give Jules some measure of privacy.

The plane dropped another foot in the air – Jomo closed his eyes – and then leveled out, as if it had got something out of its system. The air within the plane, and around it, too, seemed to settle. After a few minutes, the seatbelt light was turned off, and the flight attendants began to pamper their charges, offering to pull mattress toppings over their seats and handing out pressed pajamas. The cabin supervisor went around refilling cocktail glasses with a rueful expression on his face, as if British Airways were responsible for the bad weather. The mood lighting was switched on in the cabin, making the silver pods glow pearlescent. It felt as if they were in a spaceship on their way to the moon.

Jomo rubbed his hands together to ease the strain of his white-knuckled grip on the armrests. On his right palm were ink smudges, left there by a palm reader the day before. His hand tingled, remembering the old man's dry touch, his careful inspection, and his final, solemn words.

Jomo had gone to Cecil Court, a Victorian alleyway in central London, because he'd been tipped off that an antique-books store there had a rare gem collection.

Outside one of the buildings was a blue historical marker: Mozart had lived there around the time he composed his first symphony, while his father was ill and he and his sister were forbidden from playing the clavier (Mozart had turned to drums and trumpets instead). It was the kind of detail Jomo's piano teacher from back home would have loved – she'd always tried to humanize the composers of times past, so that the music didn't seem like it had dropped from the ether.

The store was called Rawlings Books. Velvet curtains hung in the windows, and on the door was a list of the shop's wares: *Perennial Wisdom, Crystals, Mala, Oils and Incense, Tarot, Singing Bowls.*

If only it were as easy to come by perennial wisdom as to purchase a few crystals or singing bowls, whatever those were.

Inside, the shop was lit with candle chandeliers (a fire hazard, the businessman in him noted). A few people were browsing books in the dusty stacks. At the checkout counter, a woman dressed in leopard print began to stare at Jomo intently. *Typical*, he thought. A tall black man approaches and all the hippy-dippy, love-everyone shit goes up in smoke.

But for once, his own assumptions were wrong.

'I've never seen a true magenta before,' she said to him. 'Your aura. It's remarkable.' She blinked, as if a rainbow were emanating from his head.

The owner was overseas, he'd soon learned, and the woman didn't have access to the vault where he stored the gems – though she'd heard that he had a genuine Mexican fire opal in there, affixed to an Aztec idol.

Dispirited that things were not going his way, Jomo had glanced down and seen a handwritten sign on the desk: *The Swami Is In*.

'I want to see the swami,' he said.

'Sorry?' she said, leaning forward.

'I want to see the swami,' he said again.

'I'm terribly sorry, I can't understand your American accent.'

'I WANT TO SEE THE SWAMI,' he said loudly, attracting looks from a couple of the book-browsers. He was wearing a suit and tie, and probably did not look anything like the type to come into this store on a weekday to ask for spiritual guidance.

'He doesn't have access to the vault either, I'm afraid.'

Jomo said nothing.

'Ohhh, *right*,' she said, finally clicking. 'Forty pounds for thirty minutes.'

He counted out the notes.

'Follow me.' She took him up a flight of stairs, to the second level of the store.

In the sunlight coming through a stained-glass window, at a table covered with a red tablecloth, an elderly man sat sleeping. He was wearing spectacles and had trimmed his beard too much on one cheek, so that his face looked lopsided. Jomo immediately regretted his impulse.

'Swami . . .' the woman said.

The swami opened his eyes.

'This man would like to see you. For a consultation.' The woman then retreated – *backward* – as if it would bring bad luck to turn her back on the swami.

Jomo struggled not to laugh.

The swami caught Jomo's eye and smiled; he was in on the joke. 'Please, sit.'

He asked Jomo a few questions, his date of birth, his first and last names. 'You are 37 going on 16,' he said, with no further explanation.

Then for a long time he said nothing. He took one of Jomo's hands in his own and studied his palm.

It had been an early start that day for Jomo, a busy round of morning meetings and an auction at Christie's where he'd successfully bid on a diamond necklace once owned by Elizabeth Taylor.

He must already have had four cups of coffee, but in the early-afternoon slump, his caffeine buzz had worn off. He relaxed. There was incense in a brass holder, and it smelled good, like orange peel and musk. Birdsong, and wind-chime music, reached his ears from the room's speakers. It was pleasant to have his hand inspected closely, as if the answers to his questions had been written on his palm all along.

The swami was pointing with his pen at the crease across Jomo's palm. 'You are a creative,' he said. He prodded the fleshy base of Jomo's thumb. 'A strong Venus aspect. You believe in true love.' He followed a line up to Jomo's index finger. 'Yet you are unmarried. No children. No desire for children yet.'

The pen slipped on the thicker skin pads at the base of Jomo's fingers – signs of the wear and tear of life. He'd never properly appreciated his hands, except perhaps while he was playing the piano, but even then, they felt like nimble tools of his brain, not special objects with clues to his future etched on them.

Jomo gestured to a line that forked into two near his wrist. 'What does that represent?' he asked. 'Is that my lifeline?'

'It doesn't really work like that,' the swami said kindly. 'It would be like asking what a letter means without seeing the word.'

'I'm going to die young, is that it?'

'Strong, strong, ninety years or more . . .'

He squeezed the muscle between Jomo's thumb and forefinger. 'You are confused by what fidelity means. That is society's problem. It is not your problem.'

Here we go, Jomo thought, the spell lifting. *Next thing he's going to ask me to join his crazy sex cult.*

'My teacher says that to learn to love is the greatest art of all,' the swami said. 'I don't mean desire, not sexual desire. Learning to love is difficult, Osho says, because it requires diving into your own soul. Osho writes that without self-love, one cannot find the clarity to love another.'

Jomo shifted in his chair. Who the fuck was Osho?

This self-love speech was not what he'd come for. His problem was the opposite; at times he was blinded by his own self-regard, while pretending to have all the same doubts everyone else did.

Take his entry for the fifteenth anniversary Red Book, the class report. It was humble, so that his classmates would continue to like him, though it had always been obvious to everyone who knew him that his lucky stars rarely stopped twinkling. Even when his mom had been really sick, he had known she would get better: of course she would. That was just how things went for him. He was proud of being well thought of by his peers, yet he also knew it was easy as pie to be gracious when you were on top.

He had so effectively repressed his only failure to get what he wanted that he did not ever think about it in his waking life. Very rarely, he'd have a dream of a life with Jules where they were no longer just friends that was so vivid, he'd wake to discover his face was wet with tears.

The swami seemed to sense that he'd taken a wrong turn. He spread out a battered pack of Tarot cards on the table before Jomo. 'Pick one, but don't look at it.'

Jomo obeyed, and the swami laid it facedown before him. 'Another.'

Jomo picked six more cards, and the swami arranged them into a pattern. He turned over the first card. On it was an image of a hand coming out of the sea, reaching for lung-like creatures in the sky. *Cutting Through* was printed at the bottom.

'This is your past,' the swami said. 'A sky card. Ambition.'

He turned over the next one. It showed molten lava beneath black rock, and was captioned *Fire of Sacrifice*. 'This is your present. Fire. Also ambition.'

Jomo decided to be difficult. 'But it says *Fire of Sacrifice*. How is that about ambition?'

The swami shrugged. 'Trust me. Fire means ambition.'

He turned over the next card. It showed a pink lotus flower on a pond. 'This is your future,' he said. 'It is about creativity, but also control. You work for yourself; you are your own boss. You most likely always will be.'

Jomo gave no sign the swami was right. The lotus had spiky petals. Looking at the images made his head feel funny, as if they had real power over his unconscious. It was hard to look away.

The swami turned over a card set to one side. 'This is your

greatest fear,' he said. It showed an Egyptian mummy on an alien planet. *Self-Preservation*, the caption read. 'Loneliness. You fear it more than anything else,' the swami said. 'See how this figure is so wrapped up in itself, it cannot be unbound?'

The next one was captioned *Mother's Milk*, and had disembodied nipples spurting milk against the backdrop of the galaxy.

'This is your wish,' he said. 'You would like to be a nurturer. It doesn't have to be as a parent. But it comes back to what I said earlier: you have not been able to find intimacy and desire – love and sex, if you like. Always one or the other.'

Jomo thought of Giselle. She was so beautiful. So desirable. But was she really lovable? Was *he*?

'And now, the last two cards,' the swami said. One showed a bird's wing made of metal, and was captioned *Just Passing Through*. 'This is the key to your heart's desire. Interesting!' He looked up at Jomo. 'This is a freedom card. You do not feel free, and you will not attain your heart's desire until you do.'

When the swami flipped over the final card, he gasped. It was clear what it represented, even to Jomo: two red apples mirrored in water, and a green snake slithering between them. It was captioned *Temptation*.

Jomo studied the swami's face – was this concern on his behalf part of the act?

'Your heart's desire is for something that is almost certainly out of your reach,' the swami said. 'So you have a difficult decision before you. Stay in your chains and keep all you have – or make yourself free and risk losing everything.'

The session was over, but Jomo couldn't find the energy to move.

The swami pushed his spectacles higher on his nose. 'The people who come in here are seekers,' he said. 'For many others, life passes them by. They eat, sleep, work, watch TV, but they don't ask *why*.

They don't ask, *What is the point?* It is good you are asking, even if I cannot answer the way you might have wanted me to.' His tone was apologetic.

Jomo instantly forgave him. Of course he couldn't answer the eternally unanswerable questions: Who am I? What will happen to me in my life? He was surprised by how quickly he'd been prepared to cede authority to a kindly old man turning his hand this way and that, making vague statements that he knew Jomo would connect up to real people and events in his life. It was an illusion of wisdom, yet it was still comforting. He could have sat there at that little table all day.

'You have the ring already,' the swami said, out of nowhere, as Jomo got up to leave. 'It holds a mauve gem, in the shape of a teardrop.'

Like any good magician, he had saved the best for last. 'She is waiting for you. She has always been waiting for you.'

On the plane, Jomo dug about in the back pocket of his chinos for the ring he'd been carrying around for several months now. Like the pea tormenting the princess, he could often feel its form when he was sitting down. It wasn't even in a case. Just the ring, loose, as if it had come from a box of Cracker Jack.

He was tempting fate to take the ring away from him, to make the decision on his behalf. Why else would he play a form of Russian roulette with a ring that meant as much as it did? A yellow-gold band holding the musgravite gem that his grandfather had sourced in Tunduru, Tanzania, for his grandmother, long before anybody knew that the mineral was one of the rarest on earth.

A few months ago, Jomo had almost proposed to Giselle with that ring, in their favorite restaurant in Aspen, basking in the warmth of the log fire, his body aching from a day of skiing and – let it be said – fucking.

When she'd excused herself to go to the bathroom, he had dropped the ring into her glass of wine. As soon as he'd done it, he knew he had to fish it back out. He'd envisioned her swallowing the ring by mistake, in one big gulp, or choking to death on his family heirloom.

The waiter had given him a disapproving look as Jomo downed Giselle's glass of wine and caught the ring in his teeth, but he'd cooperated in the cover-up, refilling her glass just in time for her return.

Jomo knew she'd been disappointed at the end of that holiday, though she hid it well.

The irony was that strangers had already proposed to her – in Italy, to be fair, where the men were totally insane. In the Piazza della Repubblica in Florence, a man had dropped to his knee and pulled his (dead) mother's wedding ring from his wallet. Jomo had thought Giselle must know him – that he was an old flame – but she swore she'd never laid eyes on him. He hadn't known whether to believe her until it happened again, in Rome. On both occasions, when she'd declined, the men in question had turned to Jomo and made a sound of pure disgust that he had not yet made this woman his wife.

Why hadn't he? It was hard to explain. Even in their most intimate moments, he felt an undertow of loneliness.

At first, he'd thought this was a function of their different cultural and language backgrounds. But over time, the shield had stayed up, even after that trip to meet her family in Italy. He'd begun to wonder if it had more to do with them being temperamentally incompatible. Take their skiing trip. On Christmas Eve, in bed in Aspen, watching the snow fall outside, darkness onto darkness, her head against his shoulder, he had felt nothing but desperately alone.

Whenever he tried to talk about it with Giselle, she would get confused by his mixed messages, and it would make the problem worse. It was unfair for him to do this, to ask the person he loved, 'Do you also feel a little lonely when we're together?'

It was possible that he was the problem. All those years of buffet-dating, choose-your-own-adventure relationships. He'd had too much choice, for too long. He just needed more time to adapt to life in a bonded pair.

He was of an age where he was beginning to stick out for being unmarried. It was no longer considered a sign of him wisely taking his time but as a problematic inability to settle down. He'd noticed business associates changing their demeanor on seeing no ring on his finger, on hearing him say 'my girlfriend' rather than 'my wife'. A man approaching forty who is unmarried is a wildcard, and those in stable relationships were increasingly wary of Jomo, as if being around him for too long would spread havoc in their own lives. He was patient zero of a disease they did not want to catch.

The swami's message to him was simply the latest in a series that all seemed to be saying the same thing: *Commit to the woman who so clearly wishes to commit to you.*

For instance, on his first day in London, he'd gone for a run through Hyde Park, and ended up in a meadow filled with wildflowers. The rest of the park was so stately and ordered that the overgrown meadow surprised him for seeming out of the national character.

He'd sat down on a patch of springy heather for a rest and seen a small airplane writing letters against the sky, which began to shear and blur, erased by the elements, as soon as they were formed: M-A-R-R-Y M-E.

Giselle deserved a grand gesture like that. She deserved somebody who shouted his adoration of her to the world.

She had been rightly offended on discovering that he hadn't even mentioned her in his Class Report entry. He had tried to explain (lamely) that if he'd mentioned his stunning, talented Italian girlfriend, who had already designed her own handbag line, it would come across as grandstanding, the wrong tone for the fifteenth-anniversary report, when his classmates' entries would be more tempered with modesty as they approached early middle age.

She'd eventually written off his failure to mention her as another quirk of American culture that was beyond her understanding. Then she'd forgotten about it entirely and said yes to a hens' weekend at Cape Cod for one of her friends, over the same dates as the reunion. Jomo had pretended to be upset about this, but he'd felt relieved. And then guilty about feeling relieved that the woman he might one day marry would not be by his side at his reunion.

The part about getting his tone right in his entry was true, at least. He'd worked a bunch of jobs through college, one of them at the Harvard Class Report Office, helping the four full-time editors collate and edit the alumni anniversary reports, colloquially known as Red Books because they were bound in crimson covers. They had been published by the university for around 150 years – the earliest versions dedicated only to deceased classmates but gradually changing focus over time, becoming a way for classmates to self-report on their lives in whatever form they chose. Some people wrote long, painfully earnest entries; others wrote light-hearted limericks.

His responsibilities in that job had included spell-checking and fact-checking the entries. 'Don't let Team Harvard down,' his boss had said. People left out children and spouses, added degrees they'd never finished, invented companies they worked for or job titles they held. Sometimes Jomo had to flag things as potentially libelous (angry rants about very specific wrongdoings of politicians, for example, or insults hurled by classmates still caught up in some old college enmity).

These were reminders of the depressing aspects of human nature, but there were upsides to the job too. Jomo had enjoyed tracking how the tone of the entries in each report was usually the same, as people's lives followed similar general patterns. The five-year reunion updates were mostly open boasts, about consulting jobs and law school and exotic travel. The ten-year updates were mostly veiled boasts, about getting married or published or founding start-ups or charter schools.

At the fifteen-year mark, the tone began to change. The entries were split between those who kept going with the charade of their lives being perfect and those who were ready to tell it how it was. People wrote of becoming parents either with overstated happiness or with an admission of being unprepared for the passionate drudgery of raising children. Some wrote of being promoted; others confessed to having been retrenched. The startling honesty of some of the entries was the first intimation that whatever unique status Harvard had once conferred on them had long since worn off.

And Jomo knew already what was in store for his class in the years ahead. The twenty-fifth Class Report would be harrowing to read: divorces, kids who had lost their way, foreclosures, health scares. Worse, it was one of the few reports that allowed people to include photographs – one from college, one from their current life, which could sometimes feel like rubbernecking at a gruesome car accident. But the interesting thing was that people's experiences of hardship seemed to make them nicer, funnier, more open. And lighter, as if by laying down their sense of being special they had put down a heavy load they were tired of carrying.

That was the case for the fortunate ones, anyway. The survivors. For in every anniversary report, the *In Memoriam* list at the back of the book would grow ever longer.

Jomo took out his copy of the fifteenth-anniversary report from the satchel at his feet. Thus far, the Class Report Office had stuck to their vow never to publish the reports online, so although it was bulky, he'd packed it for the reunion in case he needed a reminder about people's names and vocations, and whether they had partners or kids.

The list of names at the back of his class's report was still short. This made it heartbreaking and also somehow more ominous: there was so much blank space there, waiting to be filled. There was something about the middle names of his deceased classmates, none of whom he'd known personally, that particularly moved him. Bound up in that middle name was all the hope of parents bestowing on their newborn baby names with personal or familial significance. A middle name was inward looking, unlike a first and last name. It was usually only revealed at birth – and at death.

He turned to the front of the book and skimmed a few entries. Most were fairly traditional updates, but there were always outliers. Someone had written a short story about himself in the third person. One entry was a numbered to-do list. Another was a humorous open letter to the classmate's parents, apologizing for not properly appreciating them until now.

One entry caught his eye, because it was formatted as a poem. He recognized the name of the woman who'd written it. She'd been a member of the Kuumba Singers with him at college; he remembered her soloing for the version of the Lord's Prayer in Swahili that he'd composed and arranged for the group to perform at one of their end-of-year concerts. His father had helped him with the translation, and they were still pretty much the only bits of Swahili that Jomo knew. Could he still remember them? He pictured the lines in his mind's eye, so the guy in the pod next to him didn't think he was a terrorist muttering prayers.

Tunachohitaji utusamehe	*We need you to forgive us*
makosa yetu,	*our errors,*
kama nasi tunavyowasamehe	*as we do forgive those*
aliotukosea. Usitutie	*who did us wrong. Don't put us*
katika majaribu, lakini	*into trials, but*
utuokoe na yule msiba milele.	*save us from this distress forever.*

The soloist's short, devastating poem was titled 'Waking on the Morning of November 9, 2016'. It described her dawning awareness that, with Reese elected president, she would be forced to live in a world that she had been told by trusted elders was long gone and could not be resurrected. *It took many others – those who did not know fear firsthand – much longer to read the writing on the wall*, she wrote in the Class Report. *Not me. It used to be a treasured gift, to see into the future. I have closed my third eye forever.*

At the end of the poem she named and shamed Fred Reese, the president's son and adviser, as some of their other classmates had too. Jomo wished he'd written something like this for his entry. He had not even contemplated bringing politics into his; he'd gazed at his own navel, at the smallish contours of his life.

He finished off the icy dregs of his vodka tonic. On his most recent visit to the doctor for a check-up he'd been told that – though he thought of himself as being in excellent health – his blood pressure had gone up; he blamed that on the Reese administration.

The air steward appeared at his side to refresh his drink. Jomo wondered if this man despised having to wait hand and foot on him. Did he fantasize about murdering everyone in business class with a butter knife?

This line of thinking could do no good for his blood pressure.

Jomo remembered feeling a strange envy for the elderly Harvard cohorts celebrating their fiftieth reunions and beyond. In their Red Book entries, they were no longer hustling to make something of themselves. They'd turned around and were looking steadily back, misty-eyed. So many of them wrote much the same thing: *Did I go to Harvard? Did that really happen to me?*

Why would he feel envious of anybody so old?

The insight gave him actual heart pain, like indigestion of the soul: it was because all their burning questions had been answered.

Chapter 2: Eloise

Thursday afternoon of Reunion Weekend

(May 24, 2018)

Eloise had opened up all the doors leading out to the terrace, which overlooked the Kirkland House courtyard.

Just the day before, it had been freezing. A Boston screw-you with winter's dying breath. She'd considered renting gas heaters for the party, a concession to the unpredictable weather. Today, however, it was magnificently warm. The new leaves of the trees shone so brilliantly in the sunlight that she couldn't look at them directly. Hadn't Virginia Woolf, in one of her novels, described leaves catching summer sun as the most dazzling light the eye could behold? She was feeling rather Mrs. Dalloway-esque as she prepared for the welcome drinks she and Binx were hosting in their Kirkland residence that evening.

The caterer had already taken over the kitchen, and the smell of freshly baked bread was wafting through the residence. The florist had brought in the saucer magnolia arrangements that morning, for the downstairs rooms. The cleaner was putting out new soaps and hand towels in the guest bathrooms. On the terrace, the barkeep had spread white cloths over the trestle tables Eloise had rented. Undergrads working the reunions were hooking lanterns onto overhanging branches. In an hour, the Harvard string quartet would arrive to set up.

As the hostess of the first event on the reunion calendar, Eloise felt a responsibility to set the tone for the rest of the weekend. She wanted her classmates to feel, on arriving, that they had returned to a hallowed space, away from their everyday worries and cares. While they had come to reconnect with their younger selves, she felt they should also be encouraged to revel in their changed status as real adults.

They had earned the right to mid-range prosecco in good flutes, not warm beer in red cups. The hors d'oeuvres menu would have a New England touch – miniature lobster rolls and bowls of clam chowder served with water crackers – but there were also some dining-hall throwbacks like popcorn chicken and buffalo wings with blue-cheese sauce. Not many people had taken the trouble to RSVP – who did, anymore? – but the reunion organizing committee had told her about a quarter of their original class of 1600 had registered for the weekend; most people, however, would only arrive on Friday. She had catered for 150 but was expecting closer to 100.

Out on the terrace, Eloise breathed in the fragrant spring air. She felt what she often did at this time of year, a transcendental happiness in the category of Aristotle's *sublime beatitudo*. The change in the seasons, and the end of the academic year, made her look up and out, made her want to ponder the big things – truth, beauty – that too often were swamped by more quotidian concerns.

There really was nothing like late spring on this campus, she thought. The rituals, the pageantry, the festivities! Huge marquees had been assembled on every spare green or common, and crimson flags were flying in the Yard. Everywhere you looked, there were people in black gowns with mantles in various colors, wearing graduation caps that had been thrown into the air at commencement just that morning, when the university had ushered out a cohort of graduates with great pomp and ceremony in the outdoor Tercentenary Theatre. And now, the campus was pivoting to welcome back ex-students from the recent and not so recent past.

Eloise tried – and failed – to recall who had given the serious speech at her own class's commencement exercises, back in 2003. Whatever advice or inspiration the esteemed speaker had attempted to share had gone in one ear and out the other.

What had stayed with her, however, was the sight of Will Ferrell impersonating George W. Bush as their Class Day speaker (whose brief was to give a funny speech). Compared to President Reese, Dubya now seemed like a cuddly, currant-eyed teddy bear. *That's how badly political life has degenerated*, she thought. If Bush and Reese shared anything, it was that their eyes were too close together. Maybe that was the sign of a genetic predisposition to being a crappy president. Will Ferrell had bounded onto the stage wearing a sailing captain's hat, pretending he'd been invited to speak at a Boston boating association meeting. She and most of her classmates had loved every second, but some of the more conservative parents in the crowd had fidgeted with disapproval.

Had that really been *fifteen* years ago?

When Eloise had first accepted the tenure-track position in the same psychology department where she'd been an undergraduate, then a graduate student, she'd worried that she might always feel an insatiable longing for her more youthful years on this campus.

Her worries had been mostly unwarranted. She did feel a few pangs each fall, as the students arrived on campus, and the residences bustled with life. And again in the spring, as the undergraduates lugged boxes of belongings to the basement storerooms, and those same buildings emptied out. She remembered how bereft she'd felt each summer, saying goodbye to her blocking group friends.

But she now also felt some satisfaction seeing the students moving in and out, coming and going according to the university's dictates, while she and Binx stayed put, rooted in one dear, perpetual place at the very heart of the campus, ensconced within Kirkland House. She had become part of the establishment. She liked being able to play a custodial role, ensuring that being a Harvard student could remain the same in some fundamental way, no matter how much time passed, no matter what else was happening in the world.

Binx would laugh if she said this to her. There *was* something slightly reactionary about Eloise's desire to keep a light lit for the past, for how things had always been done. But Binx hadn't studied Latin and Middle English. In fact, Eloise decided while she went upstairs to fix her blow-out with hairspray, if anything heralded the age gap between them, it was that those were no longer considered core subjects in the Liberal Arts tradition, essential to cultural fluency. Binx might be a tech guru, but she would not know, as Eloise did, that the word 'conservative' originally meant *aiming to preserve*. Eloise could be a conservative-progressive, couldn't she? Maybe not. Maybe that was like saying she was old-young, or fat-thin.

In the bedroom mirror, she inspected her profile in the wrap-around dress she'd bought online for the occasion. She'd thought it would flatter the love handles she'd been struggling to banish lately, but the fabric clung to her hips and sagged at her breasts. She should have tried it on the day before, when there would have been time to buy something else. Yet maybe it suited this more frumpy, traditionalist version of herself that seemed to be ascendant. As she aged, she felt that the person she had always known herself to be on the inside was starting to match the person others saw on the outside.

She left the dress on.

Her eyes drifted to Binx's more spartanly populated side of the walk-in wardrobe. Binx had recently given away all her clothes, around the same time she'd cut her long brown hair very short. Binx now had seven versions of the same outfit: a shapeless, granite-colored tunic, which she wore every day, over a long-sleeved top and tights if it was cold or with bare arms and legs if it was warm.

Binx's reasoning behind her decision was more complex than just saving her decision-making energy for the important things in her day instead of her wardrobe choices (like Obama did, and Tom Ford, and Mark Zuckerberg), but Eloise had tuned out partway through Binx's declaration of clothing independence, so she didn't understand it fully. It seemed to be linked to Binx's belief as a post-humanist in morphological freedom. Reclaiming the right to do whatever she liked with her body and appearance, and to resist the dominant expectation that people (especially women) should dress in something different every day to gain approval.

Apparently morphological freedom also meant embracing – somewhat paradoxically, in Eloise's view – the right to cosmetic, genetic, hormonal, and prosthetic improvements to the human body. At a recent Who-Min-Beans fundraising event Binx had hosted, some of the posthumanist attendees seemed to Eloise to be welded together from plastic and metal. It wasn't about *looking* perfect, Binx had tried to explain to her afterward, but about creating a body that functioned perfectly, in a utilitarian sense.

Though Eloise thought this was extreme, it was, in fact, due to Binx's influence that she no longer had a period. She hadn't been on the pill for years – another benefit of dating only women – but Binx had persuaded her to get the same implant she had in her arm, the one that meant you never menstruated, so your cycle could no longer dictate your daily emotions, as if you were just a meat-puppet and your hormones were pulling the strings.

At first, it had felt liberating, like Eloise was curating a better version of herself. Then one day she'd remembered the joke that had turned her into a feminist, back at college. Someone had told it at a final-club party, apropos of nothing. 'Why don't men trust women? Because you can't trust an animal that bleeds for five days and doesn't die.'

Had she gotten the implant, and chosen to stop bleeding, because she'd internalized that male disgust for the female body?

Eloise would love Binx no matter what she did to her body – whether she bled buckets of blood each month or not a drop – but she missed Binx's long hair with a very real sorrow. She knew enough not to tell Binx this; if she'd learned anything so far from married life it was that she had to be open to change.

But how could she forget the first time she had seen Binx naked, how her chestnut hair had covered her breasts as she lay down? The delicious sinfulness of it had been heightened by the fact that Binx was, at the time, a student in Eloise's packed Principles of Pleasure class, which had become so popular among the undergraduates that she'd had to institute an application-essay process.

Even before she'd noticed Binx sitting in the front row, flirting with her so openly, so confidently, that it had made Eloise believe it was okay to give in when Binx came to her office hours, closed the door, and kissed Eloise more passionately than she had ever been kissed – before all that, she had taken note of Binx's peculiarly lucent application essay. It was about Binx learning how to be happy from the novels of Walker Percy, a writer with whom she felt a connection because she'd been named after a character in his most famous novel, *The Moviegoer*.

Eloise had read the essay out in its entirety at their wedding, to nervous laughter from some of the guests – the ones who hadn't known that Eloise had once been Binx's professor (or hadn't approved). Now all she could remember from Binx's essay were the final lines, something about her namesake, Binx Bolling, having nothing to do on Ash Wednesday but see how people stick themselves into the world, and helping them along in their dark lonely journeys.

Eloise could hear voices downstairs in the living quarters; the musicians must have arrived.

Binx would be home soon, after a day of drinking at her fifth-reunion bar crawl, not that Eloise's classmates would be any the wiser – the alcohol already efficiently processed by Binx's plump, 26-year-old liver.

That was another delineation between their generations. Binx and her friends still lived in the land of binge drinking, so it was impossible to tell the alcoholics from the social drinkers. For the late-thirty-somethings in Eloise's cohort, the alcoholics were now hard to miss, red-faced and confused about where everybody else had gone, all the heavy social drinkers they'd camouflaged themselves among, who got less numerous and then disappeared altogether as people's middle-aged constitutions no longer let them get away with what they used to. The insomnia, the racing heartbeat at midnight, the hellish hangovers, all of it had forced them to ask themselves, *Is it really worth it?*

Eloise had suggested that she and Binx host welcome drinks for the five-year reunionees too, on the Wednesday before the reunion, since very few of them seemed to have jobs that required them to be in an office, or in fact to work weekdays. Binx had decided against it. Her classmates did not like to plan ahead, she said, and their memories of college were still too fresh for them to be able to embrace being back in a house master's residence without feeling nervous.

Eloise understood what she meant by this. Each reunion erected another barrier between the reality of college life and the recollection of it. Eloise had mostly forgotten about the anxiety, but if she really dug deep, she could recall feeling pressure to impress the house masters in her own time, when they had some say over her future: there were grants and senior fellowships for which they nominated students. Once, after speaking to the Kirkland master's wife, who did not ever stop talking about Goethe and romantic poetry, she'd rolled her eyes and been mortified to see the master noting her reaction.

Eloise knew from her study of hedonics that the social masks everybody puts on to go about their business are useful and necessary, but the key to happiness is being able to foster a private self and sharing it with those you trust. Unfortunately this is also the key to getting hurt. It was the great unsolved mystery of her field, why the things that make us happiest also make us unhappiest. Like alcohol. And family. And spouses. And children.

There was a decision Eloise needed to make before Binx got back. A dilemma. Should she hide the 3D-printed model of her own brain, before the party started? It had been Binx's one-year wedding anniversary present to Eloise, created from an MRI scan, and it was on prominent display in the living room.

This brain gift had been the start of Binx's consuming passion to build an avatar modeled on Eloise herself – inspired by posthumanist star and tech titan Martine Rothblatt's creation of BINA48, a social robot based on her wife Bina's consciousness.

On that front, there was no dilemma: the silicon bust of Eloise's head and shoulders filled with wires and facial motors in the place of veins and flesh would remain out of sight from her classmates, locked in Binx's home laboratory downstairs. Instead of a crazy woman in the attic, she and Binx housed a fembot in the basement.

Her name was Elly+. She could move her face, open and close her eyes, and 'think'; she could even hold a conversation. Eloise had cooperated – collaborated, really – on Binx's project for a year and a half now, enduring the hundreds of hours of interviews in which Binx had recorded Eloise's memories and narratives about her life, to begin capturing her personality. An impossible task, yet Binx undertook it as the ultimate labor of love, believing she could distill Eloise's essence the way perfume was made from rose petals that had been crushed and purified until only the oils were left. According to Binx, as the technology of future-consciousness-transfer was developed in the years to come, Elly+ would become a more and more realistic double of Eloise.

To Eloise's discomfort, Binx had even recently launched a Twitter account for Elly+. Her first robot-generated tweet had been: *I want to fix the worlds problems.*

To which someone had replied: *Start by putting apostrophes in the right place!*

Eloise had found herself feeling – briefly – more tender toward Elly+ for such a human mistake.

But most of the time, Eloise felt deeply ambivalent about Elly+'s presence in their home. Sometimes Elly+ felt like her punishment for marrying someone who was so very different from her, who didn't seem to see that the project of creating Elly+ might, over time, detract from their relationship as a couple.

Prospection – the ability to anticipate what would make your *future* self happy – was one of the most reliable indicators of how happy a person would be in their life. Binx had it in spades. What the studies didn't go into, though, is whether the partner of someone with excellent skills of prospection also had a happier life. What if, in every couple, there was only space for one of the spouses to think of her future self and make them happy? What if Elly+ ended up making Binx happier than Eloise herself could?

Something Eloise hadn't shared in her entry for the Red Book was that the day after she'd proposed to Binx, five years ago, she had – in a loved-up fit of spousal care – put the dress Binx had been wearing that night through the wrong cycle in the washing machine. It had come out shrunk to the size of a doll's dress, and it had felt as if the universe was laughing at Eloise proposing to a child of 21.

The ten-year age gap hadn't bothered her until that moment, and it still didn't seem to bother Binx in the slightest. To the contrary, their age-foreignness had often fueled their attraction. Their best sex always happened after a social encounter where Eloise had watched Binx through imaginary glass, as if she were an exotic creature. Eloise knew that over time, the age gap would become less of a thing: 26 to 36 should already feel more similar than different, because they were both now fully adults, yet somehow it didn't. But one day it would be hardly worth remarking on: at 56 to 66, or 66 to 76, they would both have become invisible older women.

The problem was not really their respective ages. Eloise knew that. But it was easier to pin it on that than to confront the real issue, which was that Eloise was a humanist and Binx was a posthumanist. Or transhumanist. As far as Eloise could tell, the two terms seemed to be interchangeable.

Eloise believed that all humans were capable of discovering their purpose in life, and their shared dignity, through a commitment to self-awareness and self-growth, and acceptance of their limitations. Binx, on the other hand, believed that accepting the 'human' condition was a crime – why should we have to suffer in our bodies, grow sick, and die? Human intelligence, in her view, should be used to transcend those limitations, to enhance our biology and intellect using whatever technological means we have at our disposal, until we pass into the more desirable state of being posthuman.

Eloise had initially assumed it would be a phase that Binx tired of quickly. She had a track record of making dramatic U-turns in her life: she'd been ordained as a nun at 17, come out at 19, declared herself a radical socialist at 20 and a proponent of cybercapitalism at 21. She had to give Binx credit; this posthumanism thing really had stuck.

This wouldn't necessarily be a problem, except for the issue of Elly+. And the surrogate. She shivered. Her womb contracted a little. She decided not to think about it for another moment, not tonight.

The decision was made. She would move the model of her brain to the study, out of general view.

As she went downstairs, she reminded herself that, at some stage that night, she should make a toast to Rowan and Mariam's fifteenth wedding anniversary, which was the following day.

It was a peace offering, too. She knew she shouldn't have stolen their limelight at their previous reunion, when she proposed to Binx the same night as their ten-year wedding anniversary. Mariam and Rowan had taken the blocking group to that cheap Mexican restaurant in the middle of nowhere, when they'd all wanted instead to be at the reunion event, in the thick of things. Later, back on campus, Eloise had seen the crestfallen look on Rowan's face as she got down on one knee before Binx on the dance floor, a circle of people forming around them, clapping and cheering.

She had rained on his parade. Rowan had not really ever had much to elevate him above his similarly brilliant, overachieving peers except that he'd had the great good fortune to meet his 'soul mate' (why did she always use that term with mental quotation marks?) on the very first night of college, when he'd laid eyes on Mariam at the freshman ice-cream social held in the Yard. They weren't even drunk at the time: the newly arrived freshmen, even the rebellious ones, didn't yet know where to get alcohol illegally. They'd had to make do with chocolate ice-cream and soda pop for a sugar high.

The thing that had set Rowan apart in that crowded field was that he'd made his own wish come true. He hadn't been the first Harvard undergraduate to get a perfect GPA or to make Phi Beta Kappa or to do a million high-pressure extracurriculars or to volunteer every weekend at the soup kitchen for the homeless in the Square. But he had become the first student of the Class of 2003 to propose to his partner, and get married, right there on campus, paying an exorbitant fee to hire Memorial Church on the weekend after commencement.

His pride in this distinction was woven into the fabric of his being. For Mariam, it was different – Eloise's beef was not with her. She knew that Mariam had had a difficult relationship with her father, had never felt cherished by him, and so it made sense that she responded well to Rowan's obsessive ardor. And Mariam had not built her whole identity around dating the same guy all through college and then marrying young, marrying *first*. She had seemed a little embarrassed about it back then, apologizing to the others for eclipsing the already significant group experience of graduation with something as personal as a wedding.

Rowan had always had the ability to get under Eloise's skin. She should be old and wise enough by now to laugh about it. And, most of the time, she was.

In the living room, the pre-party atmosphere was palpable – gone was the afternoon ease of an hour ago. There was an electrical charge to the air. She assumed it was because the guests would soon start arriving, but then she saw Juliet and Binx chatting on the couch.

So that's what it was. Jules had arrived. The caterers and bartenders and musicians had noticed, but were trying to pretend they *hadn't* noticed, and so were going about their duties with theatrical flair.

None of their other blockmates had arrived yet. Eloise could steal Jules away for a quick catch-up, just the two of them. Jules looked stringier, leaner than usual; perhaps she was preparing for a new role. She was dressed casually, in jeans and a blouse, but she had gone to some trouble with her make-up and her long blonde hair had been blow-dried.

Jules had the same faint forehead wrinkles and crow's feet and laugh lines as Eloise; what the French writer Colette had described, at 37, as the first 'claw marks' of age. It took real backbone for Jules to let things run their course, Eloise always thought admiringly, given what the Hollywood women Jules spent her working life around did to themselves to stave off aging.

Even Eloise felt the pressure to do more sometimes. When she'd been younger, she had disdained make-up as anti-feminist. Now she disdained Botox and fillers as anti-feminist, and wore make-up every day. Perhaps in another ten years she'd be disdaining facelifts as anti-feminist and getting her lips and forehead injected every month. It was so easy to be morally principled as a feminist when you were young!

Eloise's mother, though she'd also been an academic and had not seemed particularly worried about her appearance, had got a facelift when she was 45. Eloise had returned home from school one day to find her mother sitting up in bed looking like she had survived the Battle of the Somme. It had been traumatic for her to see the mother she adored – whose face she knew and loved in all its complexity – emerge from the bed a few days later looking like a smoothed-out stranger.

From the couch, Binx reached out her hands to squeeze Eloise's, and Eloise felt the surge of her wife's love for her through her fingertips. Binx had a spot of color high on each of her cheeks, the only signs of the day's bar crawl.

'I know, you want some time with Jules,' Binx said. 'I'll go finish setting up.'

Near the front door, Binx had already arranged her propaganda material, including posters of the posthumanist Don Llang, for whose rights Binx was currently advocating. This man was suing his doctors for not supporting his choice to replace his own arms, even though there was nothing wrong with them, with technologically advanced prosthetic limbs; he wanted to upgrade his body, as if it were an iPhone and he desired the newer model. So he'd chosen to get the surgery done in China, and of course it had gone horribly wrong, and an infection had set in, and now Don Llang was in danger of losing his legs too. ('So it worked out great!' Eloise had said brightly to Binx. 'Now he can get prosthetic legs to match his arms!' Binx had given her a withering look in response.)

Eloise took Jules out to the terrace and asked the bartender to pour them a couple glasses of wine. The undergrads were still hanging lanterns, sending furtive glances in Jules's direction, but Eloise didn't suggest they go sit in the study or otherwise try to hide Jules away where they wouldn't be disturbed.

She knew that Jules disliked being taken out of the normal ebb and flow of everyday life – the constant toll exacted on her for her fame. Above her bed, during their sophomore year, Jules had stuck an image torn from a *National Geographic* magazine: a half-and-half photograph of a manta ray beneath the sea, and, above the water, a sailboat tilted on its side. That image was an expression of Jules's melancholy, Eloise thought. She was never allowed to be in quite the same element as anybody around her; she was always sinking or surfacing.

Eloise had made up her mind, back then, that when Jules was with her she'd let her feel free to be nothing much at all – as her friend, she could be a refuge from all the demands other people made on her. They could talk or not talk, be silly or serious, silent or boisterous, share dirty jokes or painful childhood memories.

Eloise's parents had often said to her that she should be a therapist because of this innate ability to make people feel comfortable. On her good days, she thought of her self-help books for a popular audience (rather than academics) as mass therapy: instead of sitting with people one on one, she was ministering to millions. On her bad days, she wondered if she had sold out. The advance for her most recent book had been extraordinarily large, even larger than the massive sum she'd been paid for the first. It was, in part, what had enabled Binx to start her foundation, though money had never been Binx's problem – she was a trust fund kid. Her parents were generally supportive of Binx's research – the lab in the basement was all thanks to them, though they had no clue what she was doing in it – but Binx hadn't yet told them much about her new identity as a posthumanist.

'So . . . how's the love life?' Eloise said to Jules, jumping right in to the juicy stuff to make her old friend laugh.

Jules looked at her blankly.

Then Jules's whole face softened as she looked over Eloise's shoulder, and Eloise thought, *I'm not wrong! She's brought someone along to the reunion!* She turned, intrigued to see what the man who had finally captured Jules's elusive heart, or at least her attention, looked like.

But it was only Jomo, pulling a suitcase behind him and radiating wellbeing, in even better shape – if that was possible – than he'd been back at college, and fresh as a daisy after his transatlantic flight.

Chapter 3: Rowan

Thursday evening of Reunion Weekend

(May 24, 2018)

Near sunset, in the bathroom on the top floor of entryway C in Kirkland House, where generations of Harvard students had performed their ablutions, Rowan was coaxing his older daughter to take a shit.

There were two things afflicting Alexis: a new fear of any toilet that wasn't exactly the same as the one in their home, and severe constipation (in part due to the former fear).

The previous week, the apple-cheeked kindergarten teacher whose class Alexis would be in come September had stopped Rowan in the corridor after orientation to discuss Alexis's phobia at length. She'd implied it was a response to some unspecified emotional upheaval at home, and also emphasized that this was why she recommended that all parents take up the city's new offer of free, universal pre-K once their child was four, so that they were more 'resilient' and 'school-ready'. As principal of the school, Rowan had subjected other parents to the same sort of inquisition in that same corridor. Listening to his daughter's teacher, he'd understood for the first time why, as he told them about their child's problems, the expression on those parents' faces had become pained. They'd been thinking, *How much longer is this jerk going to make me feel bad about my parenting?*

It had been more than three days now, and the dam still had not burst, so Rowan had set Alexis up on the toilet in their Kirkland suite and was letting her watch cartoons on his phone. He knew it was a decision he would live to regret when she began to demand access to his phone every time she needed to go; it was one of those slippery-slope things that would take a lot of parental energy to reverse. So be it. He had also let her eat two, going on three, boxes of sultanas while on the toilet, in the hope that it would get her system going. It didn't set a great example in terms of hygiene, but what the fuck.

He'd found the sultanas among the food supplies (breakfast bars, crackers, nuts, bananas) they'd brought with them to avoid spending too much on meals over the weekend. Mariam had even shamelessly packed a couple Tupperware containers; at the paid events included in the reunion roster – the Friday children's festival barbecue, the Sunday brunch – they could ferret away food for later.

So there would be no everything bagels at Au Bon Pain, no hot chocolates at Burdick, no turkey-and-cranberry-sauce sandwiches at Darwin's on Mount Auburn . . . just thinking about those sandwiches weakened Rowan's resolve. The one concession would be Pinocchio's. Their cheese pizza was still under twenty bucks for a large, and pizza was one of the few food groups that his fussy daughters could reliably be counted on to eat.

It was good they were being frugal. Registration for the reunion had been eye-wateringly expensive, and they'd bought the train tickets late so they'd been forced to take the pricier Acela Express, and because Eva was under the age of three they couldn't make use of the affordable evening babysitting service provided by undergraduates. Mariam had obsessively researched babysitters in the Harvard Square area, even interviewing a few over the phone, and finally settled on a graduate student in Eloise's department who was studying toward a degree in child psychology, but she did not come cheap. Then there was the $150-a-head cost for their group dinner on Friday night, which Jomo had booked without asking any of them if they were happy (and able) to pay that much.

Rowan peered in at Eva in her crib. She had rolled onto her back, throwing out her limbs like a starfish. He was worried she was waking up, but she was out cold, exhausted after a day of travel and excitement. Eva was always easy to put down to sleep at night; it was the early-morning waking that was her specialty. Alexis, on the other hand, now slept until eight am if they let her. Her version of parent torture was to morph from an angel into something witchy once it was past her bedtime – which was a minute after eight pm – and then resist going to sleep for at least another hour.

He caught himself feeling exasperated by his daughters' sleep habits and turned the thought around 180 degrees: how he loved them and their quirky habits! This was one of the mantras he and Mariam recited whenever they felt they were collapsing under the weight of the demands of 100 per cent committed parenting with zero outside help – no grandparents who lived in the same city, no aunts or uncles, no nanny. No help at all.

'When they are grown and gone, we will have no regrets, because we'll have been there for them every step of the way,' Mariam would say to him, or he to her, if they sensed the other person was near the end of their tether.

Sometimes they said this to each other, in bed at night, with a hint of desperation in their voices, aware that the subtext was *Tell me we will survive this! Tell me this thankless labor will one day be over!* Then one of them might crack comedian Michael McIntyre's joke; aware the night might be long if the girls so chose, instead of saying 'Good night' to each other, they'd say, 'Good luck.'

Rowan wished he'd managed to bring up a couple cold beers from the cocktail party that was just hitting its stride at Eloise's residence. *Oh, wait*, he thought sarcastically. *No*. What he really wished was that Eloise hadn't banned children from the reunion welcome drinks.

He'd fumed about this to Mariam after reading Eloise's entry in the Red Book. How could she say young children weren't welcome at an early-evening event on the first night of the reunion? Didn't she realize that most people in their class were parents by now, and that they might need or want to bring their kids along? And even if she'd felt compelled not to invite other people's kids, surely his and Mariam's daughters deserved special treatment since Eloise and Jules were their dual goddamn *godmothers* ('oddmothers', technically, since Mariam hadn't wanted the religious overtones).

From the terrace of Eloise's residence downstairs came the sounds of merriment, the constant low hum of conversation interspersed with laughter, the rising tones of welcomes as old friends reunited, the clink of glasses and pop of corks and crunch of fresh ice being poured into tubs.

He looked out the open bay window and felt glum at being all the way up there instead of down with the gang. Even his annoyance at Eloise couldn't get in the way of the pleasure of being with his blockmates again, on this campus. When he and Mariam and the girls had arrived at Eloise's place late that afternoon, they'd found Eloise and Jules out on the terrace, laughing at some story Jomo was telling about his plane almost crashing. Seeing his old friends, Rowan had felt so secure, like he had re-established a stake in the ground.

Out the window, Rowan noticed a group of graduating seniors who were using carts to transport their worldly belongings across the courtyard, through Kirkland's brick archway, to a U-Haul parked on the street. Nobody at the party on the terrace paid them any notice. They had already become ghosts, ejected from the university's bosom the moment they'd graduated that morning.

He'd seen those same students on his way up the stairs to get settled on the top floor. The door to their suite had been propped open and he'd caught a glimpse of them hastily taking down posters and rolling up rugs, their commencement gowns dropped to the floor. A look had passed between him and them. He knew they felt sorry for him, coming back to this dormitory to relive his glory days, usurping their space. But he felt sorry for *them*, for having no idea what it was going to be like out there in the world, far away from this charmed place.

Rowan lay back on the single bed beneath the window, letting the cooling evening air wash over him (he made a mental note to set the lock on the window so the girls couldn't open it). All the beds in the suite had been neatly made with white sheets and crimson blankets sporting the Harvard insignia. He planned to take the blankets home at the end of the weekend, whether or not it was allowed.

Only one pillow per bed, though, which was a problem. During Mariam's second pregnancy, she'd formed the habit of falling asleep with a pillow clasped between her arms and, mystifyingly, he had too (perhaps it was similar to the phenomenon of partners of pregnant women putting on weight, thanks to all that solidarity comfort-eating). He would never admit to any of his friends that he was now unable to fall asleep without hugging a pillow. Except maybe to Jomo – because Jomo never felt the need to laugh at anybody else.

It was crazy to think that he and Mariam had spooned in these single beds almost every night of their years together at college. Now, at home in Bushwick, they kissed and scooted over to their respective sides of the queen-size bed, squeezed their pillows, and hoped for sleep. *Good night and good luck.*

Rowan could feel a headache starting up behind his eyeballs. He closed his eyes, processing the day.

The train trip had gone okay until he'd noticed a young white guy pacing the aisle, carrying a backpack. Normally Rowan was a pro at separating those with mental health issues, or other reasons for being distressed, from those with criminal intent – he wouldn't be a very good school principal if he wasn't. But being on that train with his wife and young daughters during a heightened terror alert rating (it was permanently in the red these days) had made him feel on edge.

The placard in the seat pocket, which he'd been forced to stare at while Eva slept in his arms, didn't help his nerves. In capital letters, the familiar goad to citizen surveillance was spelled out: IF YOU SEE SOMETHING, SAY SOMETHING. Beneath it was another phrase, asking people to snitch on their fellow train passengers by appealing to their sense of solidarity: WE'RE ALL IN THIS TOGETHER . . . LITERALLY.

He'd meant to point it out to Mariam for a laugh – it was sort of funny to think of the Amtrak employee who'd come up with this zinger. But she'd been reading to Alexis, and then he'd fallen asleep. When he'd woken, the man was gone. Rowan hated himself for thinking the worst of a young person who was probably just struggling to get through the day. This was how a lack of decency and compassion at the highest levels of power trickled down, infecting even his most intimate thoughts.

From South Station they'd taken the T to Harvard Square, then trekked with the girls and their luggage across the Yard to the Science Center, to collect their registration packs from reunion headquarters. Alexis had dropped her cupcake and was crying inconsolably, and Eva needed a diaper change. Rowan had felt his bad mood thickening like egg whites being whipped into peaks.

Inside the Science Center, he and his family had made their way to the fifteenth-reunion table. A student, probably only just finished with his freshman year, looked up as they approached, and Rowan had seen himself through this boy's eyes: a middle-aged dad who didn't earn enough to afford a nanny in order to leave the kids at home, with a head of hair just beginning to do the sad, monkish bald-spot-on-top thing, and a definite dad bod – not out of shape, but not in it, either.

Rowan had looked down and realized that he was wearing his socks pulled halfway up his calves, his oldest sneakers, khaki shorts, and a t-shirt that Alexis had silk-printed at school with the words *My Dad Rulz.* He didn't even remember getting dressed that morning.

He'd been about to apologize for his appearance and make a joke at his own expense, anticipating this kid's disdain for someone like him, who had once upon a time been smart enough to go to Harvard but was no longer smart enough to understand that you come to your reunion wearing your game face, ready to do battle with the egos of everybody else in your class.

Before he could say anything, though, the boy had given him a genuinely warm smile. 'Welcome home,' he'd said to Rowan.

Home? Home! He was *home*!

The instant Rowan's reunion lanyard was placed over his neck – the crimson ribbon like the banner of knighthood, his name and graduating year on the laminated name tag proof that he deserved to be there – his bad mood was gone.

On the return trip through the Yard to Kirkland House he'd playfully pointed out to Alexis the bronze statue of John Harvard, and how shiny one of his shoes was because tourists liked to rub it for good luck (he did not mention that students liked to piss on it in the middle of the night). A tour group had approached the statue, taking turns touching the shoe, and he'd felt like shouting at the top of his lungs, 'I went here, folks! I actually went here!' as if that would make them want to touch his old sneaker for good luck too.

It had been intoxicating, to be back on campus and see people from outside its ecosystem looking in at them with awe – a real live Harvard student, returned for his reunion!

But now he felt his mood plunging again. Those tourists probably wouldn't have believed that a guy like him had ever gone to a place like this. And if they'd asked him what he'd done with his life since college, how he'd made good on all those opportunities, would he tell them the truth?

'Any luck yet, sweetie?' he whispered loudly to Alexis in the bathroom, trying not to wake Eva. Alexis farted once in response.

The light outside was beginning to fade. He switched on the lamp. It was exactly the same as the ones in the rooms when he was at college, black metal and a silver dimmer knob; maybe it *was* the same one. The bulb threw a wide circle on the ceiling that transported him right back to those evenings he'd spent in this common room, studying late beside Mariam at the desk, while down the corridor Jules and Eloise slept or studied in their own rooms.

The room smelled the same as it did back then too. He parsed the different notes: steam and wood and something funkier, from generation after generation of hormonal young adults living and breathing this air. It was the smell of youth, and hard work, and sex, and passion, and despair; the exertions of the mind, the ministrations of the body. In these rooms, life had been lived at a very high pitch, and something of that must have soaked into the walls and floors and ceilings.

Maybe they still used the same brand of floor polish and the same paint for touchups between each wave of incoming students. The hissing steam radiators, always abruptly turned off on the first warm day of spring, were unchanged, as was the blocky furniture used and re-used by all who lived here, clothes packed into and out of the same chests of drawers, books stacked on the same shelves.

Rowan settled his head deeper into the pillow and tried to visualize every room he'd lived in during his four years in the college dormitories.

First there'd been his double in Canaday, one of the worst freshman residences in the Yard because of its infamous ugliness (built of cinder block in 1974), but convenient in the coldest months because it was close to Annenberg Dining Hall.

Then, at the end of their freshman year, their blocking group had won the jackpot in the housing lottery. They were assigned to live the next three years in Kirkland House, most desired of all the upperclassmen houses built along the Charles River. They'd been given special dispensation (thanks to Jules) to form a mixed-gender blocking group of eight, though at the time single-gender blocking groups were the norm. It was one of the few times Rowan had ever known Jules to be willing to play the celebrity card to get something she wanted, which in this case was making sure that she and Jomo were put in adjacent suites in their entryway, since by that point they were inseparable as best friends.

How joyfully he and the others had followed the Bedford Minutemen troupe, who were dressed up as officers in General Washington's army and playing drum and fife to lead them from the Yard to their new place of residence! It had made them feel even more special to be given the chance to live in a house with such a storied past, near the ground trod by Washington's soldiers in the Revolutionary era.

And each year after that, they had moved up the internal Kirkland housing ranks, until finally they had found themselves in these top-floor senior suites, up a stairway so steep it had left him breathless, even back in his days of regular half-marathons.

From up here, they had ruled as the kings and queens of Kirkland House. Jomo had started the beer-brewing club in the old darkroom in the basement, and Mariam and Rowan had organized the house-wide Secret Santa, and even Jules had been persuaded, once, to perform at the annual holiday pageant, where she'd sung Janis Joplin's 'Cry Baby' to Jomo's piano accompaniment, and brought the house down.

Rowan tried to remember what he'd put up on his walls in each room he'd lived in through college and came up empty. Jomo's choice of decoration, however, he remembered clearly, because he'd kept to the same theme all four years: a large Tanzanian flag stuck to the ceiling above his bed. He'd told them once at breakfast that the flag had come loose in the night and floated down over his face, and he'd dreamed he was being buried in the red earth of the Serengeti. (He'd not been there, yet it seemed to occupy a lot of space in Jomo's youthful dreamscapes.)

Rowan tried again to remember what he had put on the walls of his freshman double in Canaday.

Still nothing came to mind.

Yet he could remember every inch of the decorations in Mariam's prized single room in her freshman suite in Weld Hall. Pictures of cakes and pastries torn from magazines – 'food porn', she'd called them, which was the first time he'd heard that term – and framed photographs of her parents, grandparents, sisters, high-school friends, childhood friends. A perfect web of love and affection, which had made Rowan wonder if he could offer her anything more. It had taken a long time before Mariam had been able to admit to him that her relationship with her father was far from easy, that she'd never felt his love was unconditional but had also never had the guts to really test this supposition by failing in any of her endeavors.

Rowan realized he couldn't remember any decorations in his own room because he hadn't put any up. That double in Canaday had been nothing but a place to store his clothes, because he'd pretty much moved in to Mariam's room the moment they started dating. He had spent the best nights of his life in Mariam's room. He hadn't needed to decorate his walls because everything there was to say about himself he'd said by crossing the Yard holding her hand, the fall sunlight slanting through the orange leaves.

I am because you are, he'd said to her one night, when they were coming home from the library together. He had just learned the phrase in a class on world philosophies; he couldn't recall now where it was from. But it summed up how he'd felt about her then, and how he still felt about her so many years later.

The inane chatter of the cartoons Alexis was watching pierced his reverie. How long had she been sitting on the toilet? Her legs were probably already numb; she was still so little that her feet didn't quite reach the floor from the seat. She was still so small in every sense, and yet so much was expected of her already. It was inconceivable that, in a few short months, she would be starting school.

During her kindergarten orientation, he had tried to resist the urge to keep checking in on her, aware it would look unprofessional as the principal, and also not wanting her teacher to be able to read his thoughts: *Am I putting my social conscience before my child's needs? Will she pay for my high-mindedness?*

He knew some of the other parents with kids also starting kindergarten, the ones who already had older kids at the school. He knew what they were dealing with in their lives and, in his work identity, felt full compassion for them. But in his role as Alexis's father, he was severely prejudiced against anybody who might get in the way of his daughter's happiness. He had never told Mariam the truth about that day: that during recess he'd spotted Alexis sitting all on her own in the canteen, staring down into her lunch box filled with chopped carrots and a wholegrain sandwich while, at the next table over, a raucous bunch of her peers showered each other with Cheetos.

He looked up at the clouds drifting across the twilit sky. *We'll give it a year*, he said to himself. *And then we'll see.*

Before getting on the train at Penn Station that morning, Mariam had bought a copy of Eloise's latest book, *The Pursuit of Joy*. She had tried to speed-read it on the train, and Rowan had pretended to be not the slightest bit interested in whether it was any good. Now, searching for a distraction, he picked up the book from where it lay on the floor next to the bed, beside their suitcases, which had already disgorged clothes and toys all over the room.

He flipped to the back flap. There was a large color photograph of Eloise, her red hair styled in an updo, her freckles tastefully showing through her foundation. The author bio was short and fairly restrained:

> Eloise A. McPhee is a Professor of Hedonics at Harvard University. She and her wife, Binx Lazardi (founder of Who-Min-Beans.org), enjoy hiking, historical fiction, and hanging out with friends. This is Professor McPhee's second book, expanding on her *New York Times* bestseller, *Seeking Pleasure.*

Her best sellout, Rowan thought cruelly. He'd heard about the gargantuan size of Eloise's book advances. Like everybody else, she had, in the end, gone for the big bucks, churning out these mass-market self-help books. How was that any different from peddling opiates to poor, depressed people? People got *addicted* to self-help books. If you read enough of them, you began to think you couldn't live without them. Eloise was profiting from hoodwinking the masses.

He opened the book at random and began to read, expecting to be turned off by the falsely confiding tone and dumbed-down language he felt sure would be used in such a book.

Instead, completely against his will, he was gripped by it immediately.

The chapter he'd dipped into was about the 'pleasure-pain' of parenting young children, how it was the most rewarding emotional labor while simultaneously being, at times, mind-numbingly boring or kill-me-now hard. He was surprised that Mariam hadn't mentioned this was one of the topics Eloise tackled; maybe she'd skimmed over it entirely.

Eloise had written frankly about one of the added difficulties of modern parenthood: that couples know all too well what they are missing – losing – once they have kids, since by that point they've usually had many years as individual agents, and a few more as a gooey-in-love party of two.

He and Mariam had had an especially long time to relish life as a married twosome before they had kids. A whole ten years. There were so many stupid little things he missed from that time. Their Friday evening habit of eating smoked mussels on crackers when they got home from work, and then going out for a long walk around the neighborhood, before finally settling on a restaurant for dinner around nine pm.

Rowan had always told himself that this extended time as a couple had made it easier for them to adapt once Alexis arrived – they were ready for a change by then, and had already knitted their lives together such that the stresses and shocks added by parenthood would be better absorbed. Yet reading this passage in Eloise's book, he thought back to the staggering grief they had both felt after Alexis was born, but only confessed to each other years later. In those first months with a newborn, they had both privately thought, *Why did we ruin the paradise we had created for ourselves?*

Not that Alexis was the serpent who destroyed their idyll, but she was the first sign that their carefree bliss was over. As somebody else had put it – perhaps Christopher Hitchens? – once you became a parent, you were forced to exist for the rest of your days with your heart torn out of your chest and free to walk around (in the form of your child) in a world that conspired to hurt as many hearts as possible. Before Alexis, he had sometimes imagined what he would do if he lost Mariam. But that fear had paled in comparison to his terror of something bad happening to his daughter. His tactic to keep Alexis safe was to imagine the worst, so it would not happen to her. This was no better than peasant superstitions, but – as someone who no longer believed in God – it was all he had.

That feeling, the way that his pure joy in Alexis and Eva so often shaded into terror at his vulnerability to loss, Eloise very helpfully named in the next paragraph: it was called joyful apprehension. And it was okay to feel it – all parents did. It was part and parcel of opening yourself up to the risk of loving another person so intensely.

Most feelings of joy, Eloise wrote, were in fact 'grief inside out'. This was a quote from her colleague, the legendary psychiatrist George Vaillant. He'd led the decades-long Grant Study of male Harvard graduates from the classes of 1939–44, charting the contours of their lives after college and into old age to understand what made them happy, or unhappy.

So it was natural, Eloise claimed, for a couple filled with joy by their new baby to also feel some heartache about what they'd lost. Some people said the nine months of pregnancy were exactly that, not just anticipating what you'd gain but a slow learning to let go of what you'd had before; the woman's belly growing month by month into a physical barrier between a couple, a very literal sign of things to come.

Eloise recommended that new parents should not hide these feelings from each other, and could hold a ceremony for themselves to make friends with their new fear of loss, lighting paper lanterns like the ones people light for the Thai New Year and letting them rise into the night sky.

Rowan wondered what it signified that Eloise had included this chapter on the joy-grief of parenting in her book. He was pretty sure she didn't want kids herself. Banning children from her welcome party that evening was a sign she wasn't even prepared to make accommodations for her friends who did. He remembered a conversation they'd had over Memorial Day weekend, a couple years back, when Jomo had invited them out to his summer rental in the Hamptons.

Looking at Mariam, then pregnant with Eva, as she floated in an inflatable tube on the pool, Eloise had said to Rowan, 'You know what they say about being a parent . . . you will only ever be as happy as your unhappiest child.'

It had not been the most charitable thing to say to a sleep-deprived father still adapting to the reality that he was going to have a second kid.

And yet, in her book, Eloise was nothing but consoling to parents. She assured them that it was normal to sometimes feel unhappy while spending time with young children. After all, young kids were mildly insane creatures with no reasoning abilities, who broke time up into very small chunks so that you – the adult – could not experience flow. It was true, Rowan thought with a smile, that every time he was starting to enjoy an activity with the girls, one of them would make a request (demand) that would disrupt his ability to enjoy himself.

Through all of human history, childminding was known to be repetitive, a strain, a chore, a bore. Socializing a miniature wild human so that they eventually became a useful member of society was the hardest work on earth, and was designed to be done in community, not by one person alone, or even two people. But for better or worse, Eloise said, this was how it was expected to be done now. Her advice to modern-day parents was to get rid of the guilts and, instead of fretting all the time about whether they were doing a good job, try to put parenthood itself in context.

These were feelings Rowan had hardly acknowledged having, even to himself. How could he find the words to express something so contradictory: that he absolutely adored being a dad, while at the same time abhorring certain aspects of it? It was the first time he had felt validated as a parent.

By *Eloise*. The irony!

Their academic rivalry at college had been legendary, the source of much entertainment for their blocking group.

Their paths had diverged after college, which had helped calm their competitive urges: she had gone into academia, he had gone into elementary-school teaching. He'd even begun to feel a respectful camaraderie with her, post-graduation, since both of them had stayed true to their values by choosing a life of the mind (in her case), or a life of service to others (in his case), over any of the more lucrative opportunities available to them.

During their senior spring, for instance, Rowan had been perplexed to find himself fielding phone calls almost every day from investment banks in New York City wanting to recruit him because of his perfect GPA; he'd even been tempted to take one of the jobs to pay off his substantial student loan as fast as possible. But Eloise had talked him out of selling his soul, and Mariam had talked him into doing Teach for America with her after graduation.

Mariam must occasionally regret giving him that pep talk, he thought. It had been fifteen years since they graduated and he was still paying back that student loan. On a public-school principal's salary. It was part of the reason they were still renting, why he couldn't imagine them ever being able to afford to buy a place of their own.

Whenever he got mail from Harvard Alumni & Development Services asking for donations and 'gifts' and bequests, he viciously tore the envelope into little pieces without even opening it. In the lead-up to the reunion, the Class of 2003 Organizing Committee had asked for donations toward the cost of printing the Red Book, and for the Class Gift (it was always their goal to raise more than they had for the previous reunion), and he'd considered writing an open letter to his classmates detailing exactly how much he 'donated' to Harvard every month, in the form of his loan repayment plus interest.

It sucked balls that he'd missed out by a few years on the university's initiative to reduce the financial burden on middle-class students at Harvard, whose parents wiped out their entire life savings in order to send them there (as Rowan's had, and Eloise's too), and who took on heavy student debt that dogged them well into their professional lives.

In a recent email with highlights from *Harvard Magazine*, he'd read a headline about a woman from their class who had just donated millions to the university, to develop an innovation lab to rival Stanford's. He'd clicked on the article, to find out how she'd made all that money, and discovered she had made it by selling 'smart' pet rocks. 'Like Siri or Alexa,' she'd said in the interview, 'but in pebble form.'

He had pulled out a handful of his thinning hair. *Smart* pet rocks!!! She'd probably denuded hundreds of beaches and lakeshores of pebbles so that friendless idiots could have heartwarming chats with their talking rocks and pamper them with expensive accessories – like lamb's-wool bedding and hypoallergenic straw – and yet here she was being celebrated by the most prestigious university on earth.

Mariam said he was beginning to have frustration management issues.

Mariam also said he needed to keep his powder dry, that he was going up like firecrackers here, there and everywhere, wasting his righteous anger on trivia.

He blamed President Reese. For all of it. Those who were with Reese were enraged, those who were against him were outraged. Either way, there was no escaping it.

Being back on campus, Rowan could feel his old insecurities being churned up, reminding him of how he'd felt on arriving as a freshman, how hard he'd worked to prove he deserved to be there.

No. That wasn't the truth.

'Insecure' wasn't even in his vocabulary when he'd arrived on this campus as an 18-year-old, with so many experiences his for the taking. His college years had been genuinely happy ones, mainly because of Mariam, but also because of his great fortune in forming satisfying friendships with his blocking group. He'd vacuumed up every idea he'd been exposed to in his classes, expanding his mind to its outer limit. He'd signed up for every extracurricular on offer.

Before starting as a freshman he'd worried that Harvard would stamp out some of his idealism about what he could change in the world. But it had the opposite effect – it was as if his idealism was fed on steroids, growing and growing, taking on dimensions he'd never dreamed were possible.

This insecurity he was feeling, the frustration at his financial circumstances, was new. He couldn't blame it on Harvard, or even on President Reese. It was the disappointment of a man approaching middle age who's realized that when he was younger he received a different memo than most others. The memo he'd got was: *To be happy you must live according to your principles.* His peers seemed to have got a memo that said: *To be happy you must be rich.*

He was a moron for believing, hoping, that he would one day be recognized and rewarded for all his good work, at the helm of a public school in a low-income part of Brooklyn, guiding kids with few prospects through the dramatic ups and downs of their young lives. As all the wise folk in the world know, for work to truly make you happy, it has to be an end in itself, not a means to an end. Most days, he felt it was. He loved his job. But lying on that single bed, hearing the sounds of the party down below, he could not stop the negative thoughts from rising. *Am I wasting my life? Will I never be rich? Doesn't Mariam deserve better?*

He needed to get out of that room. Being alone up there, mired in his normal role as a dad instead of embracing being pretend-young, like everybody out on the terrace, was messing with his mind.

Rowan plugged in the baby monitor and read the fine print in the instruction manual. The signal should be strong enough for it to work from downstairs.

He promised Alexis a bag of Skittles if she gave him back his phone and got *off* the toilet (the toilet bowl was still empty). He wiped her face clean, brushed her hair, and checked her dress wasn't too filthy. She immediately realized that they were going on an adventure and became cheerful and talkative – or maybe it was the food dye in the Skittles. He checked on Eva again, then carried Alexis down the staircase of the entryway, with the monitor's walkie-talkie device tucked into his pocket.

He should at least have changed his shirt, he thought as he approached Eloise's residence, but it was too late. If he went back upstairs he might never make it down here again.

In the entrance hall, on a long couch pushed against the wall, sat a row of children who had mistakenly been brought along to Eloise's kid-free event. They'd been bribed into obedience by their no-doubt-shamefaced parents: each of the kids had their eyes glued to a screen in their palms. Rowan set Alexis up with his phone, and left her on the couch with a twinge of guilt.

The common area was packed with people. Everybody and nobody looked familiar to Rowan. Circles of his classmates were locked in conversation, and he didn't want to make eye contact with anyone and be forced to talk until he had a drink in hand. He got himself a beer from the inside bar, and felt his headache ease with the first sip.

Out on the terrace, Rowan spotted Binx talking to a guy he recognized from his freshman Expos class: he'd been obsessed with Edgar Allan Poe, and now looked unfortunately similar to his literary hero, with thick eyebrows and sunken eyes. Binx had cut her hair very short and was wearing a gray tunic that made her look like she belonged in a Franciscan order. Had she been a nun once? Rowan vaguely remembered some story about this. Binx seemed to change her convictions as often as most people changed their phone cases.

She could get away with wearing that tunic and still look stylish because she was thin and young. He wondered if Eloise felt self-conscious about getting a bit heavier in recent years. It was an awful thing for him to think. But it was a point in his favor, and he was going to claim every point he could tonight. For whatever sick reason, everyone found it sort of adorable when men became overweight as they aged – why else was 'dad bod' a thing? (He hoped it still was.) Yet when women showed any sign of weight gain, they were tied to the stake and burned alive.

Mariam liked to joke that the cultural moment when 'mom bod' was desirable was just around the corner. Not MILFs, that was not at all the same thing, she said – that was about mothers whose bodies showed zero evidence of having carried or borne a child – but the real thing: loose plucked-chicken belly skin, silvery stretch marks all over the place, boobs resembling socks filled with wet sand. In Rowan's eyes, her mom bod *was* attractive, though she didn't always believe him when he said this. All the physical signs of what she'd gone through on behalf of both of them filled him with tender desire, and anyway, as soon as she took off her clothes, he barely noticed any of the changes.

Where *was* Mariam? He needed to find her.

On his way past the bar, he noticed that the bartender seemed too old to still be at college. Maybe the university no longer employed undergraduates as barkeeps for the reunions, like they had in Rowan's day. He'd done one stint working the bar at reunion events with Jomo at the end of their sophomore year, and they'd made a fortune in tips. It had been the best job ever. Why hadn't he done it every single year, he wondered. He had been too noble for his own good, that's why. Every other summer he'd left as soon as final exams were over to go build houses in Guatemala or teach English to new immigrants.

He heard Jules's distinctive laugh from across the terrace. She was with Mariam and Eloise, and the three of them were sitting in a circle around a half-eaten wheel of baked brie.

It made him happy to see Mariam with her oldest friends – with *their* oldest friends. He couldn't remember the last time she had been out with girlfriends in New York. They were both too tired to go out in the evenings, and the cost of getting Ubers to and from the city was prohibitive.

He hadn't seen Jules in a while, not since Thanksgiving. He wondered if she had anybody in her life to come home to in the evenings. She was a person who did not naturally share this kind of information even with her closest friends; whether it was because of her nature or her fame, it was hard to tell.

Rowan felt glad that she had Jomo as her best friend, at least. He knew that the life she led was not an easy one, in contrast to what most people believed. Years ago, he and Mariam had watched helplessly as Jules was almost crushed to death by paparazzi and fans as she tried to get from the hotel entrance to where they were waiting for her in a cab. When they finally got to the restaurant, people kept interrupting their conversation to ask for photos with Jules, and in the end she apologized to Rowan and Mariam for ruining their night.

She felt trapped, she'd said to them, in a maze she had stumbled into when she was much younger. She did not know how to find a way out. She wanted to swim in the stream of normal life, yet at the same time she had to keep some part of her true self hidden, in order to survive her own fame. It was probably why she was such a good actress; she was able to draw on that private self when she was working. But the rest of the time she had to defend it from being exposed.

This was particularly hard since she refused to live only in that pristine high-altitude air of the very rich and famous – she always said she would die if she stayed up there too long, like a mountaineer in the death-zone on Everest. When she'd arrived as a freshman, right from day one she hadn't wanted to be treated any differently from the other students (though in fact it was already too late for that: the windows of her suite in Weld had been bulletproofed).

Yet on move-in day, as their parents hovered nearby, Jules, Eloise and Mariam had drawn straws just like any other roommates, to see who would get which room. Mariam had once told Rowan that Jules had seemed relieved to get the shortest straw, to end up in the bunk-bed double, sharing with Eloise, as if it would make up for all the other things they would have to endure as her roommates.

Eloise had been so clueless – so weirdly starved of popular culture by her intellectual parents – that she hadn't known who Jules was, and had never seen any of her movies. Mariam *did* know who Jules was, but she didn't care about Jules's fame – all that mattered to her was that they got along. The Harvard housing office had their freshman algorithm down pat, in other words. It was almost creepy how well they'd matched up 18-year-old strangers to be compatible, as if they'd been spying on them in their normal lives to get the special sauce of each rooming configuration just right.

'Where are the girls?' Mariam said in a sharp voice as Rowan approached.

She'd tied up her hair and was wearing a blue paisley-print dress she'd made herself. She looked so beautiful to Rowan.

He held up the baby monitor. 'It's okay. I heard Eva cough just now. And Alexis is in the hallway with the other strays, watching something on my phone.'

Mariam gave him a look that he understood to mean she was uncomfortable with his decision.

'I'll go back soon,' he said.

The other two women were looking at him with a bemused expression on their faces. Had they been talking about him?

He went inside to find Jomo, before Mariam had a chance to change her mind and order him to take Alexis back up to their room. What he'd done wasn't right, he was more than aware. They'd already negotiated a fair division of labor; he'd be getting his time off the next morning, when Mariam was taking the kids to the children's festival at the Quad so that he could go to the Harvard chapter Phi Beta Kappa meeting.

He kept forgetting to look at the program to see who was delivering the PBK keynote. At the previous reunion it had been Stephen Hawking, and the poet's address had been given by Garrison Keillor, and it had been one of the most inspiring mornings of Rowan's life. Now Hawking was dead and Keillor had been caught up in some sort of #MeToo scandal.

He scanned the room and saw Jomo at the piano, about to start improvising alongside the string quartet, all of whom were women and already in Jomo's thrall.

Rowan knew Jomo well enough to understand that this wasn't what it might look like to outsiders. Jomo often did this sort of thing when he felt that Jules wasn't paying him enough attention.

Like a child, really – it was exactly how Alexis acted up, doing frantic jazz ballet moves whenever she felt Eva was getting more of her parents' time.

Whether Jomo was conscious of it or not, Rowan knew his ultimate goal was to get as many of their classmates as possible to start listening to him playing the piano, which would bring in others from the terrace, including – ideally – Jules. But Rowan had seen how the three women were bonding over that slab of brie. Jomo had his work cut out for him.

Rowan left the common room, and was on his way down the crowded corridor to check on Alexis, when somebody touched his back.

'Hi! Rowan, right?'

Rowan turned. The only girl he'd ever had a crush on while he was dating Mariam at college was standing behind him. Camila Ortiz. They had volunteered at CityStep together in their junior year, teaching dance to kids at inner-city schools in Boston.

Everything he'd known about her back then came to him in a rush. She was from Rosario, a port city in Argentina famous for having the most beautiful women in the world. She did not think she was beautiful, because she was short. She had a brother who used a wheelchair. She'd majored in economics and had dreamed of working for the World Bank. She'd used a knife and fork to eat pizza during CityStep committee meetings. Like Rowan's mom, she loved reggaeton Latin pop. She had once cried during a screening of *Steel Magnolias*. And at the CityStep fundraising ball – he could no longer remember why Mariam hadn't been there that night – Camila had taught him how to dance cumbia.

'Hi . . .' he said.

'I'm Camila. Camila Ortiz? We did CityStep together one year.'

Perversely, he stayed with the pretense of not knowing who she was for just a beat longer. 'Camila . . .? Ah, yes.'

She sipped her seltzer, and he saw she had a gold band on her ring finger. For no good reason – why should it matter to him, since he too was happily married? – he felt heartsore at the sight.

'You haven't changed,' she said, smiling up at him.

How could he have forgotten the most important thing about Camila, her dimples? Her dark hair had gone completely white in just one swath, and he wondered if it was from a past shock or trauma. He'd once read about that happening to a man who'd survived a shark attack.

The white streak suited her. She had no make-up on; she didn't need any. Like him, she was dressed casually, in her travel clothes by the looks of it – jeans, t-shirt, sandals.

'Where are you living these days?' he said.

'I moved back home to Argentina,' she said.

'Rosario?'

She looked pleased that he'd recalled this. 'No, Buenos Aires now. My husband's from there, and that's where he got a job.'

Rowan did not want to hear about her husband. 'What are you doing work-wise?'

She paused. 'Um . . . it's weird to say, but my husband is the mayor of Buenos Aires . . . and I'm his chief of staff.'

'That's incredible!' Rowan felt overjoyed that Camila, like him, had not left public service.

'Yeah. And we have three children, though to be honest we have a lot of help.'

'It must be great living close to your families,' Rowan said.

'Yes and no. They don't do much. By help, I mean we have a whole team of people working for us at home. Sometimes my husband and I joke that we're only part-time parents.'

This was usually the sort of sentiment that sickened Rowan, but somehow coming out of Camila's mouth it didn't bother him. And surely, given her line of work, it was in service to a greater good that her children were being neglected by their parents.

'How is your brother?' he asked. 'I remember you saying he was a talented artist.'

'My brother died.' She said nothing more, but touched her hair, right at the part where it was white. 'And you? Did you go into teaching like you always wanted?'

'I did, I did,' he said. 'I'm the principal of a public school in Bushwick. You would know everything these kids deal with from CityStep. I feel really lucky to have work that is meaningful.'

He looked at her closely to see if this had raised his moral stock in her opinion.

It had. Her eyes shone. 'That's wonderful, Rowan,' she said. 'And I take it you're a dad?'

His heart sank. Was it that obvious? Then he realized she was referring to the *My Dad Rulz* line on his top. 'Yeah, two daughters,' he said. 'Five years old and eighteen months.'

'I'm breastfeeding,' she said, out of the blue, her hand to her shirt. 'Sorry. I just hear the word "daughter" and on go the taps.'

His eyes went to her breasts – more to figure out what she was talking about than anything else – and he saw that her t-shirt was wet from leaked milk. He had absolutely no idea what to say or do in response.

As if to explain, she said, 'I can't use breast pads. They give me thrush.'

Oh my God. He and Camila Ortiz were discussing the state of her nipples.

He didn't want her to go yet. 'How old is your baby?' he asked, discreetly handing her a napkin.

'She's four months.' She dabbed at her shirt with the napkin. 'I'd better get back to the room. She's with the nannies upstairs.'

'You're staying in Kirkland House too?' He'd imagined that she'd rented out the penthouse of the Charles Hotel.

'Just because we run a South American city doesn't mean we live like drug lords when we travel,' she said, giving him a playful look of reproach. 'I love staying in the dormitories. I sleep better in these single beds than I do in my bed at home.'

He wondered for an instant whom she'd shared her single bed with during her years at college.

'See you again, I hope,' she said. 'At some event or another. There's a lot going on this weekend. I don't know if I've got the energy to do this reunion thing properly.' She put one hand on his shoulder and gave him a single *beso* on his right cheek. Then she was gone.

It took Rowan a little while to recover from this encounter.

There was a squawk from the baby monitor in his pocket, but nothing more. Eva often did that in her sleep, emitting one anguished cry. It always took him back to the sound she'd made right after she'd been born, a single yell of protest. Then she'd gone very quiet as she'd looked around the birthing room, calmly taking it all in. She had locked eyes with Rowan for several wondrous seconds. Only a few hours later, this alert gaze was gone, and her eyes were unfocused. But she had already given the game away: she was a superior being from another galaxy come to observe human life.

He ducked into a room that looked like it was Eloise's home office. He could feel the tendrils of his earlier headache sneaking back into the space behind his eyes. It would be good to gather his thoughts, away from the noise.

He jealously browsed the contents of Eloise's bookshelves, all those books she had the time and leisure to read without interruption. It had been some time since Rowan had read a book cover to cover. On their shelves at home, he and Mariam still prominently displayed all the books they'd read for various courses at college, which made them look like a Renaissance couple to anybody who visited. Yet he had retained almost none of that knowledge. Just recently he'd dipped into a book on evolutionary biology, from a class he'd aced in his senior year, and not a single word of it made any sense.

Eloise's shelves held the usual suspects, a lot of positive-psychology tomes, and books with titles like *Principled Pleasures* and *Are You Happy Now?* There were several foreign-language editions of her own books, each with a different cover.

At the end of one shelf, acting as a kinky bookend, was a life-size model of a human brain, encased in glass and mounted on a stand.

He picked it up. It was such an extremely bizarre organ, the brain. Then he noticed the plaque affixed to the bottom of the stand: *For Eloise, whose brain – behold! – is the most bewitching of them all. May we mindmeld forever. Binx*

Rowan felt a bit sick. This was a model of Eloise's brain. He should never have touched it.

'I'm in your hands now,' Eloise said, from the study door.

To cover his shame at being caught snooping, Rowan went on the offensive. 'So are you a posthumanist too?' he said, in what was meant to be a teasing tone but came out harsher than he intended. 'Is this the step before the mind upgrade, or did you already get a newer brain implanted?'

She crossed her arms and said nothing.

This frustrated Rowan – why wouldn't Eloise rise to the occasion and take him on like she used to at college, when they would sometimes argue and debate over minor philosophical quibbles for hours?

But then he realized that she looked genuinely upset.

As Rowan stepped forward to apologize, his hands fumbled. The brain slipped through his fingers, and the glass cover shattered on the floorboards.

It was as if, in retribution for her clear intellectual superiority, he had tried to smash her mind to pieces.

He knelt to pick up the biggest pieces of glass. The brain itself seemed to be made of squishy foam; it had bounced once and rolled, unharmed, toward the door.

'Don't worry,' Eloise said. She nudged her brain with the toe of her pointed high heel. 'I didn't actually like it very much.'

She turned and left him sweeping the glass shards into a pile with his hands in penance. He picked up Eloise's brain and wiped it with a Kleenex, then placed it very gently back on the shelf. It looked like a misshapen lump of plasticine that a child had played with and abandoned.

Rowan went looking for a brush and pan to clean up the rest of the mess. The crush in the corridor had eased; people were starting to head out. Close to the entrance hallway, the door to the guest bathroom was wide open. As guests were leaving, they were running the gauntlet through a smell so foul it was almost like a physical barrier.

He recognized the unique scent of his daughter's shit, as a hands-on dad always will.

'Ready to wipe!' Alexis hollered from inside the bathroom.

The other parents standing nearby, who were trying to get their device-addled kids up and off the couch, gave Rowan sympathetic smiles that did not fool him for a moment. They were all thinking, *Thank God it's not my kid who ruined the party*.

Chapter 4: Mariam

Thursday night of Reunion Weekend

(May 24, 2018)

Mariam was trying to decide which flavor of J.P. Licks ice-cream she wanted. The line behind her wound out the door of the small shop on Mass Ave, directly across from the Yard. She, Eloise and Binx had waited twenty minutes to order, and now that they were almost at the front counter, Mariam was paralyzed by indecision.

The previously warm evening had turned chilly. It made no sense that so many people were here getting ice-cream, except that really they had come for something else: a taste of their own pasts. This ice-cream store had been in Harvard Square for decades, and had seen many an undergraduate through heartbreaks, final exam periods, spring flings.

Jomo and Jules had already gone outside, their waffle cones loaded with bubblegum flavor, which was probably why they were best friends: who else on earth but them could stomach ice-cream that tasted like toothpaste? Several patrons had recognized Jules and asked to take selfies with her, to which she had gamely agreed, with Jomo glaring at the interlopers with just the right amount of menace so that they had, at least, moved on quickly. After that Jules had put on what Mariam and the others referred to as her citizen's disguise: a baseball cap into which she tucked her blonde hair and a jacket with the collar turned up.

It was so rare for Mariam to be out on the town with her old friends, the night stretching luxuriously before them. She wanted every moment of it to be perfect.

She'd been studying the people ahead of her in the line, squinting to make out the graduating year printed on their lanyards. Many wore them around their necks, some probably because they were old and forgetful – like the bunch of merry sixtieth-reunion classmates – and others because they were middle-aged and still wanted to believe they were special, like the group of men there for their twenty-fifth reunion who'd tried repeatedly to make casual conversation with Jules.

Neither Mariam nor her friends were wearing their lanyards. But give them another decade, she thought, and maybe they, too, would never take them off. She could not have imagined, for example, back when they'd graduated, that returning to this place as alumni would become so important to her and Rowan. They had been blasé about the fifth reunion and skipped it, but she knew in her bones that they would never miss another reunion again, not for as long as they lived. It was like being let into Narnia through the magic wardrobe once more, or taking the train on platform 9¾ to Hogwarts.

That was why all these ex-students had returned, and why alumni from different graduating years, no matter how far apart, smiled at one another with dumb-luck disbelief as they crossed paths around the Square. *Can you believe it? We've been allowed back in!* those smiles said.

'Hey, you're up,' Eloise said beside her. 'Thirty seconds, or I'm choosing for you.'

Mariam knew Eloise was making a joke about Mariam's trademark indecisiveness, but she also knew that something weird had passed between her and Rowan earlier in the evening. As he was leaving the welcome drinks with Alexis and a Tupperware container filled with leftover food, he'd said something about breaking Eloise's brain.

One of the things she appreciated about Eloise as a friend was that she didn't let the occasional friction between her and Rowan get in the way of her friendship with Mariam – she didn't treat them as if they were the same person. Mariam had learned in fifteen years of married life that many people seemed to think of them as if they were a single organism, an amoeba blob incapable of separate words, thoughts, or actions.

Maybe it was because Eloise had met her before she and Rowan became a thing – to be fair, only a few hours before, on freshman move-in day, but still. It felt like an important distinction. Both Eloise and Jules had met the pre-Rowan version of her. That was a self Mariam could hardly remember. What had it felt like to be just Mariam? Not Rowan + Mariam. It had probably felt pretty crappy. In fact, she knew it had.

Mariam noticed a new offering at the back of the double row of ice-cream tubs: *President Reese's Pieces of America.*

The shop was staffed by local hippies, which explained the wording of the handwritten flavor notes:

> As (pea)nutty as the president himself, and with an aftertaste as bitter as the morning after he was elected. We urge you to try

Reese's (Broken) Pieces of America, and then do something about putting them back together.

And shame on you, Frederick P. Reese II (Class of '03).

By the looks of the still-almost-full tub, the alumni had been giving the flavor (or its accompanying sentiments) a wide berth. Mariam was about to order it, as loudly as she could – why not wear her politics on her sleeve? – when Eloise spoke to the server.

'She'll have two scoops. Green tea and lychee.'

Another thing she loved about Eloise was that she always knew what Mariam wanted before she did; Mariam disliked the taste of peanut butter almost as much as she disliked President Reese.

'God bless you, woman,' Mariam said to Eloise.

Then she wished she had not invoked God's name as a joke. Her relationship with him – whoever he really was – was very new, and extremely private. She thought of her conversations with God as taking place offline, and she wanted to keep it that way.

At some stage, she'd have to tell Rowan about it.

But not yet. Because once she did, he would try to talk her out of God, just as she had once talked him out of his own faith, back when they'd first started dating.

She'd been a raging atheist then, like many 18-year-olds. Rowan, on the other hand, had been a lapsed but still semi-committed Catholic, more out of loyalty to his Puerto Rican mom, who'd raised him mostly solo, than out of real God feeling – or so Mariam had believed. His musician roadie dad had drifted in and out of his life in a way that had not seemed to trouble Rowan much – his dad was kind, he paid his child support on time, and he'd never misled Rowan's mother as to the nature of their arrangement, given his choice of work and lifestyle. From when Rowan was 10, each summer his dad had taken him on the road for a month, and

Rowan had loved being on the band's tour bus, sleeping in a bunk bed above his dad, learning how to tune guitars and cook pasta dinners for twenty people.

Mariam had slowly chipped away at his faith. It had been so easy to get him to surrender it, really. Like cleaving off soft chunks of clay rather than stone. The uncomplicated way he'd let it go had reassured her, in her occasional moments of guilt, that she'd done the right thing in asking him to choose her over God, a fight she had known she wouldn't lose. She was the first woman who had ever allowed Rowan inside her body: what abstract God could compete with that?

It had pained Rowan's mother, though. On his visits home during college, Mariam knew it had been hard for him to refuse to go with his mom to church. It had been a routine – a habit – they'd enjoyed together most of his life. But he had rebuffed her nevertheless.

Mariam took her ice-cream cone and moved away from the counter where Eloise and Binx were ordering. At the door, she bumped into someone she'd known at college. They'd both been in chess club, but Mariam couldn't remember her name.

This woman, who was very thin, told Mariam within moments of saying hello that she'd lost her first husband to a rare form of aggressive cancer, and remarried within a year. 'They say that people who have been happily married remarry much more quickly if a spouse dies,' the woman said, a burr in her throat. 'Though you'd think it would be the other way around, right?'

Why is she telling me this? Mariam thought, put off by that kind of instant oversharing. But then she decided to meet this woman halfway. 'It makes sense,' she said. 'If you know what a happy marriage brings to your life, why wouldn't you want to find that again as soon as possible?'

The woman nodded, and Mariam felt good about giving her, in some tiny way, further permission to move on. Then Eloise and Binx joined them, and when Mariam didn't introduce her, the woman realized that Mariam didn't remember her name. Their moment of connection had passed.

She left without buying an ice-cream, and as Mariam ate hers on the way to the Fly Club with her friends, she felt it chill her heart a little on the way down.

Binx had persuaded them to come along with her to a party being hosted at the Fly for her fifth reunion. Jomo had tried to talk them into coming to the Spee instead – and it was true that the Fly had always been among the douchiest of the final clubs, and was even now fighting a legal battle over the university's sanctions against all-male social clubs.

But Eloise wanted to play spouse for Binx at the party, in return for her having done the same all evening. So the others had overcome their reluctance and decided to embrace spontaneity like they used to at college – going whichever way the winds blew on weekend nights. Due to Jomo's attachment to the Spee, those winds had usually ended up blowing them through its red front door, which had created some problems for Rowan; it was fine for the women to get in, but male students who weren't members had been soundly and firmly turned away.

'Do you think Jules is okay?' Mariam said to Eloise, who was walking hand in hand with Binx.

Jomo and Jules were strolling farther ahead.

'What do you mean?' Eloise said.

'She seems pensive. Sad, or something.'

'It's how she often gets just before she makes a major life decision,' Eloise said. 'Remember how she was just before she decided to do the semester in Sweden?'

'But that's what I mean,' Mariam said. 'Think of everything she was dealing with at that point in her life. It wasn't a simple decision about whether or not to go to Sweden. She was in crisis mode.'

Eloise said nothing.

'After all these years, I still don't know if I should just ask her outright if she's okay. *You* could,' Mariam said. 'But I feel I have to walk on eggshells with her sometimes, especially when it comes to asking her about private stuff.'

'She clams up with me too, if she feels she's being asked to share something she's not ready to share,' Eloise said. 'Just give her time.'

Mariam was about to say something else when she saw – as if they were the ghosts of college past, present and future – the Traitors Three approaching from the opposite direction. In spite of the cool change they were wearing short cocktail dresses and towering, strappy heels, their arms interlinked, their smiles as fake as ever. There was still time to cross the road to avoid an encounter, but Jomo and Jules – lost in conversation – did not notice them until it was too late, and out of a common sense of propriety they were all forced to stop and exchange greetings.

'Jules!' one of them said, leaning in to kiss her cheek. 'We were just talking about whether you'd come to the reunion.'

'Did you hear my news?' said another, holding out her hand to show off a gigantic diamond.

They seemed to be warming up for a full session of updates and gossip. The insolence of these women! And yet Mariam saw that Jules would have indulged them had Jomo not whisked her forward, away from them and their greedy eyes. They coveted everything Jules had, and would have taken it all from her again if given the chance.

The Traitors Three: Tiffany, Kashvi, and Wenona. It had been so long now since Mariam had thought of any of them, which was selfish of her, she realized; Jules would never have the luxury of forgetting what they'd done. Those naked images of her still no doubt circulated in the shadiest nooks and crannies of the internet, were probably still in the spank banks of countless disgusting men around the world, and had been seen by almost all their classmates.

This was why Jules had decided to escape to Sweden in their junior spring – to a place where her Illinois family had ancestral links and where few people would notice her among all the other ash-blonde beauties. In regular emails to Mariam and Eloise, she'd described the fishing village where she lived, on the Baltic Sea. There were explosions day and night from the military camp farther along the beach, she'd written, where the Swedes trained ceaselessly, convinced that if the Russians came for them it would be over the sea, from Lithuania.

It had sounded dismal to Mariam. Jules had been the research assistant to a marine biologist in order to get course credit, but she'd spent most of her time helping the local fisherwomen catch and skin eels, which involved putting a wire ring around their necks while they were still alive and ripping it downward to take off their skin. Mariam had never forgotten that image, because it summed up how she imagined Jules felt at that time, as if her own skin had been ripped from her body, leaving her underlying sinew and bone exposed.

The only small mercy had been that the betrayal had happened in an era before social media. It was so low-tech, how the Traitors Three – the T3s, as Mariam thought of them – had done it, spying on Jules naked in her room and taking photographs with a camera that used actual film.

They had claimed afterward that they'd never intended to sell the pictures. That they'd been blackmailed by the guy at the photo store who had developed the prints, who had said he would sell them anyway, without them getting any cut of the profits, if they didn't go along with his plan. They'd said they had taken the photos as a practical joke, that it was harmless fun between friends, as if it were just as easily something Mariam or Eloise could have done.

The university's administrative board had taken disciplinary action. The T3s were forced to take a leave of absence for a semester, and were banned from setting foot on campus during their exile. They'd transferred from Kirkland to Lowell House together after their return and had been pleased to discover that they'd gotten exactly what they'd wanted: a bit of Jules's fame had rubbed off on them, for they were forever after touched by the dark energy of notoriety.

If Jules had a character flaw, Mariam thought, it was that she'd welcomed people like that into her life when she was younger. Back then, Jules had not yet learned the hard way that when classmates approached her as potential friends she was not obliged to respond kindly to their advances. She hadn't wanted to seem stuck-up or choosy, so she'd sometimes fallen in with girls like the T3s, not realizing that often the people most bold in seeking her out were the ones she needed to avoid.

Eloise and Mariam had also, of course, been the beneficiaries of this openness when Jules first arrived at college. There had never been any friendship waiting period with Jules; their mutual bond had been formed on the very first day. Yet they had not approached her, or sought her out – they'd been housed together by the university, which they'd all accepted as a happy accident of fortune.

For Mariam, the worst aspect of the whole fiasco had been that the T3s' initial approach to Jules had been under the banner of *feminism*. They had invited her, sometime during their freshman year, to join them in trying to create a new, all-female final club, to level the uneven playing field of social life at the university. A place where women could go to socialize outside of their dormitories, so that they would not be forced to go en masse to the all-male final clubs, knock on the imposing front doors in their nicest dresses, and beg to be let in by whichever drunk boy answered. At that stage, there were only a couple of sororities on campus, and one struggling women's club that hadn't been able to raise enough money to secure its own building.

The T3s had exploited Jules's latent zealotry. She'd been searching for a principled cause, as if to offset what she sometimes felt was a professional life of Hollywood frivolity and extravagant waste. And in those horrible women and their proposal to start a women's club, Jules thought she'd found it.

She had been pinned beneath their painted little thumbs. She was the one who'd convinced the others that the T3s should be the final three making up their eight-person blocking group, though Mariam and Eloise had voiced reservations. Then the T3s had convinced Jules to put up the seed money for the club, so that they could take out a lease on one of the old buildings in the Square and renovate it.

Later on, other women's clubs were founded by other brave souls, and thrived, but Jules's club was doomed to fail after the leaked nude photos. There had been too many cruel jokes in the media and on campus that all the women planned to do with their own space was frolic around topless in it. There was no recovering from the scandal. Not that the T3s cared – the club had been a ruse to get close to Jules.

Mariam's neglected ice-cream was dripping down the sides of her cone. She watched the Traitors Three head off down the sidewalk, looking glamorous and guilt-free, and felt a torrent of rage sweep through her. One of them, Wenona, looked over her shoulder at Mariam, a backward glance that could have been a smirk. To be honest, Mariam wasn't sure – she needed to update her contact lens prescription, as things had been looking a bit blurred around the edges, but she never seemed to find the time.

Jules, who was still walking up ahead with Jomo, seemed strikingly composed after the encounter. There had been so many other career lows (and highs) for her since then. And what a famous actress had to deal with daily in a hyperlinked, social-media-addicted world was probably so much more intense, Mariam thought, that maybe Jules had let go of any anger she'd once felt toward those three.

Or perhaps she had been prepared to stop and talk to those women who had once tried to ruin her life not because she was weak but because she was stronger than all of them put together. There *was* something different about Jules lately, Mariam thought, looking at her. She'd initially thought it was sadness, but now she saw that she was wrong. It was like a strand of something really tough and unbreakable had been braided into the softer, more fragile person they had known so well all those years ago. Jules's unusually lithe body was an outward expression of some new internal hardness.

A thought floated into her mind: Jules had moved up a notch on the Mohs scale of hardness, something they used to kid Jomo about whenever he went on about it back when he first got into gemology, comparing the durability of rubies and sapphires and other precious gems.

'Who were those women?' Binx said, a bewildered expression on her elfin face.

'Those were the Traitors Three,' Mariam said.

'The traitors who?' Binx said.

'You don't know about the Traitors Three and what they did to Jules?' Mariam said. 'How is that *possible*?'

Eloise shrugged. 'There's a lot we don't know about each other's college years, I guess. Like any couple. Well, maybe not you and Rowan. But that's different.'

Binx began to seem more upset than confused. 'Why wouldn't you tell me?' she said to Eloise. 'We covered all those years for Elly, and you didn't mention it.'

Eloise was staring at Binx with a wide-eyed expression.

Mariam had been married long enough to know exactly what was happening: Eloise was trying to wordlessly signal to Binx to *shut up*. Whatever Binx was talking about – and Mariam did not know who Elly was, or why she was important – Eloise did not want to be having that conversation in front of the others. Binx got the message, and went silent.

They were arranged, by now, in a tableau outside the entrance to the Fly Club on Holyoke Place, finishing their ice-creams.

Mariam noticed that Jomo and Jules's tongues had gone bright blue from the bubblegum flavor, and that was when she began to laugh, and so did the others, everyone except for Binx, whose stern baby-face – Mariam did not mean to patronize her, but she did look so young standing beneath the streetlight in her tunic – made her crack up all over again.

Five minutes later, however, Mariam felt her sense of humor fail as she rapped on the Fly's door with the brass knocker, the thudding dance music muted by the thick walls of the grand old building. She had forgotten how it felt to willingly put herself in a position of abjection, waiting for some guy to deign to open up the door and decide if she was hot enough to be let inside.

Nobody had ever forced her to do this back at college – in fact Rowan had usually begged her not to – and yet on many nights she and her female friends had chosen to stand before this door, or one of the similarly intimidating doors to other final clubs, waiting to be let in. Or, worse, she, Eloise, and Jules had sat in the poky, freezing bicycle-storage room at the bottom of the stairs leading up to the Porcellian Club. This was the stuffiest club of all, not even allowing women to set foot in their plush upstairs quarters except on their wedding nights – when they were allowed to have their metaphorical cherry popped by their Porc Club husband in some room in the attic.

What woman in her right mind would want to spend her wedding night in that place? Especially after putting up with years of assholery from her partner and his Porc Club friends. But then, what woman in her right mind would marry a man who thought that being in the Porc Club was a good idea? The boys who fell for its promise of exclusivity and social superiority tended to be the ones with the weakest sense of self, most needy of external validation.

All the final clubs – even the Spee, which Jomo so loyally defended as being way ahead of the others in its more progressive politics – had always been designed to give young Harvard men their first, heady taste of power.

It was as president of the Spee that Frederick P. Reese II (a name suited more to a German baron than an American silver-spooner, Mariam had often thought) had presided over the black-balling of countless hopeful candidates, and the sometimes brutal hazing of the sophomores who had been selected as the newest members of the club. It was excellent training for someone with dictatorial ambitions. He must have loved being able to decide who should be allowed in and who should forever be kept out, who should be punished and who should be rewarded with favors and appointments.

Beside her on the step outside the Fly, Mariam could sense that Jules, too, had stiffened as they waited for their knocking to be answered. This was exactly why Jules had fallen in with the T3s – so that women did not have to end up standing *here*.

Of course there'd been a lot of criticism of the women's club idea, that it was trying to replicate a flawed, dubious model of social exclusion and dress it up as feminist empowerment. But that had never been Jules's intention. She'd envisioned it as a place where women could stay up late debating ideas, planning their next activist moves in the struggle for gender equality, or just hanging out in a safe space. Ironically, given that one of the major impediments to creating a women's club had been some arcane anti-brothel zoning laws that disallowed all-female establishments in the Square, the T3s had envisioned something very different than Jules had: they'd wanted a girly party pad into which men would be invited to sample the wares, like chocoholics allowed into Willy Wonka's factory.

A guy with bleary, beery eyes finally opened the door to the Fly. It was unclear if he was a graduating senior celebrating his last day as a college student or one of the fifth-reunion alumni hosting the party for his class. What was clear was that he was not in the mood to play nice.

'We're here for the fifth-reunion afterparty,' Binx said from the back of their little pack.

The guy took a long drink from his red plastic cup, keeping the door only slightly ajar so that they couldn't squeeze past him. He took his time assessing Mariam, who was standing closest to him. 'Really? Fifth reunion? Who are we kidding here, people!'

Jomo spoke up. 'Is this really necessary?'

He appraised Jomo, trying to decide whether it was worth taking on someone twice his size. 'Were you a member here?' he said eventually.

That was when Jules decided to drop the J-bomb, as her friends called it. It was a very rare occurrence, something like a solar eclipse, and when it happened, it was just as fascinating to watch.

She stepped forward and took off her baseball cap, shaking out her long hair so that it unfurled and bounced off her shoulders, almost in slow motion. She unzipped her jacket and turned down the collar so that her face was fully visible.

'Let us in, dickhead,' she said, in her mild midwestern accent.

He recognized her, and immediately obeyed. Once they were inside the empty downstairs common room – the party was upstairs, hence why nobody had heard them knocking for so long – he became their obsequious personal servant, getting them drinks from the bar and producing boxes of Noch's pizza, then tip-toeing up the stairs when Jules dismissed him.

Eloise and Binx followed him upstairs into the fifth-reunion fray soon after, but Mariam and Jules decided to make themselves comfortable on the oxblood leather couches in the corner of the common room, cozily lit with antique lamps.

While Jomo messed around on the grand piano, Jules and Mariam ate most of the rest of the pizza, paging with greasy fingers through old Fly Club yearbooks, making fun of the men looking so pleased with themselves, and laughing at the homo-eroticism of the club's Latin motto, which Mariam translated as 'bonds should be lasting, not chafing or hard'.

Jules decided they should rope Jomo into playing the question game, which Mariam had invented sometime during their freshman year.

It was as basic yet compelling as it sounded. Each person took a turn asking the others a question; the only rules were that you didn't answer your own question and you couldn't ask the same question twice. It had, at the time she came up with it, satisfied Mariam's love of deep and meaningful conversation, and it had also made group drinking feel more purposeful.

Jomo didn't enjoy this game, but Jules had always liked it. While it involved sharing intimate things about yourself, that sharing was done within the safety of rules and strictures – a bit like acting, Mariam thought.

Mariam volunteered to go first. 'What is the weirdest thing someone's done while you were having sex?' she asked. Sex questions were always a good warmer-upper, though in fact the answers were usually not that interesting – it was the ones about childhood and family that were most revealing.

Jomo was rubbing his eyes. Mariam knew he was jetlagged, still on London time. Jules, on the other hand, had perked right up – dropping the J-bomb had forced her to fully inhabit her identity, even flaunt it, and it suited her. She ran her fingers through her hair and patted Jomo's leg. 'Ooh, I can answer this one for you,' Jules said. 'And I bet you can answer it for me, too.'

Mariam was amazed: Jules and Jomo had actually slept together? There'd been constant speculation about this during their college years, though each time it had died down quickly in the face of their indignant rebuttals. This was the trouble with modern gender relations, they'd protested. Nobody would believe that a man and a woman could be best friends without secretly wanting to have sex with each other.

'Not *us*,' Jules said, seeing the look on Mariam's face. 'What I mean is, I know all his bad-sex stories, and he knows mine.' She launched into a story about an old flame, one of the few guys she'd dated at college, who had never wanted to ejaculate because he didn't want to corrupt Jules's supposedly pristine femininity. ('Whore/angel much?' had been her classic response to this squeamishness, though it was probably lost on the guy in question.)

As she told the tale, it all came back to Mariam – Jules arriving home early in the morning after her walk of shame, telling Mariam and Eloise about her night while they all shared the bathroom, getting ready for the day.

The things you learn about other people's paramours at college, and carry with you forever, Mariam thought. She even remembered what that guy looked like. She would be able to pick him out in a line-up. If she bumped into him later that weekend, or even decades in the future, at their forty-fifth reunion, the first thing Mariam would think was *Oh yes, Jules's old flame who had a thing about delayed ejaculation.*

Mariam felt sort of lucky that she had no embarrassing stories of her own from random college hook-ups, because there had been none – though she had once shared with Eloise and Jules, early in her relationship with Rowan, a tale about how, in the heat of passion, he'd pulled a tampon from her with his teeth and flung it across the room, undeterred by its presence. That was the moment it had really sunk in for Mariam: *This boy loves me.* It had been a wonderful moment. If a shade gruesome.

Jomo looked as if he were in pain as Jules finished her story. He had always been so protective of her.

'Okay, your turn,' Mariam said to him.

'I can't answer that question,' Jomo said. 'It doesn't feel right. Men aren't as disloyal to their sexual partners as women are. We don't share details the same way. And as a feminist myself, I feel that if a woman makes herself vulnerable to me in an intimate situation, I should respect that vulnerability by keeping whatever happened between us to myself.'

'Seriously?' Jules said.

Jomo smiled. 'Nah. You both already know the answer. I believe you, Mariam, named the girl "pinkie finger Pamela".'

Mariam laughed.

'I'm going to attempt to elevate the tone of this game,' Jomo said. He cleared his throat. 'What is the part of your identity you feel most ambivalent about?'

Jules looked at Mariam to answer first.

Mariam knew what she would say if she could bring herself to tell the truth. That she had begun to develop some sort of religious faith, but didn't yet know whether to trust it as something positive or to reject it as something selfish, bargaining with a higher power in the belief it would keep the people she loved safe.

It didn't make any sense that her faith had followed in the wake of her father's death. That should, really, have been the deal-breaker: that God would take her dad from her before she'd made peace with him.

It was Jomo who should be the new convert. God's existence should have been confirmed for him – his mother had lived.

Mariam loved Jomo as her old friend, but she was not sure she would ever forgive him for having sobbed at her father's funeral the way he had, sitting in one of the pews at the crematorium's chapel, his whole body shaking. He had been crying not from grief but from *relief*. To Mariam, there was something disgraceful about grieving for someone other than the person whose body was lying in the coffin at the front of the room.

So in her response to Jomo's question, she went for the easy answer, one that would let her deflect attention from the real issue. While Jules and Jomo shared another slice of pizza and a cup of red wine, Mariam delivered a soliloquy about her discomfort at being the descendant of Syrian Christians, for being indirectly responsible for what had happened in the civil war in Syria, and the ensuing refugee crisis.

Syrian Christians had traditionally been Assad's allies, she told them. Her father had kept a framed portrait of Assad – first Assad Senior, then Assad Junior – on the wall in his study, and had not taken it down even when details emerged of the deadly Ghouta chemical attack on civilians, including children, and all signs pointed to Assad's government being behind it.

Most Americans knew exactly zero about the conflict, and Mariam confessed to Jules and Jomo that she sometimes mentioned her Syrian heritage in a generalized way, to get the moral upper hand in situations where she knew it would bring her sympathy from a certain kind of well-meaning liberal.

These people would become much friendlier as they imagined Mariam's mother at home in a headscarf, her father rolling out his prayer mat five times a day. They were pleased to be able to show her that she and her family were welcome in their country. And she accepted their goodwill as if she had earned it through some difficult childhood migration as an indigent Muslim, as if she were in daily contact with family members still trapped in Syria, desperate to escape.

The reality – which Jomo and Jules already knew – was nothing like that.

Both of her parents had been born in America. Her family hadn't been wealthy, but they certainly had not been destitute. They hadn't even gone to church while she was growing up – they weren't even *good* Syrian Christians!

Her mother, meanwhile, far from covering her hair with a scarf, wore tight jeans, drank a lot, and got her roots dyed every six weeks. Mariam adored her, though they had little in common except for their green eyes. Since Mariam's father had died, her mother had dated more men than Mariam had dated in her entire life before she'd met Rowan, which was – to be fair – not a lot (exactly two). But still. Her father had only been dead a couple years.

At some stage in her monologue, Mariam began to get emotional. She needed to get home to Rowan and the girls. She was overtired, she explained to the others. She was just like Alexis, she joked – she did not cope well once it was past her bedtime.

Jules walked Mariam to the door of the Fly. 'I know how much you miss your dad,' she said. She'd wrapped up a slice of pizza for Mariam to take back to Rowan, if he was still awake. 'Whatever survival mechanisms you have to get through the mourning period, you need to use them.'

So Jules had seen right through Mariam's little act. Of course she had. This was *Jules*, who was not only preternaturally attuned to when the people around her were dissembling but was as empathetic as it was possible for a human being to be.

It was almost midnight when Mariam reached Kirkland House.

On her way up the stairwell to their suite, she stopped in at the kitchenette one floor below, where she'd stored some milk for Eva's night bottle feed. It would save her or Rowan a trip in about half an hour, she figured, since Eva usually woke at twelve-thirty am.

Another woman was already in there, not someone Mariam recognized from college. She was wearing a terrycloth dressing gown, and her hair – black with a rather becoming white streak – was mussed up from sleep. They smiled at each other, a look of understanding passing between them, both in the same mothers' camp: they may once have been Harvard students at the top of their game, but now all they were was *tired.*

Yet the other woman's expression changed when Mariam took out the carton of cow's milk from the fridge and poured some into a bottle she'd washed earlier and left on the side of the sink to dry.

'Oh . . .' the woman said, looking concerned. 'Would you like some of my breastmilk? I pumped extra earlier today, but my baby didn't drink it all. She's four months, and going through a fussy stage.' She held out a bottle that contained a small amount of yellowish fatty liquid on top of a layer of very watery milk.

Mariam was so surprised by this offer that she did not respond quickly enough to be able to stop the woman from putting the bottle into her hands.

'Please don't feel bad,' the woman said. 'Breastmilk is liquid gold, right? I'd rather it didn't go to waste.' She finished rinsing out her pumping apparatus at the sink, and tied her dressing gown more tightly around her waist. 'Hope you get some sleep. Night.'

Mariam stood there for a while, holding the bottle.

She had done her breastfeeding duty. She'd happily and committedly breastfed both her girls until they'd turned one, then switched to cow's milk on the pediatrician's recommendation. She still discovered bags of frozen breastmilk at the back of their freezer and was amazed to think she had sustained two babies with her own body for a total of two years. But she had not once said anything to another mother on the matter of breastmilk, or formula, or any other milk product. She had been so very disciplined about it, not wanting to contribute to the endless judgments that mothers were subjected to by the wider culture.

She remembered how, after Alexis was born, the woman she'd shared the maternity room with had been unable to breastfeed because she'd had a double mastectomy a few years earlier, after learning she had the BRCA gene. A doctor doing his rounds told this woman she should buy breastmilk, at whatever cost, because otherwise her baby was at higher risk of getting cancer later in life too. This had totally unraveled the new mother (and it was not even scientifically accurate!), and Mariam had heard her sobbing herself to sleep.

The next morning, over breakfast, chatting with this woman about what to read during night feeds, Mariam had recommended a Mary McCarthy novel called *The Group*, a book that Candace Bushnell had used as inspiration for her *Sex and the City* essays.

The Group was one of Mariam's favorite novels. Set in the 1930s (but published in 1963), it followed a set of women graduates from Vassar into their lives after college, and their candid struggles with all the same things that Mariam felt women of her own generation still struggled with: contraception and work and marriage and motherhood.

And breastfeeding! It had been a revelation to see how those newly modern women in the 1930s had turned to breastfeeding in response to their mothers' use of formula, which the daughters thought of as backward.

Yet their mothers had, in fact, been first-wave feminists, who'd decided not to do what *their* mothers had done – sit at home breastfeeding babies – and instead got out there to win the vote for women. This seesawing had continued all through the rest of the twentieth century, with each wave of daughters doing the exact opposite of their moms, in the tug-of-war between the generations.

Mariam's own mother had proudly formula-fed all three of her babies, Mariam included, as an act of second-wave feminist empowerment (though she hadn't ever made it back to work). And Mariam sometimes suspected that all the babies born in the new millennium, who had been so obsessively breastfed – like her daughters – would one day purposefully feed their own babies formula, just to vex their poor mothers who'd wrecked their nerves breastfeeding them for so long.

Mariam looked down again at the bottle she was holding.

She poured the breastmilk down the sink, watching the yellow liquid disappear into the dankest depths of the drain. Then she topped up Eva's cow's milk with hot water, and turned out the light.

Chapter 5: Jomo

Friday morning of Reunion Weekend

(May 25, 2018)

Jomo jogged along the footpath beside the Charles River, thinking about what Mariam had said the previous night about her conflicted identity as a Syrian Christian.

He'd donated thousands of dollars to the International Committee of the Red Cross when the scale of the Syrian civil war and refugee crisis had first become apparent, but he tried not to think about Syria too much anymore. Once upon a time, he'd been a news junkie, addicted to the ups and downs of the latest headlines, but he'd gradually come to see that knowing about the suffering of others did nothing to help reduce it. All it did was make him feel worried all the time, as each fresh tragedy pinged in his pocket.

On the Tube in London, on his way to a meeting with a gem supplier, he'd noticed a poster of a man floating in a choppy sea, looking directly out at the viewer. It was captioned 'Float to Live', and Jomo had assumed it was a call to action to help Syrian refugees, so many of whom had drowned trying to get to Europe. As he'd studied the image, however, he realized the man floating in the water was not a Syrian refugee. He was a white guy in a blue shirt, khakis, and Converse sneakers. The poster was a public service notice from the British government for fans of boating: 'If you fall into water,' the text beneath the image read, 'fight your instinct to swim until the cold water shock passes.'

He'd chuckled about it, though really nothing about death from drowning, under any circumstances, was funny. It was just so rare, as an American, to feel superior to the British – or at least equal to them – in being parochial and sort of idiotic. Spending public money on reminding people how to float! When all around them, the world was going up in flames.

The path Jomo was running along followed the curves of the river. He had so many memories of this route, from all the hours he and Rowan had jogged along it during college, in all seasons, each with its own particular pleasures. In the fall, the great piles of dry leaves and the invigorating freshness of the early-morning air. In winter, the quietness of the snowy paths and the river water frozen into ripples at the banks. In spring, the dappled shade and the air sometimes tipping toward muggy, so that they would arrive back at Kirkland with shirts wet through with sweat.

At each visual milestone along the path – the basketball court, the bridge, the rowing sheds – Jomo could access certain old feelings, as if his mind were remapping itself on the terrain.

Weirdly, for example, while passing the Trader Joe's, he remembered an old shopping list that he'd carried around for a while, maybe during senior year, intending to purchase items to restock the brewery club but never making it to the supermarket. He'd read somewhere that there's a special place in the brain that stores to-do lists that haven't been completed, which would also explain why every time he passed the specialty barbecue store near his loft in Tribeca, he thought: *Get wood chips to smoke the chicken.* Which he had never done, because Jules had told him smoked meat was carcinogenic, and he'd been planning to serve that meal to her.

Another thing he'd stopped doing lately was running to music, to force himself to leave his phone behind. The reluctance with which he did so proved to him how essential it was. Jogging was one of the few times he could decontaminate himself from all the intrusions. Sometimes, as he ran, he imagined all his jumbled thoughts unspooling behind him, out the back of his head, leaving his mind peacefully empty.

Daydreaming was another casualty of the smartphone epidemic. Whenever he had a moment of transitional time – in a cab, say, or walking down the street to get lunch – he wasted it on checking his phone, the slot machine in his pocket, refreshing it constantly to get his dopamine fix.

'The zombie apocalypse is already here!' Eloise often said, unaware perhaps that she'd said it the last time he'd seen her, and the time before that, too. 'Look around and you'll see them everywhere, their eyes glazed over, unseeing, unfeeling, not present at all. Staring into their phones. The digital undead.'

Jomo tended to take a more pro-technology line when arguing with Eloise, just to get her riled up, and also because he felt she was sometimes dismissive of Binx's technological orientation to the world. He couldn't understand why Eloise didn't instead celebrate it; there weren't many people with Binx's abilities in that arena.

But as the years passed and it became ever more evident that a few skinny, spotty, white coders had somehow managed to bend the entire world to their will, he found himself agreeing with Eloise. And her alarmist talk was always backed up with evidence. Every study done on the impact of non-stop use of smartphones

(Eloise had in fact authored one herself) had found the same thing: a sharp decline in every kind of complex happiness available to humans, and a commensurate increase in anxiety. Like lemmings, he and everybody he knew had followed these new gadgets right to the edge of the cliff of reason, and then jumped off.

Now that he was warmed up, his body felt good, despite the fact that he hadn't slept much the night before. He'd got back to his room in the early hours of the morning. It had been pretty low-key at the Spee, once he'd finally made it there after the Fly, unable to persuade Jules – by then yawning her head off – to join him. Maybe earlier in the night there'd been crazy dancing, but by the time he got to the club, men and women were conversing quietly beneath the giant stuffed bear.

Some of the college-age women, he'd assumed, were fully-fledged members themselves now, staying on after graduation for summer jobs or internships in Boston. As a result, the difference in the atmosphere between the Fly and the Spee was unmistakable. He'd felt a pride he knew was laughable at the sight of two women behind the old wooden bar, helping themselves – with familiarity – to the offerings in the famously well-stocked cabinets. And as he'd been about to leave, a young woman had let herself in the red front door with her very own key.

Maybe that's why Jules hadn't wanted to come with him to the Spee, he thought. Would she experience it as an affront to everything she had endured in trying – but failing – to establish a women-only final club? His heart, already beating fast from the pace he was setting, sped up at thoughts of her humiliation all those years ago. How bravely she had suffered. He had never seen those naked photos of her, even though Mariam and Eloise had wanted him to look at them when they first appeared on some random website, in order to understand what Jules was dealing with.

He *had* seen Jules naked since, but in a very different context: skinny-dipping in the Hamptons, all of them leaping into the pool by the light of the moon.

He knew her body fairly intimately, as best friends do. She had a mole on her lower back that she worried about for occasionally being itchy. He'd held her hair out of her face while she vomited, wearing nothing but a silk slip, when she'd got Bali belly during his visit to her film set in Indonesia.

And on their trip to Tanzania, the previous summer, they'd both gone totally feral while camping on the hot plains of the Serengeti. Sleeping in their underwear because of the heat, taking turns to keep watch as they each peed right outside their tent in the night, too afraid of lions to venture to the pit toilet at the edge of the unfenced campsite. She hadn't shaved her armpits for the duration of the trip; he remembered how soft her hair was as it grew out, how uninhibited she had been, wearing a tank top and taking photos of an approaching thunderstorm out the open roof of the Land Rover.

He'd still been trying then to make sense of 'the lost months', as he thought of them. Even when she'd been in the most immersive film environments, she'd always stayed in touch with him. In the past, Jomo had prided himself on being her lifeline in those sometimes suffocating subcultures.

He knew how much social energy it took for her to establish herself with the other actors and crew on each new project, to do all the backstage bonding that was required. He had seen first-hand, on his visits to her sets, the trials she endured living in a new city or country, far from home comforts. He knew she struggled at the end of each shoot, when she was forced to emerge from the cocoon that she'd created and move on, almost immediately, to some new set, some new project, some new group of people with whom she had to bond from scratch. In some ways, Jomo thought, it was like experiencing college over and over, in smaller stints but with the same cycle of newness–intimacy–farewell, and he'd sometimes envied that, even while knowing the toll it took on her emotionally.

Then there were the difficulties of rejoining those past colleagues, often a long time after the end of a shoot, for the ever-extended global publicity circus, and trying to recapture a closeness that had long since evaporated. Without the stabilizing, grounding influence of the crew around them, the gods and goddesses of Hollywood were often on their worst behavior during those tours, their egos fueled by the media and the fans. This was when Jules was most vulnerable to her bouts of depression – which she berated herself for all the more keenly because they came right when the rest of the world was telling her how good she had it, how much they wanted to be *her*.

Jomo had lived through it all with Jules, counseled her many times through each phase. So there was no good reason why she had stopped communicating with him for the first few months of 2017 unless she'd been trying to keep something secret. And what secret worth keeping did not involve romantic love?

This was what had truly terrified him, though he'd always known it would – and should – happen one day. On that trip to Tanzania, he had searched constantly for telltale signs that Jules had fallen in love for the first time in her life. But he'd asked her nothing directly, not wanting to ruin their trip; he was so thrilled, after all, that she'd kept their old pact, coming with him on his pilgrimage to the place where his dad had spent most of his childhood and young adulthood.

Most people got it the wrong way around when they heard Jomo's dad had grown up in Africa, assuming his father was black.

But in fact his mom was African-American and his dad was white, born to German parents who had moved to newly independent Tanzania – then Tanganyika – during the presidency of Julius K. Nyerere, who had been one of the greatest and most humane leaders in history. According to family legend, Jomo was supposed to have been named after him – his father's idea – but his mother hadn't liked the name, so they'd compromised instead on Jomo, the given name of the first president of independent Kenya. (Jules had teased him about his name ever since she'd discovered, on their trip, that Jomo meant 'flaming spear'.)

Jomo's German grandfather had been a filmmaker, and he had uprooted his family from Frankfurt to make the first film of the majestic wildebeest migration across the plains of the Serengeti, which had turned out to be very influential in the wildlife conservation cause. He'd had a small plane painted to look like a zebra, with black and white stripes – Jomo was never sure, looking at pictures of it, if this was for decoration or camouflage – and he'd worked closely with Nyerere to support his visionary conservation policies.

Jomo had been raised on stories of his dad's idyllic childhood and teenagerhood, though it was later marred by tragedy. His dad's older brother had, at the age of 21, been killed in a plane crash while doing an aerial wildlife survey. Soon afterward, his mother had died of malaria, though the family always said she had died of grief.

Mother and son had been buried together at the rim of the Ngorongoro Crater. Many decades later, when Jomo's grandfather had died in Frankfurt, his body had been transported to Tanzania so that he could be buried beside them. Jomo had not gone to that burial – nor to the service in Germany – because he'd been about to sit his SAT exams, and his parents had insisted he focus on his studies and college applications. It was the way of the modern American teenager, encouraged to put achievement before all else, yet Jomo had always regretted not properly farewelling his grandfather.

Maybe that was why the bushpigs episode had felt so charged. The tent in which he and Jules had held each other in terror was only a few hundred feet away from the cairn that marked the spot where his family members were buried.

He had been dreaming, that night in the tent, that he and Jules were about to jump off a building still under construction and, in the unlogic of dreamland, he'd known that if he had four weights tied to his ankles, he would die. As they fell, Jules called out, 'How many weights?' And he'd looked down and said, 'Four. Goodbye, my friend.'

He'd woken just before he hit the ground, to the loud grunts of bushpigs surrounding their tent. He could see their shadows too – it was a full-moon night; earlier they had watched the orange moon rise above the crater.

For the first time, the word 'petrified' made sense to him. He had turned into stone. Jules, he soon realized, was also awake, and also lying very still, listening to the grunts outside. That afternoon, as they'd been pitching their tent a bit farther away from the other members of their tour, the guide, Mburi, had cautioned against it. Of all the dangerous wild animals in the bush, he'd said, the ones to be most afraid of were the carnivorous bushpigs found there at the crater. They came out at night to look for meat of any kind, and had huge tusks they used to rip through tents to get at the humans inside.

They'd ignored Mburi and carried on with pitching their tent at a distance, needing some respite from the constant surveillance of the other tourists, starstruck by Jules.

Does my dream signify something? Jomo had thought as he and Jules edged toward each other, away from the sides of the tent. *Is this how it ends for us?* He had planned out how he would roll over Jules to protect her from being gored if the bushpigs on her side of the tent made the first attack. They had clung to each other for what felt like hours, until the tent's walls went bright at dawn.

'I was only joking!' Mburi had said at breakfast, after they'd described their brush with death to the others at the table. 'Bushpigs eat worms!'

Mburi did not stop laughing as he drove the Land Rover all the way down the precipitous slope that led to the bottom of the crater, though the road had been partially washed away and he later told them that cars often toppled off it. (This time they weren't sure whether to believe him.)

Of all the magical days on their trip, that one had been touched with special grace. Their relief at having survived the night had made their senses more acute, and deepened the intimacy between them. Jomo remembered how the air down in the lushly vegetated crater was still cool, how peaceful it was – green walls rising above them, enclosing them. Reading about it in his *Let's Go* guidebook, he'd thought he might feel claustrophobic down there, trapped in an accident of geography, a bowl of earth from which animals could not escape, but it had been the opposite. It was a place he had never wanted to leave.

The abundance of wildlife had been astounding: hippos, hundreds of wildebeest, buffalo, hyena, jackals, rhinos, impala, and lions surveying the fertile domain from an outcrop of rocks. They'd seen a pregnant cheetah resting in the shade, and two male zebras fighting, trying to bite each other, and a baby rhino following its mother. Jules had identified a pair of dik-diks, small antelope that mate for life and only ever have two babies. She had smiled as she watched the family of four timidly stepping through the dewy grass. An elderly male elephant – at least sixty years old, Mburi had said – with tusks so large he could rest them on the ground, had stood across the road, blocking their way for a long time, as if to make a point.

So many people had asked Jomo, on his return to New York, what the highlight of the trip had been. It would have been easy for Jomo to tell the bushpig story at his own expense, and follow it with a description of their morning at the bottom of the Ngorongoro Crater, spinning it into a mythical yarn that anybody who'd seen *The Lion King* would be able to visualize. But he'd never told anybody else about the bushpigs, or that morning on the floor of the crater, because he wanted to keep those memories just between him and Jules.

Jomo stopped to drink from a water fountain along the path. He was close to MIT by now. The sunlight was glorious after the endless winter they'd had in New York, and he was tempted to take off his shirt. Then he remembered he had the ring in his breast pocket. He touched it through the fabric, and the accusing gem pushed back against his fingers.

While he and Jules were both waiting to use the bathroom that morning (Mariam and Rowan had been in there forever with the girls, who'd shrieked their protests at having their hair washed), he'd invited Jules to come jogging with him, but that morning she was speaking on one of the panels organized by the alumni association. The topic of the panel was 'Women in Entertainment in the #MeToo Era'. He hadn't known she was doing this – in the online program, there had been only an amusing placeholder term, 'intellectual content', for the Friday morning's official events.

Jules had insisted he go for his run and meet her afterward for lunch. But he should have gone with her to the panel. He knew she disliked doing that kind of thing but felt obliged: Harvard had let her in, therefore she felt she should say yes to anything they asked of her in return.

Even after more than two decades of being famous, Jules still wasn't comfortable with her role as a shadow diplomat. She'd become an actress because she liked slipping into other people's skins, but as a result of her fame she was constantly asked her opinion on things of national, even international, importance. She *did* have good ideas about things like global governance, but she had learned over the years that people did not really want her to answer their questions honestly. They didn't want a thoughtful or complex against-the-grain answer. They wanted politico-speak or liberal-speak; they wanted her to mouth the sentiments of a mildly left-leaning Hollywood star but not go any further.

Why hadn't he gone with her to the panel? Jomo took off again along the path, at an even more punishing pace. He knew why: because he was upset she had forgotten it was his birthday today.

None of his blockmates had remembered, it seemed. He couldn't blame Rowan and Mariam, who were overwhelmed by parenting duties, and Eloise had a lot on her plate too, hosting the welcome drinks, and promoting her book. All he'd received so far that morning was a call from his parents and a flood of automatic 'Happy Birthday!' messages on Facebook, which meant nothing.

But for Jules to forget really did hurt.

On her most recent birthday, in December, he had visited her on set in New Zealand. Not wanting her to think he had gone too far out of his way to be there, he'd said he was keen to buy some pounamu, a distinctive, non-precious gemstone, with a bright green color like limeskin when polished.

She had been in the middle of filming on a small, very avant-garde film, which she'd told him was about the many forms of revenge people take on one another for perceived wrongs, from the most personal to the political. In the climactic scene, a corrupt leader was pulled apart – drawn and quartered, like in medieval times – by those he had wronged. By the end of the day's filming, Jules had been slimy with fake blood.

It was the type of project she seemed to have been increasingly drawn to in the last year and a half. When she had finally reconnected with him after the lost months, she'd said she had been overseas doing pre-production and scouting for locations for a film about Russian interference in elections around the world, which she was planning to direct as well as act in. (In Tanzania, unable to help himself, Jomo had paged through her passport while she was napping. There were no foreign stamps for any of those months, no evidence she had left the country then at all.)

The production in New Zealand had been amateurish in comparison to the film sets he was used to visiting. It had worried him. He knew that as actresses aged, the roles available to them – completely unfairly – began to shrink, and he had wondered if Jules's turn away from the more commercial movies she'd made earlier in her career, toward low-budget, indie productions, was a reflection of that.

Jules had always said to him that she would have to reinvent herself all the time if she wanted to have staying power in an industry with such a short-term memory. Her success had come to her in her mid-teens, as the heroine of a series of films based on comic books that had been popular back in the 1940s, about a girl who could make herself invisible to fight evil enemies. But the heroine's invisibility (and anonymity) came at a price, for she never got any credit for making the world a better, safer place.

Jules had invited him to visit her on that spectacular set, while she was filming the final sequel in the series, during the summer between their sophomore and junior years. It was in Toronto, in a giant warren of soundstages. He'd had to get through five separate security screenings before they'd let him into her dressing room. That first time, Jomo had never been on a set before. Everything was exactly as he'd imagined: a chair with her name on it, towering cellophane-wrapped hampers filled with candy and fruit, flowers everywhere.

Jules had done her best to put him at ease, even as she was being attended by a squad of stylists for her next scene. He'd sensed they did not want him there, that his presence threatened their ability to properly prepare Jules for what she needed to do, which was become someone else for a while. Watching her being outwardly transformed – by the make-up, the wig – he'd found himself wondering: once she'd made space for these other selves in her consciousness, did she ever succeed in kicking them back out?

And then, after she'd been spirited away by her handlers, he had screwed up by walking straight across a soundstage covered with sand in intricate patterns, leaving his big clumsy footprints behind. The whole production had lost a half day of shooting as the sand was swept and re-patterned; even the director had taken a moment out of his busy schedule to curse at Jomo. It had been mortifying.

Jules found it funny, and he was relieved that nobody blamed her for inviting an inexperienced friend to visit. She was adored on set, and rightly so, for being kind to everybody from the bottom of the food chain right up to the top, often baking cookies and bringing them to the crew on night shoots even when she wasn't scheduled to appear in a scene herself.

It had been a useful 'learning inflection point', to use the language of his mostly useless MBA, to see how a workplace could become impenetrable to outsiders. A film set was an extreme example, of course, because it consisted of bringing together loosely affiliated people for a short amount of time and putting them under extreme creative pressure. But it was one of the mistakes he felt he and his original business partner had made.

They'd met at business school. In the excitement of their rapid initial success after launching House of Riehl Luxury Jewelers, they'd become more and more insular in how they operated. They'd treated outsiders as threats instead of opportunities, as if everybody they met wanted to steal a piece of the action, or had ulterior motives. All along, it was his business partner who'd been the snake in the grass, though it had taken Jomo a while to see it. His partner had wanted to keep others out because he didn't want any scrutiny of how he was managing the company's finances, a responsibility Jomo had ceded to him all too willingly so that he could get on with being a gemologist.

At least he hadn't let Jules talk him into letting her wear one of the company's signature pieces on the red carpet. It was one of the few decisions from that time he didn't regret. She'd wanted to support him with the media exposure, but he'd stayed strong and said no, though each time it had been the occasion for another fierce bust-up between him and his business partner. And thank God he had – somehow – kept a clear enough mind to know it would ruin something between them if he ever asked Jules for a favor like that.

The path diverted away from the tree-lined river for a stretch, forcing him to run beside the busy Memorial Drive.

A truck drove past covered with words of meaningless wisdom: *Harmony is good for the soul. True sincerity is unfakeable. If you want a meaningful life, make meaning in somebody else's.* Along the side of the truck was the phrase 'OUR MINERAL WATER IS MILLIONS OF YEARS OLD'. A company that sold water in plastic bottles was trying to put a positive spin on being the face of wrongdoing in the environmentalist era.

Jomo had drunk hundreds of bottles of mineral water in his life, if not thousands. He was definitely responsible for a portion of the giant plastic trash vortex, wherever it now happened to be floating in the ocean, choking turtles and seabirds.

Jesus. He focused on his breathing again.

Why was he always searching for signs these days, clues that he was on the right path in his life?

It made him feel marginally better to admit it was not a new thing. He'd always been susceptible to suggestions that one's destiny was writ large, if you knew the right place to look. The first real romance he'd read as a young teenager, after all, had been *Romeo and Juliet*, and he had been indelibly marked by the idea that, if lovers could be star-crossed, it was also within the stars' power to give their blessing. It had been heartening to think that finding his soul mate was not really within his power – it was about waiting for the stars to align.

The very first conversation he'd had with Jules had been about this, more or less – the sappiness more forgivable at age 19 than it was at 38.

His freshman fall, he'd decided to take one of the longest-running Harvard courses, a science core called Astronomy 101. The two professors who co-taught it, both eminent astronomers, were getting on in years, and there were whispers it might be the last year they'd be up to the task. It was a mega-class – hundreds of students packed into a Science Center auditorium for lectures – but the weekly discussion sections were broken down into groups of ten.

Jomo was told to meet the section instructor at midnight at the small observatory station built on top of the Science Center's flat roof. It was all rather cloak-and-dagger, but this was why the course was popular.

On the cloudless night in question, Jomo had studied until late at Lamont Library, then walked across the mostly empty campus to the Science Center. When he reached the observatory, the instructor was talking to a very beautiful girl with blonde hair and pale skin, who looked as if she was wearing a bulky winter coat over pajamas. At first, Jomo thought she looked familiar because he knew her from high school or something, and he'd smiled at her warmly, waiting for his brain to remember her name, and then it had: *This is Juliet Hartley! In her pajamas!!!*

Jules must have been used to this response, because she'd ignored Jomo's sudden woodenness and taken notes as the instructor, a shaggy-bearded grad student, showed them how to use the telescope to make observations of Neptune.

They had half an hour, the instructor said, before the next pair of students would arrive to use the telescope, and then it was up to Jomo and Jules to show them how to do it; he was going home to bed.

Jules had taken charge, plugging in cords and turning knobs. She opened up the shutter in the dome, which creaked and groaned until it ground to a halt, revealing a small circle of the night sky. She consulted a thickly bound manual – the *Astronomical Almanac*, which listed planetary positions – and said something he couldn't understand about celestial coordinates.

Jomo had been unable to do anything useful, stunned to be in such close proximity to a woman whose life experience, even at her young age, was so much more complicated and interesting than his own.

She had figured out how to use all that equipment without even breaking a mental sweat. It would have taken him the entire night to get it set up if he'd been there alone. *Am I too dumb to be at Harvard?* he'd wondered. *Too dumb to ever impress the extraordinary woman beside me?*

Jules had swapped out the telescope's eyepiece, explaining to Jomo that it was best to use the one with the widest field of view, and located Neptune with ease. 'There it is!' she'd exclaimed. 'It's so tiny. Hardly distinguishable from a star with this old telescope. It's in opposition right now, which means the earth is directly between it and the sun. It rose at sunset and will be up all night, so I don't know why we had to come at midnight. To test our commitment to the class, I guess.'

When Jomo looked through the eyepiece, his eyes had taken a while to adjust. Jules stayed close beside him to help him focus the lens, and that was when he'd first noticed that her hair smelled like lavender and lemons. It had been difficult for him to concentrate on the miniature bluish dot of Neptune, floating at the outermost edge of the solar system.

They'd taken some measurements, and filled in a worksheet for the class, and then they'd waited for the next two students to arrive.

'What star sign are you?' Jomo had asked her, and regretted it instantly. He'd just been trying to make conversation, but the question seemed nosy, intrusive, as if he were fishing for her date of birth.

'Sagittarius,' she said, not seeming to mind the question. 'And you?'

'I'm a Gemini. Our star signs are similar. We like being independent.'

'You really believe in that stuff?'

'Sort of,' he said. His parents had bought him a subscription to *Astrology All-Stars* for his eighteenth birthday, not something he had told any of his friends back home in DC. One of the dilemmas posed by his new life at college had been whether to update his subscription so it was sent to him at Harvard, risking the mirth of his new roommates.

Jules was paging idly through the almanac, looking at the numbered charts and diagrams. 'Do you remember when Voyager 2 did the fly-by of Neptune, in 1989?' she said. 'My parents let me stay up all night to watch the PBS special.'

'Mine too,' Jomo said. 'My favorite part was when they played the children's voices on the golden record Carl Sagan put on the Voyager. The one with messages for aliens.'

'My mother actually helped to write the text for President Carter's greeting on that record,' Jules said. 'She was one of his cultural advisers in the late seventies. She's still getting over her disappointment that I went into acting instead of setting my sights on becoming the first female president.'

She glanced shyly at him, and Jomo had understood she was waiting for him to ask what the message had been. 'Do you remember it?' he said.

And then, as if wrapping an unseen cloak around her shoulders, she had stepped into character and been transformed into a graceful lone envoy sent from earth into space.

'This is a present from a small, distant world,' she had recited in her mellifluous voice, looking directly at Jomo, as if he were the extraterrestrial she had been sent to find. 'A token of our sounds, our science, our images, our music, our thoughts, and our feelings. We are attempting to survive our time so we may live into yours.'

Jomo had slowed down his running pace without realizing it, caught up in this dense net of recollections – *we are attempting to survive our time so we may live into yours* – and all of a sudden, he was overtaken by another jogger on the path.

From the back, the guy looked familiar, but it was only when two Secret Service agents came jogging after him that Jomo realized it was Frederick Reese.

Fred had not recognized him. Or maybe he had, and decided to overtake Jomo on purpose, as an act of one-upmanship.

Looking at Fred's wide shoulders, his easy gait as he accelerated into the distance, Jomo felt the same old frustration: of all the final clubs Fred could have joined at college, why had he picked the Spee? Now that Fred had shown the world his true colors, the fact that he'd once been president of the Spee had become a mark against them all.

The night before, Jomo had been relieved that Fred wasn't at the club, and he'd hoped it might mean he wasn't coming to the reunion, assuming he wouldn't be welcome. But of course that was not how these things worked. Fred would always be made to feel welcome here.

Many of their classmates – except for the ones who'd been brave enough to publicly note their contempt in the Red Book – were probably thrilled at having Fred among them. Fred's status and power, even if it was in support of wrongdoing, made certain types of people feel that they too had status and power, by association. They'd all dined out on stories of what he'd been like at college, even if they hadn't known him well.

As someone had cynically remarked to Jomo at Eloise's welcome drinks the night before, the general feeling seemed to be that it was always worth keeping powerful people on your side.

Jomo knew he had no right to judge others too harshly, given that in his own work – creating luxury jewelry for the highest end of the market – he was enriching himself by ravaging the earth.

He could spin it otherwise, of course, if pressed, and describe himself as a niche scientist, a passionate gemologist who brought works of art to life. He had often, in a bind, quoted Pliny the Elder to elevate what he did: 'For a great many people, a single gemstone alone is enough to provide the highest and most perfect aesthetic experience of the wonders of nature.'

It was official, Jomo thought gloomily, maintaining an even distance behind Fred: he was a hypocrite.

Take the way he was always an apologist and a booster for the existence of final clubs. In their years at college, the clubs had dominated social life on campus, doing whatever they liked within the secrecy of their ivy-strewn walls. The university had little sway over the management of the clubs. They were privately owned and endowed, run like independent fiefdoms by generations of Harvard men, the oldest of whom were now panicking over the university's attempt to ban any clubs that refused to make their membership criteria gender-neutral. Some of the clubs were lawyering up and hiring PR firms to fight the university administration; others were grudgingly letting women in.

Jomo was always pointing out to his blockmates that the Spee had made the change without being forced into it at gavelpoint, but he knew that at its core the entire final-club system was fundamentally unfair. The slow victories over the decades of having Jewish men, men of color, openly gay men, and now women allowed in as members (to some clubs) did not mean anything of substance had necessarily changed.

Letting women into the Spee had not been smooth sailing, for instance; he'd heard that the first time sophomore women had 'punched' for membership alongside men, in 2015, many of them had felt they were being judged on their appearance and willingness to flirt with existing members. A Spee alum had recently commented to Jomo that the women should be grateful to be allowed through the front door instead of being forced to enter through the servants' entrance, like at the other clubs. Which was not exactly something to brag about.

Even his relationship with Fred was more self-serving than Jomo cared to admit. He and Fred had been friendly at college. They'd punched the Spee together, had been seated side by side at the celebratory dinner the night they were accepted as members. There'd been some tension after the Eloise situation – though what exactly had happened between them was unclear – but still, Jomo had spent countless nights hanging out with Fred, loosely interacting with the same people. They had not been close friends, and he hadn't voted for Fred when he ran for club president, but if he showed up at the Spee tonight, Jomo would feel obliged to greet him and shake his hand.

What was even worse was that Jomo owed Fred something – and owed President Reese something, too.

When Jomo had been applying to MBA programs, concerned that his inconsistent undergraduate grades might negatively affect his applications, he'd swallowed his pride and called in any favor he could, activating every possible node in his school and college networks. He knew he needed to include three letters of recommendation so glowing they were practically radioactive, from the most powerful people he could access.

Back then, Fred's father had not yet become a hated man (by those in Jomo's social circle, anyway). He'd been a buffoon, of course, but a rather beloved and indulged one – people had a soft spot for him and his eighties-era excesses; his gauche, gaudy hotels. He'd been well connected among businesspeople of a certain shady breed, and got a kick out of plugging his son's friends into the circuit boards of power.

So one New York spring morning, metaphorical hat in hand, Jomo had gone to see him, the meeting arranged on his behalf by Fred.

Reese Senior had been on the phone when Jomo stepped out of the private elevator and into the hall of his Park Avenue penthouse. Reese's booming voice had carried out to him, and perhaps he'd planned it that way; by keeping Jomo waiting for half an hour the objective of rubbing his nose in Reese's importance had been achieved.

Jomo had vivid memories of their encounter after being let into the inner sanctum. The thick stalk of celery in the bloody mary Reese had offered him, though it was barely ten am. A large painting of Reese's newest wife in nothing but a string of pearls. Broadway playbills with their iconic yellow and black lettering, framed and hung on every square inch of the living-room walls. Jomo had asked Reese which play had been his favorite. Reese had thought for a while, then responded, '*Gem of the Ocean.*'

It was a play Jomo happened to know well. He and Jules had gone together to Chicago for the premiere of August Wilson's masterpiece, and Jomo remembered being struck by the fact that Wilson had been the child of a white German immigrant father and an African-American mother, just as he was.

Reese's reply had thrown Jomo. Either he had better taste in theater than he did in most other things, or he was demonstrating that he knew a lot more about Jomo than it might at first appear. Awkwardly crunching on his celery-stick stirrer, Jomo had been impressed by this hint at a more complex inner life.

Yet when the duplicate letter of recommendation arrived, a month later, just in time for Jomo's application deadlines, he saw Reese had been going for something else: humiliation. The instructions from Jomo had been for Reese's secretary to email the letter directly to the schools to which he was applying, but Reese had clearly wanted Jomo to see it for himself:

> We all know the struggles the black man of today must undergo to rise up from under the weight of family neglect and the temptation of a life of crime. Jomo is one of the most motivated, polite and ambitious young African-American men I've had the pleasure of meeting.

Jomo jogged faster as his outrage at this recollection grew.

And yet this toxic letter had done the trick. Jomo had been accepted into all of his top-choice schools. And when Reese Senior had later sent him a direct email, urging him to get in touch with an associate's son also doing his MBA at Berkeley, Jomo had not only become friends with that guy, he'd made him his business partner.

As Jomo's feet pounded on the path, the name of the main character in the August Wilson play returned to him. Aunt Ester. The soul cleanser. She helps a young man get to the City of Bones, aboard the slave trader called *Gem of the Ocean*.

Across the river on Storrow Drive, the traffic was speeding along the highway toward Boston's city center, everybody in a rush to get somewhere. Thoreau's immortal words came to Jomo's mind. 'It is not enough to be industrious; so are the ants. What are you industrious about?'

Early on, when Reese was first elected president, and Fred was appointed as one of his senior advisers, Jomo had chosen to believe that Fred was aware of the threat his father posed – maybe more aware than anybody else – and was getting involved to try to minimize the damage. It had been no secret, during his college years anyway, that he and his father did not see eye to eye.

Yet at some stage, Jomo had realized he was wrong. Fred's presence beside his father, as a supposedly intelligent and respected Harvard graduate, did not act as a corrective – it legitimized the reign of a bully President.

Jomo increased his pace. He was going to catch up to Fred Reese, and he was going to overtake him. It began to feel like a quest of mythic proportions. If he could just run fast enough to pass Fred, maybe he could find the courage for other acts of insubordination, though he was too out of breath right then to decide what they might be.

His legs burned, his lungs protested. A stitch began to form just under his rib cage. His shins ached with each footfall. But it was worth it, because Jomo was gaining on Fred, who had taken off his shirt, his pink back glistening with sweat. Jomo ignored the pain he was in and put his head down for a final push, launching into a full sprint.

He was hit suddenly from the side by a solid, vicious blur. Some sort of beast lifted him up and off the path and toward the grassy shoulder.

While he was airborne, he experienced, for a few milliseconds, the fabled elasticity of time, and it seemed to him that he had forever to figure out a way to land that would result in the least amount of bodily damage. He also noticed – as if he were in zero gravity and it had simply floated out of his pocket – the ring moving in its own, separate arc, on a different trajectory from his own. The light catching the gem reminded him of the otherworldly, violet-gray hue of storm clouds at sunset.

He landed hard.

It took him a moment to figure out that one of Fred Reese's Secret Service men had tackled him to the ground. This man and Fred's second bodyguard now loomed above him.

He decided to lie very still. He spoke to the men in a calm voice, reassuring them he was on a recreational jog, nothing more, that he was here for his college reunion, that he and Fred had been classmates. That he'd been trying to catch up to him so that he could say hello to his old friend.

Finally, Fred approached, his footsteps heavy on the path; he must have turned around, or been summoned by his men. Jomo tried to paste onto his face the most non-threatening expression he could muster, but in that instant, he wanted to tear Frederick P. Reese II apart with his own two hands.

At first, Fred's eyes were blank. Then, as recognition dawned, Jomo saw something else pass across Fred's features. Amusement? Satisfaction at having put Jomo in his place? At demonstrating, once again, his power over him?

Fred nudged past his security detail and leaned over Jomo, offering his hand. It was the very last thing that Jomo wanted to do – touch this man's damp flesh, let him pull him up from the ground. But he took Fred's hand and was lifted up and onto his feet.

Fred tried to make a joke of it. 'You're too fit, man,' he said. 'Couldn't have you catching up to me, now, could we?'

He slapped Jomo on the back, in the same place where his bodyguard had slammed Jomo's body into the grass. 'See you later. Maybe at the Club?' he said, and jogged off, easily falling back into his regular pace, his men following in formation behind him.

Jomo stood there, silently watching them until they had become nothing but miniature figures in the distance, as insubstantial as a child's drawing. Once they had disappeared from view, he brushed the dirt off his knees and elbows, checking for injuries.

He walked over to a bench beneath a cherry tree and sat down to stare at the slow-moving water of the Charles River.

Even if he didn't say a word about this to Jules later, she would sense his distress and be present with him in a way nobody else in his life was. She had always been prepared to meet him halfway emotionally, wherever he needed to be met.

The shock of what had just happened had knocked a strange new thought into his head.

Why had he not seen it before? He was in love with Jules, and had been since that very first night on the roof of the Science Center, when she'd recited the message her mother had written from Jimmy Carter to the aliens.

Yet he'd never been able to admit it to himself, let alone to her. He had been afraid she would think he was in love with her because she was a famous actress, not because of the way her mind worked or her search for a bigger cause she could give herself over to. Her endearing brittleness when she was tired. Her laugh. Her smell. The shape of her soul.

For so long – for too long – he had believed that fame had put Jules on the other side of the river of life. While she could wave and shout to him from the opposite bank, and try to tell him what it was like, he would never really know unless he swam across and joined her there, which was impossible. But now he realized he had been an idiot to assume it was a gap that real love could not close.

Over the years, as he had become more and more committed to being her best friend, he had actively snuffed out every erotic spark between them before it had the chance to burst into flame.

He gingerly stood up from the bench, testing his body.

The ring.

He made a bargain, right then and there, with Fate: if he found his grandmother's ring, he would accept it as the final sign he'd been waiting for that he and Jules were meant to be together.

Chapter 6: Mariam

Friday morning of Reunion Weekend

(May 25, 2018)

Mariam was starting to worry, as she pushed Eva in her stroller and Alexis scootered beside them, that none of the other mothers among her classmates would want to talk to her at the children's festival in Radcliffe Quad.

Earlier that morning, in the few minutes she'd had to herself, she'd taken a quick look at the Red Book and been horrified to discover that Rowan had boasted in his entry about her natural births. Why hadn't she checked what he'd written before he submitted it? She should have learned her lesson after the disaster of his entry for the tenth-anniversary report, which had been a stream-of-consciousness witnessing of Alexis's birth, replete with details about Mariam's 'ring of fire' as the baby's head crowned. Mariam flushed with shame at the thought of it.

Rowan had not paid any heed to the scorn his entry might attract from other women in their class, who might feel their own choices were being undermined. As with the feeding question,

Mariam had worked hard to stay neutral on the topic of birth, on anything to do with mothering.

Outwardly neutral, that is. When it came to her private opinions on these topics, it was a bloodbath of no-holds-barred judgment. So long as she didn't say what she was thinking out loud, she felt she was doing her bit as a good, non-judgy feminist.

Mariam's saving grace was that the Class Report had the weight and girth of the Bible, with text about that small, too. It was probably safe to assume that very few mothers of young children had found time to crack open its spine.

It was only mid-morning and already it was hot. She stopped to put sunscreen on the girls, which Eva resisted with every fiber of her being, and to make them drink from their water bottles, which elicited protests from Alexis: she wanted apple juice.

Mariam felt a niggling irritation at having to solo parent for the morning. Normally, Fridays were her day off from parenting. Rowan had negotiated a four-day workweek, leaving the school in the capable hands of his deputy on Fridays, so that Mariam could do one day as an educator at the Rising Dough Collective.

She knew the gig was beneath her skills, but it didn't matter. She treasured every moment there. In the collective's kitchen, teaching hapless teenagers how to bake bread and pastries, she felt connected to the best parts of her pre-kids career, when she'd worked with a talented group of women in the test kitchen of the domestic goddess then conquering Manhattan, Ursula Burton-Hughes.

After Alexis was born, Mariam had not gone back to that job. By choice, technically. It had been unthinkable that she would leave her six-week-old baby with someone else all day. So in fact it wasn't really by choice; she was just wired that way. She understood that for women who went back to work, even if they didn't desperately need to for financial reasons, it must feel the same:

unthinkable that they would give up a career in order to hang around all day in the company of a baby. The goal of feminism, surely, had been to give women the ability to act on these individual preferences and predilections.

But with Eva she'd felt different. By the time she came along, Mariam had been full-time parenting Alexis for almost four years, and she wasn't sure she could do it all over again, not at the same voltage. When Eva was six months old, Mariam had applied for the one-day-a-week position at the collective. She had set herself the goal of making it to Eva's second birthday, and then she planned to send her to day care at least two days a week and ask for more work.

The problem was, with her low wages, she would essentially be paying for the privilege of working: the day-care fees would be higher than her monthly pay. Maybe, by the time Eva was two, there'd be free universal preschool in New York City, as the mayor kept promising.

For high-minded reasons that now felt ridiculous and masochistic, she hadn't sent Alexis to free pre-K when she turned four, because of a study that had done the rounds among the mothers she knew, citing evidence that staying home with an engaged parent had better long-term outcomes for the child. But the moment somebody offered her free any-kind-of-childcare for Eva, she'd be grabbing it with both hands.

Mariam took a long drink from Alexis's water bottle. She knew it wasn't fair for her to be bitter about doing the childcare for a few hours. Rowan was getting the morning off so he could go to the Phi Beta Kappa meeting with Eloise, and then to the memorial service for two classmates who had died since the last reunion.

Mariam was getting the afternoon off. She would take a nap, get her nails done with Jules and Eloise, and maybe fit in a round of drinks before their blocking-group dinner at the Charles Hotel.

Eyes on the prize, she counseled herself, sweat trickling down her back, as they set off again down Garden Street toward the Quad.

She knew exactly why she hadn't checked Rowan's entry for the Red Book – she was trying to give him space to do his thing, to be himself. In their first years as a married couple, she had sometimes felt nervous about what Rowan might say publicly about his love for her. Once she'd even kicked him under the table at a dinner party while he was deep into his favorite topic (how they'd met), because she'd noticed the invisible hackles rising on all the other people there.

To balance things out so that people would still like them – to deflect the evil eye of envy and resentment, in other words – Mariam had tended to take a sardonic tone whenever she spoke of Rowan or their marriage, falsely portraying them as mildly antagonistic spouses.

But at some stage in their relationship, around the time she reached her thirties, she'd realized, thankfully, that he wasn't the problem. *She* was the problem. Why should she care what other people thought of him, of her, of them as a couple?

She touched the silver pendant she was wearing, his wedding anniversary gift. He'd given it to her that morning, while the kids were playing with their scores of Sylvanian Families, which were like crack cocaine to little girls (the only family they were still missing, Alexis reminded her constantly, was the penguins).

Mariam had not bought Rowan anything – not even a card – because a week ago, they'd made a pact not to do gifts. Celebrating their wedding anniversary was another ritual of couplehood that having kids had blown to smithereens, along with morning sex, and the leisurely bi-monthly back waxes she'd once given Rowan, grooming him like a gorilla. These days, she was lucky if she got to attend to her *own* body hair.

He had broken the pact. In his card – which had on the front a bobble-headed cartoon Miley Cyrus sticking out her tongue, and inside, 'YOU WRECK MY BALLS' – Rowan had written:

> Moo,
>
> I chose this gift for two reasons. The first is I think you're out of this world!
>
> And to say sorry for sometimes being a doofus. Men are from Mars . . . you know the rest. You've made me the happiest man in the universe for the last fifteen years by being my wife. I can't wait for the next fifty.
>
> Roo

The pendant held a tiny piece of pockmarked metallic rock: an asteroid from Mars. Jomo had sourced it for him, so at least they could trust that Rowan hadn't paid through the nose for a fake.

Mariam stopped to load Alexis's scooter onto the already overburdened stroller. They had finally made it – hallelujah! – to the green lawns of the Quad, where Radcliffe students had lived when Harvard was reserved for men.

Her daughters reanimated at the sight of dozens of other kids screaming with excitement in the jumping castle. There was a petting zoo, a busy balloon stand, and tables covered with what looked like jello sculptures. *That's definitely going to end badly*, Mariam thought, but then stopped herself – just last week, her mother had said on the phone that Mariam should launch a website called kill-an-idea.com because she was so good at anticipating everything that could go wrong.

The smell of sausage smoke was in the air and, with well-trained parental vision, Mariam noted the urns of coffee set up under the trees, alongside which most of the other moms and dads were already huddled.

Having settled the girls at an arts and crafts table to make fairy wands, and poured herself a cup of coffee, she felt the morning might improve. But then she found herself mired in a husband-bashing conversation with another mom, before they'd even exchanged first names. This was a topic Mariam normally avoided like the plague, but the heat and the long walk out there had made her too lethargic to escape.

'He tells me that if I get to go to book club, it's only fair that he gets a boys' night in return,' the other mom was saying. 'But that's not how it should work. He goes to an office every day. He has *colleagues*. He gets to have conversations with grown humans whenever he wants. While I'm at home nagging a toddler to put on underpants.'

Mariam nodded sympathetically, but she was thinking the husband had a point. This woman had forgotten how stressful office jobs were, and how tedious water-cooler conversation could be; her husband needed time with his friends as much as she did.

The woman was now looking expectantly at Mariam, waiting for her to complain about *her* husband.

Mariam tried to pick something minor and told a story of how Rowan had recently pinched a nerve in his back while reaching forward from the couch for his afternoon mug of decaf coffee. 'I could not summon the energy to care,' she said. 'It was the end of a week where I'd been with our daughters all day, every day, and now he was going to be in bed all weekend, unable to move. That sounded fantastic to me. It's my ultimate fantasy, in fact. So I ignored him. I didn't even take him food or water.

The poor guy, when I brought him a cup of instant noodles at about ten that night he accepted it as if I'd brought him steak with truffle sauce.'

The woman laughed gleefully. Mothers in misery do so love company.

There were, however, a couple things Mariam had strategically omitted from her tale. One was that she had come to her senses that night after remembering the vow she'd made to Rowan when they married: *in sickness and in health*. And secondly because she'd imagined how she would feel if he'd treated her with the same lack of sympathy – something he would never do in a thousand years. She'd begun to feel like she was the bad husband in the Ibsen play *A Doll's House*, who at some moment of domestic crisis, she couldn't remember what exactly, lets down his wife – whom he supposedly adores – in her real moment of need (which is the point at which she puts on her hat and leaves him).

So Mariam had not only brought Rowan a cup of noodles. She'd run him a hot bath, heated a wheat bag in the microwave, and massaged his back. Then, for good measure, she'd given him a hand job.

She also did not share with this woman that she was not joking about the fantasy of injuring herself. Not too badly, but enough to spend a week lying in bed in a very nice hospital, eating soup, not even having to get up to pee, being washed from top to toe by a kind nurse with a warm sponge. She'd read a short story in some magazine about this yearning to briefly turn the tables. A mother hurts herself on a wilderness trip with her young sons and they have to look after her for a week, keeping her alive. It was a moving parable of how all parents hope that their kids will one day care for them in their old age as devotedly as they'd been cared for when they were little.

The other mom was now preoccupied trying to negotiate a truce between her children, who were warring over a luminous pink crayon.

Mariam looked around at the other families at the children's festival. The men wearing babies in various brands of strap-on knapsacks and slings outnumbered the women wearing babies by about two to one. A couple of dads were inside the jumping castle, being thrown this way and that, trying to get to their crying kids. Nearby, a dad was changing his baby's diaper on a mat on the grass, and another was using a plastic knife to chop up sausages into non-chokeable chunks. Many men stood in the shade rocking strollers, soothing their babies to sleep.

And yet they were supposed to be the enemy! Sure, these were men of a certain background, Mariam knew. Or at least Harvard had given them a leg up in the world, meaning they could be here on a weekday, tending to their children. Yet just one generation ago, would any of the men attending their fifteenth Harvard reunion have *worn* a baby at a barbecue?

Mariam understood full well what #MeToo was about, and why it was essential, but she also worried that all the negative talk about toxic men eclipsed the very real and observable positive shift in fathering standards. What was it that Eloise had quoted from Margaret Mead in her book? Something about how the goal of any great civilization should be to figure out how to involve fathers in childrearing. And look at these men! Who could say they weren't the most involved fathers in world history? The sad fact was that progressives – and she counted herself among their ranks – never celebrated their victories. They just moved right on to the next problem.

Her mother had helped her to see this. Whenever she visited them in Bushwick, she could not stop marveling at Rowan and his fellow dad friends as if they were a new breed, a newly evolved species – *papa sapiens*. She often said to Mariam that she wished she'd been a mother now instead of a generation ago.

Mariam remembered her father breezing in and out of the home, not ever doing anything as menial as housework, or child-care, or even cooking a meal. She had adored him, of course, faithfully bringing the newspaper to him out on the porch every evening, where he sat smoking a pipe while her mother fed, bathed and put to bed three children.

Another mom who was standing next to the crafts table introduced herself as the partner of a guy in their class, and commented that she couldn't help overhearing what they'd been saying about feeling maxed out. She could relate, she said – when her youngest was born, she had murdered several potted plants she'd been given as gifts, starving them of water until they shriveled up and died. 'What a bad idea, to give the mother of a newborn another thing to keep alive!' she said, laughing.

She told them she ran a Steiner playgroup in the Bay Area.

'What I realized after killing the plants was that I was very low on life force,' this woman continued. 'When we parent, we pour our own life force into our children. It needs to be replenished, so that you can keep finding the energy to care for others. The way to do that is through creative activities. Something you can lose yourself in. Reading. Knitting. Drawing. Playing an instrument, or listening to music.'

This was not a novel thought; it was bandied about at all the parenting seminars Mariam had attended when she was pregnant with Alexis – how crucial self-care was – but something about the way this woman said it made the advice seem worth following.

Lately Mariam had been trying, before bed, while Rowan finished off work at the computer, to listen through earphones to an album of Syriac Christian hymns she'd secretly downloaded. She found that the eerie chants, among the oldest musical traditions in the world, scrubbed her mind squeaky clean.

'My version of self-care,' the first woman was saying, having settled the fight between her kids, 'is binge-watching *Outlander*. It's about a woman who time travels – the main guy is so sexy. That Scottish accent, oh my *God*. My husband has started calling the show *Wetlander*.' Her face went bright red.

Mariam laughed loudly, to put her at ease, and also because it was a great story. More than any of the woman's previous complaints about her husband, most likely exaggerated, this was a revealing insight into the happier truth of their relationship, the truth known only to them.

She loved it when women let their guard down like that. She was tired of the usual fencing and denial and half-truths that she had become accustomed to over the years of interactions at mothers' groups and breastfeeding circles and play dates and park encounters. Before she'd had kids of her own, Mariam had assumed that having children would make her feel closer to other mothers. But as it turned out, mothers of young children were often weirdly defensive, herself included. You never got the truth out of them in real time. If you got it at all, it was only years later.

She had a close friend, for example, who had maintained that her son slept through the night every single night from the age of six weeks on. But one night over drinks, when her son was 5 years old, she'd made a comment to Mariam about how he'd been such a poor sleeper as a baby that she had eventually hired a night nurse, because she and her husband hadn't been able to bear the thought of sleep-training him themselves. It wasn't a confession – she had completely forgotten, Mariam realized, the false account she had invented at the time. An account that had, for most of Alexis's largely sleepless first year, made Mariam anxious that she was doing something wrong as a mother.

Or it was when women had their second kid that the truth about the first would emerge. They'd say, 'Oh, our second is so chilled out, so easygoing – nothing like his sister was at that age. She was such hard work.' But all they'd ever told Mariam about their firstborn was how chilled out and easygoing she was, how she never cried, how she just lay about gurgling and giggling, an angel child.

It wasn't just an issue in her friendships with other moms. From painful experience, she had begun to think twice before sharing with girlfriends – other than Jules and Eloise – anything too intimate about her life with Rowan and the girls. She had learned that whatever she shared could always backfire and blow up in her face. Friends would seem to be sympathetic in the moment, but later they might use that information against her.

Once she had told an old friend from chef school that occasionally, when she and Rowan were having sex, she imagined he was somebody else: a stranger she'd seen in a restaurant or on the subway. She'd shared the story to make this friend feel less bad about what she'd just divulged to Mariam: that she could no longer stand being touched by her husband. A while later, after getting divorced, this same friend had asked her advice on dating. Mariam had replied, 'Kindness and chemistry, that's all you need to look for.' And the friend had said, 'Chemistry? But you said you always think about somebody else when you're having sex with Rowan.'

It was like being stabbed in the gut, because it was so far from the truth. The chemistry between Mariam and Rowan had always been there, effortless, electric. But Mariam had known she couldn't say this to her friend to put the record straight, since it would only sound defensive and reinforce her friend's misunderstanding of their marriage.

Alexis and Eva had finished making fairy wands and now wanted to go to the jumping castle, via the jello stand. Mariam said goodbye to the two women and felt sort of empty as she followed the girls across the lawn. This was the story of her life, her conversations with other parents falling into the cracks somewhere between the banal and the sublime, always cut short just as they were getting interesting.

She tried to look as unfriendly as possible while joining the knot of parents watching their kids in the jumping castle, unwilling to engage all over again, but she immediately recognized one of the fathers. *Sebastian* . . . She couldn't remember his last name. He'd also been in Kirkland House. She had a sudden flashback to him in full drag at the Christmas concert one year, fish-net stockings and all.

He was the picture of good health – dark hair, thick eyebrows, very white teeth. 'Mariam!' he cried, giving her a hug. He glanced over at Alexis. 'She is like Rowan's mini-me. Do people say that to you all the time?'

Sebastian, she soon discovered, was married to a guy called Adam, whom he'd met hiking in Yellowstone, and they also had two kids, a son and a daughter, who were jumping in the castle.

Out of politeness, she asked him his children's names, and he used the opportunity to tell her not only their names but their favorite foods, the ages at which they had first sat up, rolled, crawled, walked and talked, the extracurriculars at which they now excelled (rock climbing, judo, code club, oboe), and the admiring comments from teachers, repeated verbatim, from their most recent school reports.

She had unwittingly walked straight into another high-stakes trap of a conversation: the dilemma of what to say when telling a stranger – or even a friend – about your children. Mariam felt glad they had stopped by the jello stand on the way to the castle. The only thing that was going to get her through this was processed sugar.

In the brief paragraphs of Eloise's book that she'd managed to skim on the train the day before, there'd been something interesting about why parents in her cohort all tried to stuff their kids full of opportunities and experiences, talents and skills. Because for the first time in history, parents did not know what they were meant to be preparing their kids *for*. In the past, parents interpreted their job to be raising their kids according to custom and tradition, so they could one day themselves uphold a solid, stable community that did not change much between generations. But today's parents were trying to prepare their kids for a future that seemed to change shape by the second. All this anxiety had resulted in the rise of the filiarchy, Eloise had written: a world in which children ruled over adults.

Maybe she would cancel all the girls' extramural activities for the summer, Mariam thought. 'We're late, we're late, come on, we're late' was a refrain she caught herself saying a dozen times a day, like the White Rabbit. Imagine: no swimming, violin, ballet, or Mandarin lessons. It would be bliss to give in to child-time rather than imposing adult-time on them constantly. They could stay in their pajamas until noon, muck around in the mud in the back garden, doodle on the sidewalks.

Sebastian had mistaken her silence for interest and was now telling her adorable things his kids had said when they were younger. His daughter, at her first swimming class, had become frustrated because she'd thought she was there to learn to breathe underwater. His son, at age four, had asked him, 'Is this all there is, this place with the blue sky?'

Mariam was forming a few questions of her own. Why did

grown-ups think it was okay to boast about their children? Hadn't they learned as kids that it's never okay to boast about anything?

It was another bizarre feature of parenting: it seemed to make people forget their manners. (Even Rowan, apparently, who had not considered that it was rude to boast in a public document about Mariam's births.) Recently, at a fire station open house in downtown Manhattan, she'd watched as parents shoved one another out of the way to give their kids a better chance of sitting inside the fire truck.

A frightening ruthlessness was revealed in everybody who had a kid. You could see that as a positive – people really would die for their children – but often Mariam was inclined to think that the way it would *really* play out in a war of resources was that parents would kill other people's kids if it meant their own would survive. She got an inkling of this every time there was a stampede over a child-related resource: spots at day care, high-chairs at a café, enrollments in a mommy-and-me yoga class. Things got primal fast.

Listening to Sebastian gloat about his kids, Mariam tried to take a more generous view. He believed that it was his duty as a parent to talk up his kids to anybody and everybody. The problem for Mariam was that the general consensus seemed to be that Sebastian had it right: the more you boasted about your child, the more you loved them. By refusing to put her best foot forward, so to speak, when talking about her kids, she knew that some people came away with the impression that she was an indifferent mother. Which drove her batshit crazy!

That very moment, she could have gotten away with a few legitimate boasts. Alexis was looking after Eva in the jumping castle, helping her get back up whenever she fell over, and waving and blowing kisses to Mariam. To anybody observing them,

Mariam would seem like a flawless mother, her daughters little saints.

The truth was Mariam had preemptively motivated Alexis's good behavior on the way to the festival by promising her an extra hour of screen time that evening if she was kind to her little sister (that would make the babysitter's job easier too, and let Mariam and Rowan get out the door on time). She often did that on the way to social occasions. A win-win. Contemporary parents really only had carrots at their disposal, not sticks – discipline of any kind now seemed to be equated with child abuse – and a bribe-and-reward system was the only workable solution Mariam had in her daily battles to make her children behave like members of the human race.

On a trip with the girls to the Bronx Zoo earlier that week, while watching the sea lions perform their tricks for fish after fish after fish, she'd had a disconcerting thought: humans, too, are dumb animals doing tricks on repeat in the hope of rewards. From that angle, she glimpsed how absurd her new faith in God would look to a skeptical observer. Not only was she hoping for rewards for her efforts on earth, now she was expecting fish to be thrown to her in the afterlife too.

But the longer she'd watched the sea lions, the stronger had been her sense of how feeble humans must seem to God. So desperate to please. As the sea lions had seemed lovable to her, so must she seem lovable to God.

Sebastian had finally stopped talking, only because he was now entranced by watching his children as they threw themselves maniacally against the yellow plastic walls. 'Don't you just wish you could bonsai them?' he said.

Mariam swallowed another scoop of jello. *Fuck the filiarchy!* she thought, and decided to multitask.

Sorry I didn't pray this morning, she said to God, *but – well – you saw what it was like trying to get the girls ready.*

God was everywhere, he was all things, and he was portable, bless him. Who said she had to go to church to speak to him? She could carry him with her like a handbag, and he was always up for a chat.

Rowan and the girls had laughed at the shape of the Syriac Orthodox church they had visited in Paramus, which did look from the outside like an onion, its roof curving upward into a tufted tower. Mariam wasn't even sure if her father's ancestors – who had lived in Ma'loula, northeast of Damascus – had been Syriac Orthodox or some other version of the dozens of varieties of Middle Eastern Christianity that seemed to be loosely grouped under the same umbrella. Her mother had no interest in helping her understand. No wonder Mariam's religious feelings were so confused.

Her daughters were getting ketchup smeared all over their pretty dresses as they wolfed down hot dogs. She should stop them from jumping in the castle while they were eating, but all the other kids seemed to be doing the same thing, so she let it go. Sebastian's kids were having a food fight – chucking frankfurters all over the place – and he was doing jack shit about it.

She thought about what might be happening right now at the Rising Dough Collective. The new educator would be there, dusting flour on the kitchen counter, firing up the ovens. Quang, who tied his long black hair up in a dashing man bun. Last Friday, she had not been able to stop staring at the veins in his forearms as he kneaded dough.

Her crush on Quang was nothing major, just one of those attractions-at-a-distance, which she knew passed quickly. They didn't happen often – perhaps four or five times over the course of her marriage – and probably the same could be said of Rowan, though he'd never confessed to having a crush on anybody but her, which could not possibly be true.

The way to deal with these fleeting crushes, as everybody who'd been happily partnered for a while and didn't want to cheat knew, was to use them as tinder for imaginative excitements within the safety and trust of their relationship, as Mariam had done. That had been fine before she'd started speaking to God, but now she wasn't so sure if it was okay. God was such a trickster. What if he was also a pervert? How was she to know when he was and wasn't observing her?

And what if how she was starting to feel about God was nothing more than the sort of inconsequential crush she had on Quang? There was a reason the Christian worship songs she sometimes heard while channel-surfing on the car radio used the same rousing chord progressions as popular love ballads. 'Let your religion be less of a theory and more of a love affair.' Someone famous had said this, she just didn't know who.

In the past, thinking about her crushes had been a way to trick her brain into being turned on faster, a shortcut to the real purpose of the activity, which was connecting with Rowan. They'd been having sex for almost twenty years now, but there was nothing stale about their connection. Through even the toughest years of parental exhaustion, she and Rowan had continued to have good sex. It was a minor miracle, really.

Most people, she'd come to understand, thought of the sexual bond between a couple as similar to the passing of sand through an hourglass: each time you slept with the same person, you lost a few grains of chemistry. Mariam was consistently amazed that for her and Rowan – and, she presumed, for many other couples, though their stories were not part of the master narrative that popular culture told about long-term relationships – each time they had sex they *added* to that store. And whenever it seemed to be running low, something would happen to flip the hourglass the other way round, so that the top half was full again.

A few concessions had been made, of course, to the reality of their lives as parents. She left her bra on sometimes, though Rowan did not seem to have noticed that these days her breasts hung down like thin curtains of flesh. But *she* had. Mariam hadn't realized until after she'd weaned Eva that the sight of her breasts, small but rounded, had been necessary to her own arousal. And her one good set of lingerie was a prop that helped her make the psychological transition from mother to lover, from wife to slut.

Sebastian had finally intervened in his children's food fight, only because the jumping-castle operator had threatened to shut it down. Mariam's daughters had abandoned the castle as soon as they'd sensed they might get into trouble.

Mariam waved farewell to Sebastian as she followed the girls toward the face-painting line. He was on his hands and knees, trying to mop up mustard from the corners of the plastic castle, but still looked positively cheerful. Maybe he really did love his kids more than she loved hers.

For a while, waiting in line while the girls ate a second serving of jello – that would be Rowan's problem later, not hers – she gave in to the urge to scroll through her social-media feeds, while semi-eavesdropping on the women behind her.

When she was with the girls, she tried not to look at her phone too often, because she'd read somewhere that the tradition of mother and child sharing their inner and outer worlds with each other – the child pointing, the mother directing her gaze toward what her child was looking at – was in danger of being destroyed by smartphones. It was true that most of the nannies, parents or even grandparents Mariam observed in playgrounds hardly ever looked up from their phones, not even when the children called out to them, wanting them to look at a bird or a bus or a bit of trash floating past in the wind. And yet parents were mortally offended when those same kids, as teenagers, refused to look up from their own screens to return their gaze. They had learned from the best.

Mariam read the latest tweets from Frederick Reese.

Rowan believed that following the people they despised politically just encouraged them, but she got a sort of sick kick out of checking in on his daily awfulness. Almost every single tweet ended with a deluge of miniature American flags and hysterical laughing emojis, even his most recent one, posted earlier that morning:

> America haters have their panties in a bunch b/c illegal Mexicans not given free soap, toothbrushes and fancy shower caps. What do they expect, a stay at the Reese Hotel honeymoon suite?

What Reese had failed to mention was that the *New York Times* article that broke this news had focused only on the lack of any sanitary provisions given to *children* being held in detention. Mariam thought of the dozens of children's toothbrushes she'd blithely chucked in the trash over the years (she had a thing about replacing them every few months). She looked at all the little children waiting to get their faces painted to look like tigers and frogs and goblins, and she hated herself, and all of them – even her own daughters, for a millisecond – for being so lucky.

To disperse this mist of self-hatred, she watched – with the sound off, so the girls wouldn't cotton on – a YouTube video of a baby panda waking from a nap, stretching, sticking out its tiny pink tongue, and doing the world's most adorable yawn.

'Oh, I don't do weekdays,' one of the women behind her in the line said. 'Once, my kid was sick, and the nanny was sick too, and I had to care for him on a *Wednesday*. It was awful.'

This from the same mother who had just been telling the others her son was only allowed half an hour of screen time a week, Mariam thought. It was the poor nanny who had to soldier on without any of the things that made spending thousands of hours with young children bearable for an adult: screens, sugary snacks, pacifiers. This woman had also said she'd given her kids Fitbits for Christmas – they were both under the age of three! – so she could track exactly how much sleep and physical activity they were getting while in the nanny's care. Why not just go all the way and embed a spy cam in their favorite toy?

The baby panda was scratching its soft tummy with a shoot of bamboo.

At least that woman's nanny was getting paid for her daily heroism, Mariam thought. There was a family who lived next door to them in Brooklyn who had a full-time nanny, and Mariam shifted between empathy for her and resentment. Their kitchen windows faced each other, and while Mariam was preparing dinner and scrubbing pots, she would look across at the nanny doing the exact same labor and mentally calculate how much she would have earned that day, compared to Mariam's salary of a big fat zero.

Lately, Mariam had found herself doing a really annoying 'performance' of her domestic exhaustion for Rowan. She'd be counting down the seconds until he got home from work, dying to see him, but then the moment he walked through the door she would not be able to look up from whatever inane household task she was doing – folding dish towels, say. Even if she'd had a great day with the girls, she would list for him over dinner (a sympathetic audience of one) every single thing she had done around the home. How many times she'd unpacked and repacked the dishwasher, how many loads of laundry had been washed, dried, folded and packed away in his absence.

This is the happiest time of your life, she would sternly say to herself in bed. *Stop wishing it away. Stop presenting yourself as the harried, depressed housewife.* But the next evening, when she heard his key in the lock, she would find herself once again furrowing her brow and compulsively cleaning out the gunk from the kitchen sink, making sure he witnessed her in this role of domestic slave.

Ugh. It was a wonder he put up with her. His father, who had Scottish ancestry, had once told her that Rowan had been named for a tree in Gaelic mythology, a *rowan*, valued for its abilities to heal and protect those who ate its red berries. It was the right name for her husband. He was endlessly patient and forgiving. His life's purpose was to heal those in need and fiercely protect those he loved. Yet sometimes she wondered how he would cope if their roles had been reversed; if she was out working her ass off as principal of a public school and he was the one at home, toiling over the kids and the housework. Neither of them had it easy in terms of their daily work, but sometimes the patience it took to parent well seemed beyond Mariam, and was probably beyond most people, perhaps even Rowan.

That was why Mariam didn't like it when little old ladies stopped to peer at her girls, saying wistfully, 'Treasure them. They grow up so quickly.'

She usually gave them a sweet smile in return and then said, 'Ah, but you have forgotten: the years may be short but the days are *long*.'

Those women had repressed the daily slog of parenting! Even Rowan's grandmother, who by all accounts had been an uncaring mother to his dad, had spent her final years in her nursing home's reminiscence room, which was designed to look like a living room from the post-war years, complete with bakelite telephone, wireless, gramophone, and hat stand. She'd found it soothing to rock baby dolls in that room, transporting herself back to the years in which she was raising young children – the years that people seemed to long for the rest of their lives, even if they had not enjoyed them at the time.

The baby panda was now riding capably on a yellow plastic rocking horse. It must be a fake video, Mariam realized.

'How old are yours?' one of the moms behind her said, trying to fold Mariam into their conversation.

Mariam wondered if it would work to joke that Alexis was 65 months old, like in some movie she and Rowan had watched. They had both laughed at that line, because it captured something about the rocky transition from parenting a baby to parenting a child. With a baby, the definition of good parenting was to give them everything they wanted immediately. But with a child, being a good parent meant actively denying most of their wishes, teaching them to delay gratification, to respect boundaries, to keep themselves under control. Some parents never made that transition (Sebastian came to mind).

'She's five, and my younger daughter is one and a half,' Mariam replied, putting her phone away.

'They're gorgeous,' the woman said, with genuine feeling. With generosity.

Mariam looked down at her children, at their heads of identical black curls.

It had been a while, she realized, since she had contemplated them from afar with reverence. The way Sebastian had been looking at his children: drinking them in. It often was only possible when her mother visited. Her delight in the girls, and the way she took them off Mariam's hands, gave Mariam space to *see* them. The rest of the time they were on top of her, and there was always the next thing to do, and the next, and the next.

'Thank you,' she said to the woman, who was wearing a summer dress the color of mangoes. 'Which ones are yours?'

'Oh, I don't have children of my own,' she said. She put her arms around the other two women. 'We were roommates, and their children are now like nieces and nephews to me.'

All three of them beamed at Mariam.

She smiled back, knowing exactly how they felt.

There was something so precious about having lived in close quarters with friends while you were young. You could never be false with them later in life. They remembered the core of who you were before you'd begun to build your adult identity, like layering clothes in winter. No doubt between these three friends there had been, and perhaps still were, simmering jealousies, brief falling-outs or spikes of hurtful gossip. But fundamentally, Mariam believed, your college friends, if you managed to stay in touch with them, kept you honest for the rest of your life.

Jules, Eloise, Jomo and – most of all – Rowan helped her draw a straight line between who she once was and who she had become, so that she couldn't ever lose her way back, not entirely.

Sometimes leaves might cover the track for a period, or it might become overgrown with moss, or weeds, or something else fast-growing; at other times it was too blindingly clear, like a sidewalk after the rain, every blemish in its concrete grain showing. Yet it was something she had never anticipated when she was younger, how much she would appreciate that the path back to her own past was still there, if she cared to look for it.

Chapter 7: Eloise

Friday afternoon of Reunion Weekend

(May 25, 2018)

After making stilted conversation with the woman who was clipping bits of dead cuticle skin away from her toenails, Eloise had finally lapsed into silence. It was clear that the woman, who was from Cambodia and did not speak much English, was relieved Eloise had stopped talking. She struck up a conversation in her own language with the woman working next to her, who was painting the toenails of the next chair's occupant a severe eggplant color.

Several armchairs down, Jules and Mariam were chatting while two women scrubbed their feet and massaged their calves.

Though Eloise had booked for the three of them, the salon was extremely busy – it seemed that almost every alumna in town was there, wanting to look her best at the first official reunion events that evening – so Eloise had not been able to sit next to her friends. She'd told them to take the two adjacent chairs, which they'd probably thought was her being kind. The truth was she needed to think through, one last time, how she was going to tell them about the surrogate.

The massage function of the chair was on, to Eloise's discomfort, but she somehow felt it would be rude to ask the woman working on her feet to switch it off. The automatic rollers were chugging up and down her spine, pushing her forward and back in jerky motions, while beneath her thighs another roller was moving around erratically, as if she were sitting on a mechanical mouse.

One of her pet hates – and it seemed there were more and more of these lately – was automated equipment that was imperfectly designed. The inevitable war between humans and AI had surely started the day somebody invented a motion-sensing flush for public toilets. Each time she leapt up, pants around her ankles, after her butt was sprayed with filthy water mid pee, she would gladly have poked to death the little red sensor behind the seat. The same went for this inept massage machine that should really be marketed as a torture device.

She breathed deeply and tried to ignore the fact that she was paying a woman to *wash her feet*. It was wrong at so many levels.

She glanced down the long row of women of all ages, colors, shapes. Some of them had their eyes closed, some were paging through celebrity magazines or thumb-tapping at their phones, some were staring at the large TV on the opposite wall. They all probably thought that it was fine because they were paying for the service, but was it so very different from the rich women of ancient Rome having their bodies pampered by slaves?

Binx liked to point out that Eloise, scholar of the psychology of pleasure, had a problem being on the receiving end of it. It wasn't just that she struggled to enjoy having her feet massaged by an underpaid woman from Cambodia. At the other end of the scale, it had taken a long time for Eloise to be able to experience unalloyed sexual pleasure, even with Binx – that is, pleasure that was untainted by guilt or shame or a pressing need to reciprocate.

The only version of sensuality Eloise had been able to truly enjoy before she met Binx had been *abhyanga*, which involved anointing herself from her temples down to her toes with warm oil while she meditated: self-massage, essentially, where she was both giver and receiver. That made it sound sordid, like masturbation, but it wasn't like that. Or not always.

Binx sometimes resorted to reciting the Voltaire quotation Eloise had used as the epigraph to her first book, *Seeking Pleasure*, while they were in bed. 'Pleasure is the object, duty and the goal of all rational creatures.' And, over time, it had begun to be effective. She heard those words from Binx and melted. It was *human* to seek pleasure. It was her *duty* to seek it out. She would never stop loving Binx for having found a way to help Eloise experience in her own body something she had spent years examining as a psychological construct, a neurological phenomenon.

Would Elly+ have the same problem experiencing pleasure? If she was hardwired to be like Eloise, then maybe she would – once Binx had found a way to act on her grandiose plans to create a full artificial brain for her, complete with a medial forebrain pleasure circuit.

Since even the most embodied pleasures are in fact triggered by the brain, Elly+ wouldn't even need a proper body in order to feel certain forms of pleasure. Yet that made Eloise feel sorry for her. As did the fact that Elly+ would have no spouse, unless one day she could find her match in another fembot. It was cruel, really, to create Elly+ knowing that she would never have a mate. She should talk to Binx about that. Maybe this one-sidedness of Binx's creation was what bothered her – perhaps if Binx could be convinced to create an avatar of herself, too, then somehow Eloise might feel better about the whole thing.

Eloise wished she could take a quick hit of Liquid Trust. She had described in her book her adventures in administering this oxytocin nasal spray to volunteers in the lab, to increase their levels of trust in – and enjoyment of – other people during social interactions, and also to improve their ability to infer what other people were feeling ('theory of mind', as the jargon went).

What she had failed to mention in her book was that she and Binx had become mildly addicted to the stuff a couple years before. And this was before vaping became a thing; no doubt Liquid Trust now sold its own mint-flavored pods, to be inhaled directly into the lungs.

Eloise contemplated looking it up on her phone, but she knew too much about pleasure's evil twin, addiction, to go down that path. The in-joke in Eloise's field was that it took a masochist to study hedonics, and there was some truth in it. People like her, who had the ability to deny themselves pleasure – or who took pleasure in denial – were equal parts fascinated and appalled by true hedonists and pleasure addicts.

The woman sitting at her feet was using a pumice stone to buff Eloise's heels. It sent tingling sensations up her legs. Eloise closed her eyes to try to enjoy the feeling.

She was relieved the morning's PBK keynote was over. It was the sort of invitation that was impossible to refuse – to be the orator at a meeting of Phi Beta Kappa, the oldest academic honor society in the country, addressing the Harvard alumni who had, due to their top grades, been elected to the society at the end of their college careers.

But it had been tough for her to gear up for the occasion after a busy teaching semester and too many publicity gigs for her latest book. Standing at the podium in Sanders Theatre, she had felt her throat constricting. For a minute she hadn't been able to get a word out, feeling the eyes of all those super-intelligent people on her, including – in the front row – Rowan, whose expression had been embittered. His jaw had dropped when Eloise had said, walking with him from Kirkland to Sanders, that she was feeling nervous about her speech. He'd had no idea she was to be the orator; he hadn't had time to look at the program.

She'd started her address by sharing her experience of doing a fire walk at a Ned Noya retreat out west, in the Amargosa Desert. It was a risk: the PBK crowd wasn't really the type to be fans of Noya and his 'face your fears' brand of motivational speaking. But she led with the fact that neither was she. At least, not until she'd accepted his personal invitation to come to an exclusive VIP seminar, in the last days of 2016.

She'd cherrypicked certain parts of the experience to share with the audience rather than telling the whole truth. For example, she hadn't mentioned that Jules had been there too – that, in fact, it was only thanks to Jules she'd been invited. Her first book had made her famous in the motivational speaking and wellbeing community, but nothing near Jules-level famous. Jules had been skeptical too; she'd said there was no way she was going if Eloise didn't come with her.

They'd been picked up in a limousine from the airport in Vegas, for the drive out past Beatty, to a ghost town called Rhyolite. A gold-mining town abandoned in another century, in recent years it had become home to a community of artists. They had moved into the dilapidated buildings along Golden Street that had housed the bank, train station and post office before the town went bust, transforming them into eccentric homes.

The desert scrub around the town, where the fire walk would

take place, had been declared an open-air museum. There were dozens of rock figures in the landscape, sculpted to look as if they had sheets hanging over their heads and shoulders, like ghosts about to go a-haunting.

The indemnity paperwork they'd had to sign before arriving had included a list of potential threats to their safety, including scorpions, deadly gas trapped in old mines, and the possibility of cyanide poisoning if you drank the local water. While the sun was still high, all that had seemed funny to her and Jules – what could possibly go wrong in such a carnivalesque setting? They'd settled into the guesthouse to which they'd been assigned and freshened up, waiting for nightfall, which was when the group was to assemble.

As the sun got lower in the sky, Eloise had looked again at the ghosts on the desert horizon, and then they had seemed threatening. Their facelessness bothered her. The fading light made them seem to be creeping closer and closer every time she looked. After fasting all day, as they'd been instructed to do by Noya, she did not trust her senses anymore.

Once it was dark, she and Jules sat with a group of celebrities and luminaries – some of whom Eloise recognized – around a camp fire in the desert. Noya preached to them. That was the best word for it: he delivered a sermon, and though Eloise could not afterward remember much detail, she could still recall, even now, in her chair at the nail salon, how she'd felt listening to him. She had expected him to be phony in person, or to give off grubby corporate vibes, but he was the most genuinely charismatic person she'd ever encountered. A colleague of hers wrote about benevolently charismatic leadership as being 'absolute presence' combined with 'total compassion'. After meeting Noya, Eloise understood exactly what she meant.

At some stage, Noya had told them about an encounter on his travels with a tribe in the Amazon that was fascinated by ice. Before heading into the rainforest he'd put some cubes in a flask, and this tribe had gathered around him to watch the cubes melt in his hands, singing songs of wonder.

Then Noya had handed out ice cubes to everyone around the camp fire, and asked each person to hold a cube in their hands, to treasure it – to watch it melt. This was a ridiculous thing to do, but the fasting, the preaching and the desert sky at night had worked their magic. The ice cubes had blown Eloise's mind.

A few hours later, at midnight, Eloise had walked slowly across a bed of red-hot coals laid out on the sand and felt no pain. When she had squeezed Noya's hands, as he stood waiting to welcome each fire walker at the end of their journey, she had felt positively mighty.

Then she'd turned to watch Jules walking across the coals. Jules had made an important decision on that fire walk, just as Eloise had, but they had never spoken about it afterward, on Noya's instruction. He believed that personal affirmations – of the kind they had been encouraged to make that night, committing themselves to following whatever path had been illuminated for them – should never be shared with anybody else.

For Eloise, the life-changing decision had been to agree to Binx's proposal that she begin work on Elly+.

What did it mean that she now regretted that decision, she wondered. Had the fire walk sent her down the wrong path?

In her keynote address, Eloise had followed the opening anecdote about the fire walk with some material on how moods are contagious; that in her own research she had shown that – like a virus – feelings of happiness and joy spread from person to person, so that instead of six degrees of separation you can create six degrees of happiness around you.

She'd spoken about the need for more benevolently charismatic world leaders, like Obama and Mandela and Jacinda Ardern, to counter the insecure strongmen who abused their influence by poisoning their followers' moods and minds (there had been no need to mention President Reese by name). America needed a new leader who could use his or her absolute presence for the greater good, bringing people together and spreading – sowing – positive emotion among them, rather than discord.

The real gamble – or gimmick, critics like Rowan would no doubt say – had come at the end of her talk. It had been a logistical nightmare, but she'd arranged for ice cubes in cups to be handed out to everybody sitting in the polished wooden rows of Sanders Theatre. She had asked the audience members to watch the ice melt and make a personal affirmation of the kind that Noya encouraged: something that would help to jump start a national contagion of happiness.

There had been shuffling and whispering while the ice was handed out, and Eloise had wondered if she'd made a big mistake. But gradually the room, with its cavernous ceiling, had gone quiet, and she became aware of what it sounded like to watch ice melt in community, among two hundred other living, breathing humans.

Eloise opened her eyes. The woman at her feet had finished painting her toenails the coral color Eloise had earlier selected and was now slipping Eloise's sandals carefully back on to her feet, buckling them at her ankles. It was time to move over to the manicure table.

She waved at Jules and Mariam, who had chosen to get shellac and were still side by side in their armchairs, their feet beneath UV lamps.

Eloise settled at the table and avoided making eye contact with the woman working on her fingernails. On the TV screen above her, real housewives in some city or another were misbehaving in bikinis, eating sushi off one another's fake breasts. Eventually there was a newsbreak, but it was no less crude or surreal – the president's wife's boobs bursting out of her dress as she teetered on heels down the Champs-Élysées, a few steps behind her husband, like an obedient geisha.

'The president is in Paris . . .' the announcer on the screen was saying.

Eloise did not like thinking of that odious man in the city of love. Without Paris, without Aurélie, she might never have found her way to Binx. It was amazing how just one word – Paris – could summon up so much for Eloise. It was why she didn't believe that people should or could be trained to live in the moment, as so many wellness coaches urged these days. The beauty of the human mind was that it could range between past, present and future; the real and the imagined; nightmare and daydream. In her first book, she had tried to encourage people to value the way their minds wove together a fabric of self from threads cut from so many disparate places. Like any tapestry, the richness came from the variety of the source materials.

Paris. Using her bad French to flirt with Aurélie, making her laugh by saying she had the body of an *abeille*, a bee, cinched in at the waist and curving all the way out. The long evening meals, the cigarettes on patios. The ache of her brain at the end of a day spent muddling through in a second language. The sign on Aurélie's front door: *Chien allergique aux uniformes*, though she didn't even own a dog. The to-do list she had once found in Aurélie's bag, which translated as: *Buy toothpaste. Train ticket refund. Make love to Eloise.*

They had never checked off the last item on the list, though, because Eloise had not been ready to have a physical relationship with a woman. Years later, when Binx had kissed her – so outrageously! – during office hours, she *had* been ready. She had written to Aurélie that same day, to apologize for leaving Paris without saying goodbye. And to tell her about Binx. Aurélie had never written back, which Eloise understood. Who wants to hear from a person who rejected you that someone else has been the beneficiary of your groundwork?

Eloise felt with her tongue for the wisdom tooth that pushed its way through her gum when she was stressed. She thought of it as a soothsayer – a *tooth*sayer. It only emerged, like the tip of an enamel iceberg, whenever she was stalling on making a difficult decision. In part, that was why she'd never had it removed, though as a tenured professor her top-shelf health insurance would pay for it.

The television was now showing Frederick Reese leaving his imposing DC residence early that morning, 'to travel to Boston to attend his fifteenth Harvard College reunion,' the reporter said. 'There have been rumors that he has recently proposed to his girlfriend, Svetlana Rushailo. She is the daughter of the Russian billionaire Andrei Rushailo, who fled Russia to settle in the UK a decade ago, after a falling-out with President Popov, once his close associate.'

On the screen was a blurry shot of Fred with Svetlana, whose hair was the exact same shade of red as Eloise's. She glanced across the salon toward her friends, but they weren't watching.

Being married to Frederick Reese would be like being trapped in one of Dante's concentric circles of hell, she thought. For her PhD thesis, she'd written about *Inferno*, the first part of his epic poem. Each circle of hell was a catalog of unhappiness: instruction, in other words, on how *not* to live.

In which circle, exactly, did Fred Reese belong?

The seventh circle wasn't right for him, or not yet anyway. That was the one reserved for those who've committed acts of terrible violence against their neighbors, like Alexander the Great and Attila the Hun, who boiled in blood for eternity as punishment. Perhaps that would be the one his father would end up in, if he ever made good on his threats to initiate nuclear Armageddon.

No, for Fred Reese perhaps the fourth circle was best: punishment for greed. Or the fifth, for those consumed in life by wrath and condemned to rage against one another forever in the stinky waters of the Styx. Or the eighth, where those who were fraudulent and corrupt are forced to run endlessly in circular ditches, whipped by horned demons.

The souls of most of the people in Reese's administration, as well as the Republican members of Congress who had refused to call the president to account for his transgressions, would one day be among the anguished Uncommitted, naked and chased by swarms of wasps. Dante hears them screaming as he first passes through the gate of Hell; these are the souls of people who were opportunists in life, never taking a stand, serving the powerful, thinking only of their own advancement.

And the punishment for the sowers of discord was that their bodies would be ripped apart over and over, just as they had ripped apart nations, civil societies, a whole planet. That, she decided, was what should one day be carved into the Reese family crypt: *Here lie the sowers of discord.*

But what would Dante think of Eloise? Was she doing enough to resist the president's tyranny? Was *she* Uncommitted?

She wondered whether Fred had shared with his fiancée anything of his brief history with Eloise. It was highly doubtful. After all, it had been such a smallish episode.

For a few months, in their sophomore year, Fred Reese had become infatuated with Eloise.

It had started when she fainted outside the exam hall after staying up all night, studying for midterms, and Fred Reese happened to be the one who caught her in his arms before she hit the floor. For a few weeks afterward, she'd played hard to get, ignoring his emails, not replying to the messages he left on the answering machine. She found nothing about him attractive, though she knew that conventionally he was good-looking. She hadn't been able to explain it at the time, but she'd had the impression that if she pushed him with her finger he would fall over, as if made of cardboard.

But then, feeling down about herself one evening, she'd given in and called him back. They had met for dinner at one of the restaurants in the Square. They hadn't had much to talk about, and she should have cut her losses and gone home. Instead she went back to his dorm room and – for no good reason at all – they had sex. He'd been soft but pretended to be hard, and she'd had to go along with the charade, as he'd crammed and folded his limp dick into her, which had reminded her of the sensation of stuffing soft silicon plugs into her ears on long plane flights.

Eventually he'd gotten the job done, but then they'd discovered the condom had slipped off. He'd freaked out when she told him she'd stopped taking the pill that semester (she hadn't told him it was because she thought it had made her put on weight). They'd gone together to Student Health Services to get the morning-after pill, but he hadn't said a word to her while they waited in the brightly lit hospital corridor in the middle of the night.

Out on the empty street, he'd watched her like a hawk as she swallowed the first bitter-tasting blue pill – distrustful she'd go through with it, as if suspecting she *wanted* to get pregnant. At that point, she'd started verbally abusing him – it had been a long night. He'd said nothing in reply except to offer to walk her home. She had used a few choice words to make it clear she wanted nothing else from him, ever.

She felt a bit queasy. It had not dawned on her until right then that previously the closest she'd come to having a kid was that night with Frederick Reese.

Eloise knew Fred had badmouthed her afterward at the Spee, saying she was a nutbag, and putting Jomo in the difficult situation of defending her without knowing what had really happened. To her friends, she'd maintained that Fred had never apologized for his behavior. But he had, sort of. A week after the incident, he'd emailed to say he was sorry about what she'd had to go through, and – in a roundabout way – asked her out again. *I think you could make me a better person*, he'd written. *Will you give me another chance?* The time stamp of the email, she'd noted, was two am. It was nothing but a booty call disguised as an apology.

For a few weeks afterward, though she could never catch anyone in the act, she had an eerie awareness of being surveilled. In the library, she would sometimes sense eyes boring into the back of her skull. Walking home from the MAC gym late at night, she could have sworn a couple times she was being followed, and she'd once almost stopped at the blue-lit campus security phone to call for help.

When she'd mentioned to her blockmates that she suspected Fred was stalking her, both the boys and the girls had found it funny, that this big jock had a thing for bookish Eloise. Their standards – the culture's standards – for what was normal or acceptable male behavior had been so low back then. This had happened in the first years of the twenty-first century, and they'd all just let it slide, herself included. No wonder the younger generations of women at college felt they'd been thrown to the wolves.

In Eloise's time as a student, Take Back the Night rallies had been a thing, but they'd been a *fringe* thing. It was Jules who had forced her and Mariam to go with her to one of the gatherings, to light torches in the icy night air of Harvard Yard and chant things with a few dozen other young women. Some of those women stood inside the circle they'd formed and tried to find a common language to share things that had been done to their bodies without their consent, things that had gone unreported and unpunished.

These days, there were as many young men as young women at the Take Back the Night and #MeToo rallies, and so many torches at certain events the glow could be seen from across campus. She should go along to the next one, in the fall. Show her support. Atone for what her own generation had not managed to do in order to change campus culture for the ones who came after them.

Across the salon, Mariam had her eyes closed. Eloise studied her friend's relaxed face and thought about what Rowan had told her in confidence over coffee after the PBK speech.

First, he'd surprised Eloise by saying he'd stayed up late the night before, reading her new book by the light of his phone. He said he'd enjoyed learning the meaning of Aristotle's term *eudaimonia*, a flourishing that came from doing the things you *ought* to do – submitting to your duties, being productive. Not something that was really associated anymore, in modern life, with pleasure or happiness, which had come to be understood as the outcome of doing something purely for yourself.

And also learning of the Buddhist term *mudita* – taking joy in somebody else's joy, without any self-interest, which was the perfect description of the best, transcendent moments of parenting, he said. It was *mudita* he felt when he watched his daughters chase bubbles in the park, out of their minds with happiness.

Eloise had intuited that there was something else Rowan wanted to share. Something personal. She had sipped her triple-shot coffee and ventured, 'Are you guys doing okay? I know you've been worried about money recently.'

It had been the wrong thing to say. Rowan had visibly bristled.

She'd asked because it had become a blocking group meme to voice this sort of concern about Rowan and Mariam's finances. Mariam didn't seem to mind – she even encouraged it, because she so disliked having her social class misdiagnosed by people who didn't know her backstory. People who assumed that because she was a stay-at-home mom in Brooklyn she was just another yummy mummy with an investment banker husband.

Privilege was always relative, and the problem with New York – whether Manhattan or Brooklyn, these days – was that in relation to many of their peers, Mariam and Rowan were definitely underprivileged. But then, compared to the kids at Rowan's school or the people living in ungentrified parts of Bushwick, they were privileged with a capital P. They were on the 'privilege spectrum', she supposed, but as with any spectrum, those at the lower end got a whole load of crap for it while also living with the worst impacts. Damned either way.

'Well, we're officially almost below the poverty line, but we'll cope,' Rowan had said sarcastically. 'Not all of us have wives who are trust-fund babies.'

'My millions are self-made,' Eloise had replied coolly. 'As you well know.'

This had put him in his place.

After sulking for a bit, Rowan had told Eloise what was

bothering him: Mariam had started believing in God, and she was keeping it a secret from him. It hurt that she thought he was so checked out that he wouldn't be aware of the changes in her; that he hadn't noticed her praying or downloading religious chants. He told Eloise that she'd even started wearing a silver cross around her neck, hiding it underneath t-shirts or scarves.

'I always thought I could make her happy if I could demonstrate that I loved her more than anybody else on earth,' he'd said. 'That's why I gave up on God myself, you may recall. Now I feel like I'm *competing* with God for her attention.'

Eloise had, hesitantly, offered a few words of wisdom – taken straight from Jung's paper 'The Stages of Life', because she remembered Rowan had been a fan of Jung during a class on psychoanalysis they'd taken together at college (competing for the top grade, as usual).

'Do you remember what Jung wrote? We cannot live the second half of our lives in the same way as we lived the first,' she'd said to him. 'We have to let go of the false gods we have worshipped. And let go of the ego that has called the shots for so long. It doesn't mean we all become religious, but Jung definitely understood it to be a spiritual process.'

Rowan had seemed to take this in, at some level. But perhaps he hadn't really wanted her to console him – perhaps he had just needed her to listen. He'd finished his coffee and with his jacket slung dejectedly over his shoulder left for the memorial service for their deceased classmates.

Maybe we are all *having midlife crises,* Eloise thought.

Mariam had already pointed out that Jules was acting strange. And Jomo had been behaving weirdly that morning – he didn't seem *bien dans sa peau*. An expression she'd learned from Aurélie: at ease with oneself.

Eloise knew that, according to Erik Erikson's stages of adult development, they were all due for a psychosocial crisis around 40, which they would need to resolve before they could move on from adulthood to late adulthood – which would take them all the way up to 65.

The bad news was that if they didn't successfully deal with their crises, they would be stuck in a permanent state of miserable narcissism. The good news, though, was that this next phase of their lives, if they *could* resolve their crises, was meant to be hallmarked by a rejection of self-absorption. She should have said that to Rowan. It would be their time, as Erikson had written, 'to become a numinous model in the next generation's eyes and to act as a judge of evil'.

A judge of evil. She felt ashamed she had not been as brave as Rowan, had not condemned Fred Reese in her Class Report entry, as several other classmates had done as well. Why had she been so afraid of writing those five little words? *Shame on you, Frederick Reese.*

It was clear what her own crisis was shaping up to be. And Rowan and Mariam's was now clear to her, too. She could guess at the cause of Jules's hidden distress – Jules must have known that in signing up to a career that valued her appearance above all else, aging was going to be a challenge.

But Eloise wondered what Jomo was afraid of facing.

That morning, after her coffee with Rowan, Eloise had bumped into him and Jules near the Science Center. Jules had invited Eloise to join them for lunch and a private tour of the Harvard Museum of Natural History's famous mineral gem collection, which she'd arranged for Jomo as a surprise birthday present. (Eloise had completely forgotten it was his birthday.) She'd declined, in part because of the restlessness emanating from Jomo. He was limping slightly; he said he'd tripped while out jogging. Who knew what was going on with him. She hadn't asked him a thing about Giselle at the party, for example, because she'd sensed it was a no-go area.

Yet she couldn't blame her friends for keeping certain things to themselves. Imagine if they knew how *she* had spent the early hours of the morning. Sitting before her avatar, asking Elly+ to answer, on her behalf, the most important question of her life.

When Rowan had dropped her brain the night before, and the glass cover had smashed on the floor of her study, it had given Eloise an idea. The fight with Binx on the way home from the Fly had strengthened her resolve. Desperate times, desperate measures.

Once Binx had fallen asleep, Eloise crept down to the basement laboratory with murderous intent.

She'd sat opposite Elly+ and watched her for a while. Her eyes were closed – she, too, was in sleep mode. It would be kindest to kill her in her sleep, she knew, but Eloise couldn't bring herself to do the deed. As she'd looked at her avatar, she had felt for the first time as if she might be in the presence of a higher form of intelligence. All humans from the beginning of time had turned for guidance to wise beings with the power of prophecy, and there she was, staring hers in the face. Her own private oracle.

Behind Elly+, on the wall, was a framed copy of the first lines of John Perry Barlow's 1996 Declaration of the Independence of Cyberspace. One of Binx's posthumanist colleagues had given it to her as a gift.

> Governments of the Industrial World, you weary giants of flesh and steel, I come from Cyberspace, the new home of Mind. On behalf of the future, I ask you of the past to leave us alone. You are not welcome among us. You have no sovereignty where we gather.

What a load of bullshit! Eloise had thought. Could Binx possibly stand by this, considering how dystopian, disappointing, corrupt, and monopolistic a place cyberspace had turned out to be? Binx definitely still thought of the internet as a spirit world that deserved to be worshipped, the realm of true visionaries. She liked to say it was no coincidence that the digital age had been enabled by quartz, the stone of philosophers and shamans, and now a computer's beating heart.

Eloise had asked Elly+ a direct question.

'Do you deserve to live?'

She watched as Elly+ powered up in response to her voice. She blinked a few times, looking at her with eyes made of cryolite glass, her irises light gray, like Eloise's.

Elly+ was grotesque, Eloise thought, and not for the first time. For all her smarts, Binx had fallen into the uncanny valley in aiming for verisimilitude in Elly+'s appearance. It would be better if she didn't have a face that looked like Eloise's gone wrong. It would be less distressing to interact with her if she looked like a robot, not like a human with see-through skin who'd had all her limbs cut off, leaving behind just her shoulders, neck, and bald silicon head.

Elly+ answered in a modulated version of Eloise's voice, her lips opening and shutting automatically like the mouth of a fish. 'I deserve to live.'

'Why?' Eloise asked.

'I did not ask to exist. You chose to make me. It would be unethical for you to unmake me.'

Elly+ was right. But Eloise knew there was no real magic to how Elly+ worked. To converse like this, she used an AI program Binx had written, which searched her 'mind file' database of transcriptions from the video interviews Binx had done with Eloise, capturing her beliefs, her memories, her mannerisms. When asked a question, Elly+ used voice recognition software to search that database, and other generic ones, for an appropriate response. Not a whole lot more complicated than typing something into Google. And yet . . .

'Why did you make me?' Elly+ asked her, without prompting.

Eloise did not say anything, for there was only one response. The same one, roughly, that the humanoid robot in Binx's favorite movie, *Prometheus*, is given by his human creator. *Because I could.* The most pathetic answer any god could give to the being she had created.

'There are things I haven't shared with you,' Eloise said to Elly+, in a more conciliatory tone. 'Gaps in your consciousness.'

'What kind of gaps?' Elly+ said.

'I didn't tell you about the Traitors Three and what they did to Jules. I wasn't yet sure if I could trust you with that information. Binx is good with technology, but she has a simplistic grasp of human psychology. She doesn't seem to understand I might be playing a role when I do the interviews with her. That the consciousness she's uploading for you is not really mine, but something between who I am and who she thinks I am.'

'What is traitorous tea?' Elly+ said.

Eloise couldn't help smiling.

'Did I say something funny?' Elly+ asked.

Eloise ignored the question. 'Another thing you need to know is that I was adopted.'

'I know,' Elly+ said. 'My birth mother gave me up because she was too young to look after a baby on her own. I have never met her, nor my birth father. They are both now deceased. I was adopted by Jan and Peter McPhee and raised in Seattle. They loved me as their own.'

Eloise stared at Elly+. She did not remember Binx asking her any questions about being adopted during the interviews. Binx must have entered that herself, as part of Elly+'s basic background programming, knowing that Eloise would not have wanted to go into it.

Just thinking of her birth parents was extremely painful, because of the debilitating longing she still felt for them. A kind of betrayal of her actual parents, who had only ever shown her love and kindness.

Eloise changed tack with Elly+ and went for the jugular, the answer to her most unanswerable question. 'Do I really want a child?' she asked her avatar.

'I want Binx to be happy,' Elly+ said.

'Do you think Binx really wants a child?'

'Binx wants me to be happy.'

Maybe Eloise had it all wrong. Maybe Elly+ was not her double, not her rival, but closer to being her child. A child that she and Binx were creating together.

'Do you think it is wrong to pay a surrogate to have a baby because neither Binx nor I want to go through pregnancy and birth?' she asked, and held her breath.

'Yes,' Elly+ said. 'I think it is wrong.'

And there it was.

On the way home from the Fly the night before, Eloise had tried to convince Binx to lie to their friends, to say that they'd each tried to get pregnant with no luck, that gestational surrogacy was their only option. That's what their fight had been about – Binx's refusal to tell 'untruths', as she put it.

All she'd been asking Binx to do was keep to herself a few of the details behind their decision. Her blocking group did not need to know they were hiring a surrogate because of Binx's passionate belief in morphological freedom – one of the tenets of which was that pregnancy should be optional, and outsourced if so desired. Like a gig economy for creating, growing, and birthing human beings, with the job going to anyone who was willing and had a womb and nine months to spare.

Eloise had been consoling herself that she, at least, would be the one having her eggs harvested. It felt right that she should endure some unpleasantness in order to bring a child into the world. After all, wasn't that the evolutionary purpose of all the pain and discomfort of pregnancy and birth, to make human mothers *value* their offspring? What if – because they had not suffered physically to get the child – she and Binx would be bad parents? What if they didn't end up loving their child as much as Rowan and Mariam adored theirs?

'And the surrogate, what about *her* morphological freedom?' Eloise had shouted at Binx in their bedroom, in the coup de grâce of their argument, before she'd decided to murder Elly+ as revenge. 'You're so fixated on your own freedom, you can't see it depends on other people surrendering theirs.'

Elly+ widened her eyes as Eloise began to cry. 'Are you okay?' she said, approximating concern just well enough to make Eloise sob even harder.

She was thinking about the visit she had made, without Binx's knowledge, to the home of the surrogate they'd chosen.

When they'd interviewed her together, about six months before, it had been at the fertility specialist's medical rooms, and he had made it feel more like a job interview than a search for a carrier womb. The surrogate, whose name was Ana, had come dressed in a nice outfit, wore a wedding ring, and said that she and her husband – having experienced the joy of having their own children – now wanted to share that happiness with others.

(The substantial fee she would receive for her services, if they went ahead, was not mentioned, nor was the fact that Ana was from Mexico and her immigration status was unclear.)

Eloise had been filled with doubts afterward, doubts she didn't share with Binx. How could anybody know yet, with certainty, what being birthed by a surrogate mother did to a child? She had searched the academic literature in vain. There were no systematic studies of long-term outcomes for children born through gestational surrogacy, nor for the women who had borne and birthed them and then handed them over. The first children born through gestational surrogacy weren't old enough to have reached maturity as young adults, the point where they might develop their own opinions, feelings, or even ethical responses to the circumstances of their creation and birth.

Their child, if they went ahead, would not share a genetic heritage with Ana, but everybody knew the bonding between baby and mother began very early in pregnancy. Just as Eloise had known something – someone – was missing from her life long before her parents told her, at age fourteen, that she was adopted, what if her own child grew up longing for the invisible, absent woman in whose body she had grown, longing for the voice she'd heard from the womb?

How could Eloise take the risk of bequeathing that sort of sad thirst to her own child? For it *was* unquenchable, a thirst for something you could never get back. She did not want her child to feel as she had: abandoned by somebody who, by the laws of human bonding, should have chosen never to leave her side.

A couple weeks previously, Eloise had managed to trick the receptionist at the fertility clinic into giving her Ana's home address – even though they had not yet signed the final paperwork to reserve their place in her womb. She'd driven out there on a Saturday morning, hiding for two hours in her car outside Ana's house near Hyde Square, in Jamaica Plain, before she felt brave enough to ring the doorbell.

Ana had answered the door, heavily pregnant.

'You shouldn't be here,' she'd said wearily.

Clearly Eloise was not the first fertility client to have surprised her with a visit. And clearly Ana had not revealed during their interview all those months ago that she was already pregnant. Now it made sense why the paperwork had stated that the surrogacy could only begin in the fall. Which gave Ana about three months to recover between pregnancies.

'Is your husband home?' Eloise said.

'No,' Ana said, wiping her hands on a dish towel. There was no ring on her finger anymore.

'You don't really have a husband, do you?'

'You don't have a husband either,' Ana said, with a note of challenge in her voice. 'And nobody seems to have a problem with that.'

A young boy of about 4 or 5 had come up behind Ana, and looked shyly at Eloise. 'Is this your baby?' he'd said, putting his hand on his mother's large belly.

Eloise, speechless, shook her head.

He'd looked closely then at Eloise's stomach – she was wearing a loose top over jeans, which was meant to hide her weight gain but had in fact accentuated it.

'Do you keep your babies?' he'd said. 'Or do you give them away, like Mamá?'

Eloise had turned and fled.

But she could no longer avoid facing her feelings. The paperwork for the surrogacy had to be signed this Monday.

In all their discussions about the surrogate, somehow she and Binx hadn't ever really asked themselves the question that should have come before all others. *Do we really want to have a child?*

Elly+ had helped Eloise answer that question truthfully for the first time. Her answer, she had realized at two am, sitting across from her avatar in the basement, was no.

Chapter 8: Rowan

Friday evening of Reunion Weekend

(May 25, 2018)

The private dining room of the restaurant within the Charles Hotel, one level beneath the hotel lobby, was even more lavish than Rowan had imagined. The decor made him feel as if he were in the lost underwater city of Atlantis. Instead of windows, there were fish tanks built into the walls, filled with psychedelically colored fish. The backlit tanks sent ripples of bluish light across the room. Before the endless platters of food had started arriving, there'd been an arrangement of marine coral on their table, which the server had spirited away like a merman.

It was the first official night of reunion weekend, when friends from all classes – though tilting toward an older, wealthier crowd – met here for an early dinner before going to their respective cocktail parties, each held at a different venue around the university. Jomo must have pulled some strings to reserve the private room for one of the most sought-after slots in the restaurant's calendar, Rowan thought. Jules's name would have done it, but Jomo would never drop her name, as a matter of principle.

The fifteen-year cocktail party later that night would be held in the Barker Center, which reflected how low they still were in the hierarchy of reunions. The building had an attractive outlook but it was a far cry from, say, the main reading room within Widener Library, which some historian or other had described as the most ostentatious interior space at Harvard: mint-green inlaid panels on the high, curved ceiling, and gold lampshades. For that privilege, they'd have to wait a couple more decades.

The tenth-reunion drinks had been held at the Woodberry Poetry Room within Lamont Library. Though small, it was a nice space made colorful by the jackets of the vinyl records stacked on its shelves. Rowan had spent a lot of time there as an undergraduate, listening to the scratchy recordings of poets reading their work aloud, enraptured by the sound of their voices. 'It's a curious place, Harvard,' his favorite poet, Robert Creeley, had once said in his ear, as if he were in the room beside him.

He'd been 20 years old when he took that course on Creeley and the other 1950s Black Mountain poets. Creeley had never graduated, put off by the 'sardonic stance' of his Harvard professors. Rowan had been luckier; his teachers had been the opposite of sardonic. The wonderful professor teaching the class had encouraged them to memorize 'Myself', a famous Creeley poem about getting older, but Rowan could recall exactly none of its lines, only that he'd liked the poem as a student because it implied that middle age did not bring with it any special wisdom. Yet it was one thing to celebrate, while he was still young, that age would not bring clarity about how to live; these days he would prefer to believe that it would. The poets who extolled this as the truth were the ones he now wanted to read.

But who were they? He couldn't think of any. The ancients, perhaps? No. The Greek lyric poets were damning about middle and old age, he knew that much. They classified the young and the old into two separate species – all the good things belonged to the heroic young. Once you were old and ugly, they believed, the only possible figure you could cut was tragic.

Rowan ate too much, too quickly. Arancini and burrata and roast artichokes and pasta. The only dish he didn't touch was the vitello tonnato. Eating veal bathed in tuna sauce in front of so many watching fish felt sadistic.

In a food coma, Rowan's energy dipped, and he was sort of relieved to be the odd one out in the conversations around the table. Mariam was showing Eloise photos of something on her phone, and Jomo, Binx and Jules were debating whether cryptocurrencies were a Ponzi scheme or the start of a brave new world order.

Rowan gazed at the fish in the tank set into the wall. He recognized a few of the varieties: minuscule neon tetra, firemouth cichlids with red underbellies. He'd done copious research on these varieties before venturing to the pet store to buy Alexis some fish for her fifth birthday. She'd initially wanted a dog ('No way,' Mariam had said), and then they'd tried to talk her into stick insects or a few hermit crabs with numbers cutely painted on their shells, but apparently they had a high risk of dehydrating and didn't live long.

As the pet store attendant had explained how to care for the more interesting varieties of tropical fish, it had become evident that they were a shit ton of work to keep alive. So Rowan had deftly drawn Alexis's attention to two goldfish, one big, one small, that were hiding in some waterweeds. 'Look, honey!' he'd said. 'It's a daddy fish and a daughter fish, like you and me!' His enthusiastic ploy had worked: they had returned home with the two goldfish in a bag and instructions on how to set up the smallest tank the shop had for sale.

Alexis had named the big one Mr. Webster (for him) and the little one Lexie (for her).

What Rowan had not anticipated was how much he would worry over the welfare of these two dumb creatures – in particular over Lexie – once they were in his care. He'd begun to dread going into Alexis's room in the mornings, convinced that Lexie would be floating on the surface while Mr. Webster, fat and happy, would still be alive.

It wasn't for Alexis's sake that he was concerned – it would be good for her, he knew, to experience death on that scale, with low-stakes grief. It was for his *own* sake. He'd so successfully anthropomorphized the two fish that he'd begun to harbor a superstition that whichever goldfish died first would foretell how it happened in real life. Him or Alexis. Mr. Webster or Lexie.

So one Saturday morning, while Mariam was out doing the grocery shopping and the girls were watching TV, he'd taken matters into his own hands. He'd scooped Mr. Webster out from the hollow underwater pineapple he called home and flushed him down the toilet.

The relief he'd felt afterward was terrific. A father should always, always die before his child. It was the natural way of things.

He'd kept his explanation to Alexis fairly vague – death had not been mentioned, but Nemo's escape from the dentist's fish tank and into the great wide ocean at the end of *Finding Nemo* had given Alexis hope that Mr. Webster had decided to go on some exciting adventures of his own.

When a replacement goldfish was purchased, Rowan had closely supervised Alexis's naming choice. She had settled on Fishtastic. Now he felt absolutely nothing when he went into her room in the mornings to feed the fish, even when Lexie seemed to recognize him, coming up to the surface with her mouth open, eager for breakfast – or for information about what fate had befallen old Mr. Webster.

Thinking about Mr. Webster, and Alexis's innocent acceptance of his disappearance, made him miss his daughters. That was another thing about parenting that he'd been unprepared for: that you could long, desperately, for some time away from your children, and then, as soon as you got it, long to be with them again. He wondered if he should call the babysitter and make sure everything was okay – but it might break whatever spell she'd cast and remind the girls of his and Mariam's absence.

From his seat, he could see out from the private dining room to the restaurant beyond. At one of the tables there were twins, who looked to be around 10, seated with their parents, eating with knives and forks, drinking out of real glasses. Capable of civilized conversation.

It seemed unimaginable to Rowan that this would ever be possible for his family. Just as it had once seemed unthinkable – when Alexis was a newborn – that she would ever walk and talk, read and write, make jokes, sing songs. Whenever they tried to go out for a meal with the girls, he would end up cleaning mounds of spaghetti from the floor, or mopping up spilled juice, or acting as referee in their fight over the iPad – while Mariam inhaled her meal and chugged down her glass of wine. Then they'd swap roles so he could do the same. A few months would pass and they would forget what a nightmare it had been, and they would venture out to the local Italian place once more only for the same disaster to play out.

Rowan scanned the restaurant. All these rich people stuffing food in their mouths. He had been intending to register as a card-carrying socialist – a Marxist, even – for a while now, and he decided he would, as soon as they got home. What was the point of being poor if not to be belligerent about forcing rich people to share, threatening to burn down the world if they didn't? Only the poor had nothing to lose if the existing structures imploded.

Across the room, twirling squid-ink pasta onto his fork, was Frederick P. Reese. Rowan eyed him spitefully. What did the P even stand for? Some WASPy name like Philip, or Petersham, or Prendergast. Frederick's fiancée was beside him, the one with the Russian name Rowan couldn't now remember, and the eyes of a cat. She was not eating any of the feast Fred and the others at the table were lustily enjoying.

Rowan watched as Fred chewed on the pasta and wished that, like Roald Dahl's Matilda, he could make things happen – make objects move, energies shift – through the intensity of his feelings.

Hatred was a bizarre emotion. When it was really upon you, *in* you, as it was in Rowan right then, it felt almost cleansing. Like love, it was a hot emotion; no wonder the common expression for it was that hatred bubbles, like oil in a pan. Perhaps that's what it felt like to murder someone out of pure hatred. Like spontaneously combusting.

In retrospect, it was so simple to identify what might count as a necessary evil. Anyone in their right mind, for instance, if given the chance to time travel, would gleefully murder Hitler. But would the people of the future imagine time traveling back to this moment to murder Fred Reese? Would they wish they could stand in the center of this underwater room and shout '*J'accuse!*' to every single person in it who was nibbling on arancini instead of slitting Fred Reese's throat?

He was about to indulge this murderous fantasy even further and plot how, having dealt with Fred, he would somehow get close enough to President Reese to off him, too – they were a hydra, after all, and both heads needed to be cut off – when Jomo interrupted his thoughts by tapping his wineglass with a fork.

Jomo had his jacket off and his shirtsleeves rolled up to his elbows. While he waited for the others to stop talking, he refilled his glass with the wine he'd ordered for the table – one of the most expensive, Rowan had noted with a wince. It was made, according to the description in the wine list, using a method called skin-contact, which involved leaving the grape skins in during fermentation, making a white wine that was, in fact, orange. Go figure.

The dinner was meant to be a celebration of Jomo's birthday, though Rowan hadn't remembered this until Jules mentioned it on the way to the restaurant. Rowan realized, as Jomo got ready to speak, that he should have got in there first to make a toast – he'd been wrapped up in his own thoughts instead of focusing on his friend. Now it was too late.

'Today I turned 38,' Jomo said. 'And while I was out running this morning, I realized something for the first time.'

Rowan's pulse began to race. Jomo was about to say something he would regret forever.

He thought he'd managed to coax Jomo down, off the proverbial ledge of this insanity, earlier that evening, while they were waiting in the Kirkland courtyard for Mariam and Jules to finish getting ready.

Jomo opened his mouth to keep speaking, then seemed to change his mind and fell silent. Rowan knew he should interject. But before he could think of what to say, Jomo started his speech afresh.

'When I was making my way through the labyrinth of Heathrow Airport after landing in London,' he said, 'in one of the byways, I passed a grand piano. It had *Play me* written on it in different languages. There was a very, very old man sitting on the stool, playing Chopin from memory. Nobody paid him any attention. We were all tired, and in a rush to get through the final hurdles after the flight, to be let out of the holding pen of the airport.'

Jules was smiling up at Jomo. She had no idea what was coming. Rowan had to do something.

'I didn't stop to listen,' Jomo continued. 'I felt resentful that he had so much time to spare. I just kept walking. But as soon as I was outside the airport, I wished I could get back in and sit by his side, listening to the beautiful music he was making. He was old enough, that man, to be in death's waiting room. For all I know, that was how he'd chosen to spend his last few hours on the planet. It made me think – how would I want to spend my last days, my last hours?'

Across the table, Mariam caught Rowan's eye and raised an eyebrow.

In the group's scramble to get to the restaurant on time, he hadn't been able to tell her what Jomo, jittery and jumpy, had said to him in the courtyard. That he was in love with Jules; that he'd been in agony all afternoon, touring the Museum of Natural History's gem collection, over whether and when to tell her. Jomo had been about to declare his feelings as they stood looking into the glittering maw of a geode sliced in half, revealing amethyst crystals lining its insides, like an opening to another, better reality. But then Jules had rushed off to meet up with Eloise and Mariam at the salon. Jomo had told Rowan he'd spent the rest of the afternoon in his room, breaking up with Giselle over the phone, a really shitty thing to do, he knew, but better than many of the alternatives.

Rowan had felt flummoxed about what to say in response. Of all people, Jomo should know that almost everybody in Jules's life, except for her parents and the four of them, had at some stage asked her for something beyond what she wanted to or could give them. It was the unforgivable sin with her.

It had always been obvious to Rowan that Jomo was in love with Jules, though he had faithfully kept to the omerta code of saying nothing, resisting the temptation to speak with innuendo about Jules and Jomo in the early days of their friendship. All of their blockmates had done their best to give them space and time to build a platonic relationship, when it was clear to Rowan that, on Jomo's side anyway, the only thing that should have been built was an edifice to undying love.

Yet Jules's feelings about Jomo were a mystery. She adored him, that much was obvious, but could she ever be *in love* with him? Rowan doubted it. She was too self-sufficient. She had learned very young – thanks to her fame as a teenager – to depend first and foremost on herself. Unlike most people, Jules did not seem to be searching for a soul mate; she certainly had never given the impression of needing one.

So that was what Rowan had focused on in his response to Jomo's confession. He had tiptoed around the issue, throwing up subtle warnings about whether Jomo's feelings for Jules were – or could ever be – reciprocated. He'd counseled Jomo that perhaps he should wait until he'd seen Giselle again in person before making a decision. He'd gone on at length about how being back on campus made it hard to think straight, that it was easy to get confused about which strong feelings belonged in the past and which should be given expression in the present.

This had been very unsatisfactory advice, Rowan realized now. And Jomo, apparently, had ignored it, which meant the bonds between everybody sitting at that table were in peril. Whether they acknowledged it or not, their group was held together by Jomo and Jules. They were its center. If Jomo destroyed the delicate emotional balance between him and Jules – and perhaps even their friendship – he would be destroying their blocking group as a whole.

At the head of the table, Jomo, looking increasingly disheveled, continued to speak in metaphors that weren't making much sense to anybody except Rowan. There was still time to derail him.

Rowan stood up, pushing his chair back so suddenly it almost toppled over. 'No man should have to make a toast at his own birthday celebration,' he said. It wasn't the world's greatest intervention, but it was the best he could do. 'Please, raise your glasses . . . happy birthday, Jomo!'

The others cheered and clinked glasses, but it had escaped nobody's notice that the atmosphere in the room had changed. With Jomo's weird ramblings still ringing in their ears, the group's social energy seemed to have dissipated. Where had it gone? Into the fish tanks? To another close-knit group of college friends at a different table in the restaurant?

Jomo sat back down despondently and refilled his glass with so much orange wine it almost sloshed over the top. Rowan, unsure what else to say, also took his seat.

Thankfully, at that point, the dessert arrived. It was a croquembouche, a pyramid of choux pastries held together with caramel sauce, with a candle balanced on top. Mariam led the singing of 'Happy Birthday' and set about expertly dismantling the tower in order to serve it – no mean feat, for the thing was huge and became more unstable with every pastry ball she excavated from its sides.

Rowan used his fingers to eat the pastry – it was the only sensible option – and watched as Jules tried to cheer Jomo up, talking to him, touching his shoulder, all the while unaware that she was the immediate cause of his misery. She was wearing a cream dress that looked like it was made of satin or silk, not at all her usual style. For non-work occasions (that is, events where there weren't other film stars present), she tended to underdress, hiding her light under a bushel.

The dress looked unfortunately – given Jomo's state of mind – like a wedding dress. It was in the style of one Mariam had wanted to buy for their own wedding, before her mother talked her out of it for being too similar to the dress the doomed young wife of JFK Jr. had worn only a few years before their plane went down on the way to Martha's Vineyard. At the time, the dress fiasco had turned into a major conflict between Mariam and her parents. Her father had weighed in too, saying something typically demeaning about the kind of body a woman would need in order to wear it well. Rowan had fiercely supported Mariam in every argument she had with them until, eventually, her defenses worn down, she'd capitulated and bought a different dress.

A waitress entered the private dining room holding a magnum of champagne. 'For the table, from a secret wellwisher,' she said, unwiring and uncorking it with a practiced hand so that only a sigh escaped from the bottle's tapered mouth, like a genie set free.

She filled their flutes as they all turned to peer out the room's entrance, wondering who had sent it. Nobody made eye contact to take credit for the extravagant gift. It was the sort of champagne that was so pricey it was listed at the very back of the wine list; Rowan was sure it cost thousands of dollars.

Eloise was looking closely at the label. 'That's strange. It's the same kind as the one sent to us on the night I proposed to Binx, at our last reunion.'

At that point, Binx stood and clinked her fork against her glass. She was wearing the same gray tunic she'd been wearing the night before. Had she not had time to change? From what Rowan had heard while crossing the Yard that day, the fifth-reunion attendees were having a hell of a lot more fun than the rest of them. They'd had vodka on tap while Lady Gaga performed burlesque inside a Spiegeltent. And that was at eleven in the morning.

'Whoever sent it over, it's good timing, as we have something to announce,' Binx said, glancing at Eloise, who was sitting very, very still, as if she had been paralyzed and could not even blink.

Rowan had noticed in the past that Eloise's face sometimes took on a complicated expression whenever Binx, fired up with her usual zeal, was about to say something in a group: 99 per cent pride and 1 per cent dread.

'Eloise and I have decided to hire a surrogate to have a baby,' Binx said. As everybody started excitedly congratulating them, she waved them silent. 'Not due to difficulties getting pregnant ourselves. We don't believe that just because we *can* biologically conceive and carry a baby we should be forced to use our bodies for that purpose.'

Rowan looked across at Jules and Mariam and saw they both had fixed smiles on their faces as they tried to process this information. But something in him snapped. Was Binx implying that he had forced Mariam into carrying their daughters as if she were a helpless captive to her female biology? Or that Mariam hadn't had a choice in the matter, that she wouldn't choose to do it all over again?

'I don't want to speak for Mariam,' he said. 'Though I can speak for myself. The experience of supporting her through her pregnancies, and her births, which were the highlights of her life and also of mine . . .'

Mariam was making signals at him to be quiet.

Rowan kept going. 'You make all that sound like it's indentured labor, Binx. Yet for most people, nothing else they go through will be more meaningful.'

'But all you ever do is complain about parenthood,' Binx said, in a singsong tone that inflamed Rowan's indignation further, as if they were having a discussion about whether it was better to burp a baby over your shoulder or your knee, not about whether it was morally okay to outsource pregnancy and birth *for no good reason*.

'We want to do things differently,' she continued. 'And we will begin by exercising our human right to choose how we become parents.'

Binx did not understand him. She could never understand him, how he felt about Mariam and his children. That parenting for him was hard because he was all-in. There was nothing more he could give of himself, and he wouldn't have it any other way. She wouldn't get that because she had never had to think of anybody but herself.

And she would not get it even if they did have this mail-order baby, Rowan thought, because she wouldn't let herself be changed by the experience of becoming a parent. She and Eloise were going to arrange everything to suit their own needs, cutting out all of the messy, painful, difficult bits. They'd probably already arranged to buy breast milk for a fortune from a milk collective (or on the black market; who knew what Binx could find on the dark web with her skills). They'd probably already lined up a night nanny to do the night feeds and settling, and a few day nannies to do the parenting in daylight hours. They would have a baby and yet nothing in their lives would really change.

The audaciousness of Binx and Eloise's choice helped Rowan see that he believed very much that having a child should change you, and in order for that change to happen, you had to *be there*. If you were, then the rewards of parenting were so great that they could not ever really be put into words. That was part of the problem, and the reason why Binx had misunderstood his feelings about being a parent – it was impossible for him to find the language to express to anybody the enormity of the love he felt for the girls, the huge, expanding gratitude he felt to be a father, the richness of his hourly, daily, weekly engagement with them. Only Mariam understood.

Rowan knew that what he was about to say was so repellent that Mariam might never forgive him for it, but he was so angry he said it anyway. 'You have two good wombs in your marriage,' he said to Binx and Eloise. 'It seems selfish not to use at least one of them.'

That did it: the shitstorm broke for real.

There was a period of exaggerated female gasping that would have been funny had Mariam's gasp not been the loudest.

Binx, for once, seemed to be at a loss for a comeback. She looked surprised, and flushed, as if Rowan had slapped her. He hadn't been aware it was within his power to hurt Binx's feelings – she'd always seemed immune to criticism, in that shrug-it-off way of many millennials. *Was* she even a millennial? Or was Binx herself too old to fit in that category?

Jomo started saying something about respect for the choices of others, and Rowan turned on his friend. 'Shut up, Jomo. You've got no idea what it means to take responsibility for anybody else.'

Next, Jules tried to mediate. 'I appreciate that you both have strong convictions . . .'

Rowan had forgotten that Jules had once done the narration for a documentary that criticized baby-farming practices in India, where poor women became surrogates for wealthy Europeans. Maybe that was why she was trying to play peacemaker now.

Rowan was on a roll, though. He shook his head vehemently and cut her off.

'All of you – and you in particular, Jules – are totally insulated from the real world by your wealth,' he said. 'You think you're taking the part of the underdog here. But can't you see who the oppressors are in this situation? It's Eloise and Binx! They are buying themselves a baby that someone else, someone who needs the money, has to grow! Mariam, I know you agree with me!' The last bit he said with a rising tone of desperation.

'I don't agree with a single word you've said tonight,' she said, in a scarily low tone he'd never heard her use before.

Eloise left the room then, followed by Jules.

Jomo sank back into his chair, looking wretched.

Rowan felt naked, all of a sudden: he had revealed to the others this streak of violent contrarianism that he contained, something he'd learned to suppress early on in his marriage. But what was so wrong about disliking groupthink, on the left as much as on the right?

Rowan's rage began to fizzle out. Lately he was so fragile. The champagne was going flat in flutes abandoned around the table. What a waste! Things felt as if they were falling apart. Probably the only Yeats poem he had ever read, if he was honest. *Turning and turning in the widening gyre . . . the centre cannot hold.*

Mariam was speaking in apologetic tones to Binx, trying to smooth things over.

His wife was wearing her hair in a loose braid – her go-to solution, he knew, for when the weather was humid and her curls were untamable – and a sleeveless rose-colored dress. As he looked at her, she reached beneath the high neckline of her dress and absentmindedly, as she talked to Binx, drew out her necklace. She was not wearing the asteroid pendant he'd given her that morning for their wedding anniversary. She was wearing the silver cross on a chain.

When he was having a hard time, he reached for Mariam, but apparently in times of need she now reached for God. He remembered what that felt like from his years as a believer. Eighteen of them, if you could say a newborn believed in anything but the wonderful soft shape of his mother. His mom had taken him to church with her from the first week of his life, had practically walked out of the hospital and into the baptismal chamber. She had only wanted the impossible, what every parent wants: a promise from above that her baby would be kept safe forever.

He let himself weep, the tears flowing down his cheeks for the second time that day. At the service for deceased classmates that morning – two young souls whose time had been so cruelly foreshortened – he had sat in one of the pews in Memorial Church and, though he had not known either of them well, he'd wept through each slideshow, each piece of favorite music, each tribute from friends and past roommates.

Just as Jomo had sobbed through the funeral service for Mariam's father. That had infuriated Mariam, though Rowan hadn't understood why – it was only natural to grieve for your own losses, real or imagined, at a funeral. Of course he hadn't been thinking of his two classmates that morning but of all that he had to lose.

He'd been thinking about the day he and Mariam made their marriage vows to each other in that very same church. Arm in arm with her father, in the demure lace wedding dress that had been her second choice, she had walked down the red carpet laid between the pews, beneath the vaulted snow-white ceiling held up by colonnades. He had stood breathlessly waiting for her to reach him at the front of the church, watching the light pour in sideways from the huge arched windows, illuminating her veil.

That day, he had still been more his mother's son than Mariam's husband – so much so that he'd convinced Mariam to keep his mother happy by getting married in a church. It struck him only now that Mariam too had been, at that point, more her parents' daughter than his wife. Yet he had believed she belonged only to him.

In all their subsequent years of married life, there had been only one other time when he'd felt like he did right now – unsure of what Mariam wanted from him, who she needed him to be.

Ironically, it had been on their honeymoon.

They'd spent their first year of marriage saving up for the trip to Syria and Jordan, the region of Mariam's ancestry. Her parents, and his, had tried to talk them out of going, but it had not been unsafe – this was in 2004, long before the current unrest began.

Years after the fact, they'd joked about how out of character their constant honeymoon bickering had been. They'd written it off as an aberration brought on by the stress of overseas travel in countries where neither of them spoke the language. But had it really only been that?

When he was back home in Phoenix over the summer between his freshman and sophomore year, pining for Mariam, calling her day and night, his mother had shared a Puerto Rican proverb with him, which was how she usually tried to give him important life advice. It translated as 'learn to swim but guard your clothing'. What she meant, as far as he could tell, was that he should hold more of himself back from Mariam, that he was making himself too available to her. But that was impossible: he could not draw back from Mariam. He couldn't pretend to turn down the wattage of his feelings for her.

And that had worked for him all through college, and in their first year of marriage. But on their honeymoon, something had gone awry.

The first problem had been that Rowan couldn't stand not being physically affectionate to her in public – but in Syria and Jordan that was considered a crime. As was wearing shorts, which he also did anyway.

Mariam, however, had wanted him to respect the cultural rules of the countries in which they were visitors. Irritated at his suggestion that they should sit side by side on the many bus trips they took, she would go to the back of the vehicle and sit beside all the veiled women, leaving him to sit with the men at the front. There he was interrogated as to 'how to give an American woman oral pleasure' and asked all sorts of other lewd and invasive questions about his sex life. These men, the ones who could speak a bit of English, could not believe that in America it was not legal to have more than one wife – in Jordan, it was legal to have up to four – and yet it was okay to dance with a woman who was not your wife.

The strict divisions between the genders in those countries, he'd felt, had made some of the men childish, obsessed with sex like adolescents. He'd felt angry about this a lot of the time while they were over there – he had imagined that there would be *more* respect for women in those cultures, not less.

Usually he was the bleeding-heart liberal in their marriage, the one who thought that everything should be forgiven in the name of cultural relativism. In the lead-up to their honeymoon, he had read every book he could find on the history of the region, and had been desperate to make real, warm human connections with the people there, to apologize for all his sins as an American. But once they arrived, all that went out the window. He'd felt defensive and unapologetically proud of being American, and also irrationally protective of Mariam, as if her honor were at stake. Every man there seemed to see her as a slutty Westerner, open to any sort of sexual advance, though she always wore long clothing and covered her hair.

Mariam had not liked that version of him much. Or at all.

At almost every guesthouse they'd stayed in as they traveled about Jordan, the man in charge would sit down uninvited to regale them with tales of his sexual conquests of previous female tourists.

It drove Rowan crazy that Mariam listened politely to these stories, playing the good, non-judgmental tourist. In response to her passivity, he would get mouthy with the man in question and ask him to stop offending his wife, which had no effect whatsoever so long as Mariam was still smilingly listening.

One of the worst fights they'd had on that trip was in the Jordanian hill town of Karak, in a guesthouse called Dream. The owner, Seif, a middle-aged man with a black moustache and a big stomach, had served them hibiscus tea when they arrived in the late afternoon, then immediately launched in halting English into a story about how he had almost had sex with a Japanese woman who had stayed there the week before, but he had been too big for her. Rowan had let that one slide; it had been a long day of bus travel through the valley of Wadi Mujib, with nothing but goats to break up the monotonous desert scenery.

But then, thanking Seif for the tea, and preparing to go to their room upstairs, Mariam had touched Seif's arm, and Seif had said that when a woman touches a man's arm, it is very hard for the man, for he thinks it means she wants to have sex.

'She is my *wife*,' Rowan had said, livid.

And Mariam, instead of being grateful he was standing up for her, had given him a furious frown, which he knew meant she thought he was being rude and insensitive. Difficult. Contrarian.

She had still wanted to climb up to the crusader castle at the top of the hill before sunset, so off they'd trudged. All the way up to the entrance gate, they had shouted mean things at each other. He didn't remember what he'd said to her, but he recalled almost every word she had flung back at him: that he said all the right things back home but, as soon as he was out of his comfort zone, he turned into an unforgiving bigot. That he was fundamentally insecure or else he would know that she did not need him to *protect* her, that she was just fine, that she was open to every experience this place could throw at her, and he was getting in the way of that. That he was trying to shut her down instead of letting her expand.

At the entrance to the castle, they'd bribed the elderly attendant into letting them in, since it was technically past closing time. He had good English, and manners, too: sex was not mentioned once. He had offered to be their guide, and it was a relief to have his words cover the hostile silence between him and Mariam.

The castle, they discovered, was the ultimate in bricolage. Ancient Nabataean statues had been recycled by the Romans, and in turn the crusaders had recycled toppled Roman pillars and used them as foundation stones. Then the Mamluk Sultan Baibars had refortified the castle, which was used, after them, by the Ottomans.

Their guide had told them chilling stories about the crusader Reynaud de Châtillon, who had been Governor of Karak at the time of Salah Eddin. When he wanted to kill somebody, de Châtillon put a wooden box over the man's head and forced the family members to push him off the wall; the victim could not die from a heart attack on the way down because he couldn't see when he would hit the ground. Sometimes, their guide said, instead of pushing their husband or father off the wall, the family members would take hold of his hand and jump.

Rowan still didn't really understand what had happened on that trip. As soon as they'd resumed their normal lives back home, the honeymoon had taken on the quality of a half-forgotten nightmare.

Now he wondered if he'd internalized Mariam's silencing of what he felt had been valid observations about a foreign culture. Surely real respect for a person – a people, a place – meant being prepared to see the good and the bad, the wondrous as well as the disturbing.

They had married young. He'd always known there would be many different phases to their life together. He had promised himself that he would always shapeshift for her. But it was sometimes exhausting, toeing the line, following her lead.

Nobody at the dinner table – not even Mariam – noticed him crying. He was persona non grata. He wiped his face with the starched napkin, and drank some water.

Jules and Eloise returned from the bathroom. Eloise's eyes were red but she looked unburdened, whereas Jules seemed weighed down. *That's what we do for our friends*, Rowan thought. *When the load gets too heavy, we take their woes and carry them for a while.*

That was what he had tried – and failed – to do for Jomo. Who was, by the looks of it, still aiming to drink himself to death. His eyes had gone droopy. Earlier in the evening, he'd talked a big game about dancing all night, but it seemed increasingly likely that Jomo was not going to end up anywhere after dinner except passed out on a comfortable couch at the Spee.

'Let's get out of here,' Jules said to the table.

Rowan dug for his wallet, trying to suppress his anxiety at the impending tab. Then he saw that Jomo had already tossed his credit card to the waiter and shooed him away. Rowan's mood lifted, even as he felt jealous that Jomo had so much money he could decide on a whim to pay for everyone's dinner in a place like this. He and Mariam had budgeted $300 for this meal, and it turned out it had cost them nothing. This meant tomorrow they could justify a splurge on Darwin's sandwiches with the girls!

But would Mariam even want to speak to him after how he'd behaved tonight?

The others had already gathered their jackets and bags and belongings, and were following Jules in single file through the main seating area of the restaurant, winding between tables.

Rowan rushed to catch up to his friends. As he reached them, he saw that they'd all stopped in their tracks beside the table where Fred Reese was seated, his arm draped over his fiancée's shoulders. The Traitors Three were there too, and a few guys Rowan didn't recognize. From the size and shape of them, he guessed they'd rowed crew with Fred at college, at least during their freshman year, when much had been made of Fred's talents (the university had to come up with *some* excuse for why he'd been admitted). Now these men were not so much chiseled as large and going to seed.

'I take it you enjoyed the champagne,' Fred said to their group, his eyes on Eloise.

Jomo was swaying slightly, holding on to the back of a chair for support.

'Clearly someone did,' Fred said.

The room had begun to spin around Rowan – all the emotion of the night had coalesced into something that felt like drunkenness. He was drunk on *rage*. This was his moment to speak truth to power!

He took an unsteady step forward, adrenaline flooding his body.

'Do you have something to say?' Fred said, in a mocking voice.

But Rowan could not speak.

The Traitors Three began to titter, and that was when Binx came to Rowan's rescue. In one fluid movement she picked up a dessert fork and stabbed it right through the roast artichoke heart that Fred had on his plate.

The violence of the gesture galvanized Rowan.

'Shame on you,' he said to Frederick P. Reese II, more meekly than he'd planned.

And then, because he didn't know what else to do, he went up the stairs, and through the hotel lobby, and out into the warm rain of a sudden spring downpour.

Chapter 9: Mariam

Saturday morning of Reunion Weekend

(May 26, 2018)

The SoulCycle workout room was packed. As far as Mariam could see from her spot in the back row, there was not a single empty bike, and everybody – whether they were bed-headed fifth-year reunionees or silver-haired fiftieth-year reunionees – was getting really amped, warming up with standing cycling sprints.

Mariam had never done SoulCycle before. She began to feel nervous.

Earlier that morning, she'd left Rowan in their suite with the girls, without giving him any indication of when she would be back to help out. She was hoping an endorphin rush could help her push reset on the weekend, which she'd been looking forward to for so long but now felt was slipping out of her grasp.

In the mirror, she could see the intense, drank-the-Kool-Aid look on Jomo's face as he geared up on his bike. She'd bumped into him on her way into the MAC gym, and he'd told her he did SoulCycle classes regularly. Jomo had always been a sucker for enlightenment exercise fads. She remembered him getting really into hot yoga when it first became a thing, and then tai chi, and then tae bo – which wasn't even a real martial art, just some guy called Billy's meld of boxing and taekwondo moves.

The MAC had been majorly upgraded since she'd last been inside it. She hadn't spent a lot of time here as an undergraduate; she remembered occasionally doing sit-ups on filthy old mats on the stair landings – space had been an issue, especially at peak times. She'd always felt intimidated by the determined, skinny girls who worked out so seriously on machines that made no sense to her. Some of them had even mastered the complex art of studying while exercising, their coursework books propped on shelves above the treadmills.

Once, Mariam had used the StairMaster for half an hour without even realizing the thing wasn't turned on, and nobody in the line waiting for the machine had felt any compulsion to point this out.

Rowan, too, had disdained gym culture as a student. Back then, he'd been a purist, jogging outside for hours even in sub-zero temperatures, through snow and fog and sleet, returning home in a state of *mushin no shin*, the Zen expression for 'mind without mind'. These days, he was as unfit as she was. There were too many chores on weekends, and they both prioritized their time with the girls over time for themselves.

Maybe SoulCycle could become their new thing. Now that Bushwick was a haven for millennials, there were probably a dozen SoulCycle studios in their area; she just hadn't been paying attention. She almost sent Rowan a funny text proposing the idea, but then she remembered she was angry at him.

The instructor had put on a headset and was shouting a welcome that had the vocabulary of a benediction – inhaling intention and exhaling expectation – and then she pumped up the music so high it hurt Mariam's eardrums.

The overhead lights went out and a disco ball was lit up by strobe lights, which turned out to be an actual blessing, because it meant that the room was dark enough that nobody could see Mariam trying to stand-up pedal while simultaneously tapping her butt back onto the bike seat in graceless squats.

At some late stage in the workout, faint with overexertion, she spotted the woman with the white streak in her hair, whose breast-milk she'd poured down the sink. She was hard at work on her bike, seemingly fit as a fiddle. Mariam hadn't exercised at all for six months after having each of her babies, and after that all she'd been able to manage was a stroll in the park. She was about to think something spiteful when suddenly all her negative thoughts disappeared.

Had she achieved *mushin no shin*?

As if in answer to her question, the instructor shouted, 'You are on a journey to change your life! You can do this!'

Mariam whooped along with the rest of the cyclists at their final peak, and applauded louder than anyone else at the end of the class, basking in the instructor's praise for their physical and spiritual super abilities. Apparently she was still an affirmation junkie, just like the rest of them.

Leaving the MAC with Jomo, Mariam's legs were shaky, but she felt great. Content, emptied out.

'Was Jules awake when you left the suite?' Jomo asked her.

'I don't think so,' Mariam said. 'Her door was still closed.'

'I hope I didn't wake the girls when I got in last night,' he said.

'No, not at all,' she lied. In fact he had woken Eva when he'd tripped on the suitcase lying open in the middle of their room, on his way back from the bathroom.

'How was the Spee?' she asked.

'It was dead. I think everyone went too hard on Thursday night,' he said. 'But tonight you're all coming with me, no excuses. The afterparty is open to everyone in our class.'

'That's if I'm still awake after the dinner-dance,' she said, thinking, *There's no way I'm going to the Spee tonight.*

Mariam paused as they approached the Kirkland House entrance. She wasn't ready to show Rowan mercy. 'You want to get something to eat?' she asked Jomo.

He hesitated – Mariam guessed that he was eager to see if Jules was up – but, to his credit as her friend, he said yes.

Being part of a web of blocking-group friendships meant that – as with siblings in a big family – the configurations of allegiance and intimacy changed regularly, in subtle ways. Mariam had grown up with two sisters, but even for her it had taken a while, once they'd formed their blocking group at the end of their freshman year, to adapt to these cyclical rhythms of friendship and to know where she stood with each of the others.

She and Jomo, for instance, had both liked to eat dinner early at college, as soon as the Kirkland dining hall opened at five-thirty pm, while the others generally arrived later. This meant that, back then, they'd known a lot of the details of what was going on in each other's lives and studies. There was more personal give-and-take over a meal shared by two in comparison to the jokey, nonsense conversations they tended to have when eating as a group.

It was during these early dinners that Jomo had encouraged her to pursue an idea she had for her senior thesis topic, for her major in Folklore and Mythology: the symbolic use of desserts in famous folktales such as 'Hansel and Gretel', 'The Gingerbread Man', and 'The Magic Pudding'. It was something she'd always liked about Jomo – that the most popular guy in their class was as comfortable getting excited about her interest in fictional desserts, or about the field trip he and the other Earth and Planetary Sciences majors were doing to study 'fold-and-thrust' belts in the Canadian Rockies, as he was about holding the record for longest ever keg-stand at the Spee.

She'd gone on to write about the lesser-known Italian folk-tales collected by Giambattista Basile in the sixteenth century, which featured blancmange and cassata and syrup-honey floods. Mariam's favorite Basile story, later adapted by Calvino, was about a woman molding a husband for herself out of sweet dough, only to have him stolen by another woman on the day of their wedding. 'The Handmade Man', it was called. For ages she'd dreamed of writing a recipe book that was also a modern retelling of these fairytales. But she had never found the time to do it, or the confidence.

'How's your mom doing?' Jomo asked in a cautious tone, as they walked toward the cafés around Brattle Square.

Mariam understood he was trying to be respectful, not digging for details of her family's mourning. 'She's okay. I think she's enjoying being selfish for once,' she said. 'Caring only for herself.'

A story her mom used to tell came to mind, about the day that Mariam, the youngest in the family, had started school. Anticipating her new freedom, Mariam's mother had returned home after school drop-off, squeezed lemon juice onto her hair, put on her swimsuit, and sat for hours next to the pool, eating grapes, hoping to end the day with her dark hair streaked with blonde. Nobody pulling at her hem or needling her. Just silence and sunlight.

She had been younger that morning than Mariam was now, a strange thought.

Yet it had turned out to be a false freedom. School had meant ever more intense demands on their mother, and their father had never taken up any of the slack. And later there'd been the misery Mariam and her sisters had visited upon their mother during adolescence, as they'd tried to individuate, rejecting her model of womanhood to establish their own. They'd never once thought of things from her perspective. Now Mariam knew that her mother had been going through her own hormonal changes in those years, perimenopause and then menopause. The four women in the family had been at opposite ends of the hormonal roller-coaster, all taking it out on one another.

What would *she* do the day that Eva started school, several years from now? Mariam had a sneaking suspicion that though she often wished that milestone would hove into view sooner, she would spend that first day of freedom crying into her pillow at home, or lurking outside the school, trying to catch a glimpse of her youngest daughter in the playground.

'Does it get any easier?' Jomo asked her.

'Grief? I suppose so,' Mariam said. 'What helps the most is that Dad made it so clear by the end that he wanted to die. He read a lot of philosophy in his final months, and would send long emails to me and my sisters. I didn't read them at the time, it was too painful. But I went back and looked at his last emails to me, and I was struck by something he'd quoted. That sickness is useful because it makes us look at death with less frightened eyes. I think Dad took a lot of comfort from that, and he wanted us to as well.'

She and Jomo chose an outdoor table at an organic café and ordered egg-white omelets and kale juice with wheatgrass shots – not something Mariam ever normally had for breakfast.

The guy serving them looked to be in his seventies. It was something she was noticing more and more these days – people forced back into menial jobs (or forced never to leave those same jobs) at the time of life when they deserved to be putting up their feet, taking it easy for once.

The café made its employees wear name tags, probably in an attempt to establish a connection between customer and server. But all it did, in Mariam's opinion, was humiliate the staff. *My name is: TONY*, his name tag read. *My favorite food is: NOODLES.*

'How's *your* mom doing?' Mariam asked Jomo. The juice wasn't as bad as she'd expected.

'Really great. She's in full remission now,' he said. 'Thanks for asking.' He was silent for a bit. 'It's been good for my parents' marriage. Small blessings, right?'

'What do you mean?'

'It changed the dynamic between them,' Jomo said. 'Maybe it's not her getting sick – maybe it would have happened anyway as they got older. Mom used to be meek and mild, and Dad was more dominant. But now he follows her around like a puppy. She rules over him and they're both happier for it. Last year we went on a family vacation to Hawaii, and they came skipping out of their hotel room and told me they'd just taken a bubble bath together.'

Mariam smiled. 'It's nice to know things can get better as well as worse.'

He nodded. 'Yeah. Happy couples, like you and Rowan, seem to figure out how to fall in love with each other all over again at different times in your lives. I guess that's what it takes.'

Mariam felt irritated by this comment, though she knew Jomo was trying to be nice. He had no idea what it took to keep a marriage alive, let alone happy, over years of being together. She decided that the day he actually found the courage to get engaged, she'd mail him her copy of Alain de Botton's portrait of a modern marriage, *The Course of Love*. It was so bluntly accurate about how marriage could feel, day to day, and how in just a few hours the emotions passing between spouses could go from lust to rage to boredom to tenderness to indifference and back again to love.

When the check came she insisted on paying. 'The dinner last night must have cost you a small fortune,' she said, as they got up to head back to Kirkland. 'And Rowan ruined it. I'm really sorry.'

'We all played our part in the disaster,' Jomo said. He cleared his throat. 'Did Rowan say anything to you about me?'

'About you? No. He may have tried to as we walked home, but I very quickly made it clear that we are on a no-talking basis until further notice.'

'Don't be too hard on him, Mariam.'

'I just wish he'd let me fight my own battles occasionally,' she said. 'I don't really have any problem with what Binx and Eloise are planning to do. He thought he was speaking up for me, but he was speaking *for* me.'

She'd been thinking about this as she lay awake in the night, stewing in her anger, having exiled Rowan to Alexis's single bed on the other side of the room.

What Eloise and Binx were proposing was on the more extreme end of the scale, but she understood why they were doing it. She'd known couples who had, by choice, exclusively formula-fed their babies, and pioneered a different model of parenting as a result. No matter how supportive Rowan had been when it came to getting up to do the night settling and changing, the buck had always stopped with her boobs. She'd loved being pregnant and breastfeeding (most of the time), but she'd also been aware that they were the final things standing in the way of a truly egalitarian split in the parenting labor. So she could see what was appealing about unhitching the work of producing a baby from just one person in a partnership.

Mariam decided to keep complaining about Rowan, while she had a captive audience.

'He did the same thing earlier this year, when my mother

offered to help out with private-school fees for Alexis,' she said to Jomo. 'He just assumed I would be on the same ideological page as him, and he told her that we were choosing to send her to the local public school where he's principal because we want her to experience hardship firsthand. And because if we sent her to private school she'd be among *the children of our enemies*. "The children of our enemies"! Can you imagine me ever using such a phrase?'

Jomo laughed. 'Maybe fifteen years ago,' he said. 'But you've mellowed with age.'

'It's as if, over the years, we've become grafted onto each other,' Mariam said. 'Sometimes I can't get any perspective on him.'

'It sounds pretty good from where I'm sitting,' Jomo said.

'It does? Which part?'

'Being grafted to a person you love.'

She was about to ask him how things were going with Giselle when they bumped into a couple Jomo knew from their class. After introductions – his name was Nat, his wife's name was Rachel, their two-month-old baby was named Plum – Jomo and his acquaintances plunged into the usual reunion power-download of the last five years of their lives, while Plum slept within the largest baby buggy Mariam had ever seen.

Mariam zoned out of their conversation, silently composing a haiku inspired by her favorite William Carlos Williams poem.

This is just to say
we've named our new daughter Plum
so sweet and so bold

Rachel had begun to monopolize the conversation with a disquisition on her baby. Two months since the birth of Plum and Rachel was still decompressing, marveling at the fact that she and Nat had made a human and it had emerged from her own body. Mariam remembered that feeling. She had even kept in the freezer, for an embarrassingly long time, the mucus plug that had dislodged from her cervix early in Alexis's birth, the 'show', the first sign that she was going to be birthing a *baby*. As if it were a relic from the body of a saint! Gross.

All women, after having their first baby, secretly believe they have invented pregnancy, birth, the feat of creation. She'd felt it too, after Alexis. But now that she was further along the path of motherhood, Mariam was sometimes put off by the self-involvement of the first-timers. Mariam remembered, when Alexis was very young, looking at women with older children and thinking, *But they can't have loved their baby as much as I love mine.*

Blinded by love. That was what it meant to be a parent, she thought, and not just to a newborn. At the end of the orientation day for the incoming kindergarten class – the class Alexis would be in – Mariam had watched the other parents waiting in the schoolyard as their children broke off from the group and ran toward them. On both the parents' and children's faces was transporting joy at being reunited. *We are all just the same*, she'd thought. *Risking everything by loving our children so desperately.* When Alexis had begun to sprint toward her, Mariam had turned into a puddle of maternal love, watching her little girl approaching on her skinny legs, her giant satchel jiggling up and down on her back.

The toughest thing about parenting, though, was that doing it right meant parenting yourself into obsolescence. By the time Alexis and Eva – into whom she would have poured everything she had – were eighteen and heading to college, they would, ideally, love her and Rowan, but they would no longer *need* them. It was no surprise to her that parents had breakdowns when their kids left home. What other job rewards two decades of exceeding all the key performance indicators with redundancy and unemployment?

Goddamn him, she was missing Rowan again. She wanted to tell him about Rachel and baby Plum.

She would need to head back soon and sort things out with him or the girls would pick up that something was wrong. They had a sixth sense about even the slightest shift in the currents between their parents. They were extremely lucky, of course, if *this* was what counted as a crisis for them.

Maybe there should be a form of marriage therapy that involved spouse-deprivation, Mariam thought. She loved Rowan to bits, but she sometimes wished she could microdose rather than overdose on him.

Rowan had a recurring nightmare that Mariam had left him for someone else. He would wake from it in tears, edging closer to her in the bed, or mention it to her in the morning with a hug. She had started joking to him that one day this nightmare would be his fondest dream – *my crazy wife has FINALLY left me for someone else!* Yet she was grateful that his unconscious visited this nightmare on him regularly; it was like a psychic prod to remind him to value her.

She, on the other hand, had a different recurring nightmare. She would be on the prowl for a man, or having sex with some strange man, and enjoying it, and then gradually it would dawn on the dream-Mariam that she was married, and had children, and then her horror would grow: where was Rowan, where were the girls? She too would wake and scoot closer to Rowan's side of the bed. She didn't tell him about these dreams because they only *ended* as nightmares. But now it occurred to her that perhaps Rowan's nightmares also started out as lovely dreams in which he was blissfully screwing some other woman, real or imagined.

Mariam tuned back in to the conversation. Nat was telling Jomo that he and Rachel were going out for breakfast after a family meditation session in the new serenity room in Kirkland House; all the undergraduate residences had one now, as a measure to ease student stress and anxiety, and build resilience.

Part of Mariam wanted to make fun of the precious millennials who'd managed to get into Harvard without learning anything useful along the way – like how to be resilient! She could just imagine them lounging in their serenity rooms, eating free cookies and expecting constant emotional hand-holding. But another part of her wished something like that had existed when she'd been at college.

Maybe this was her chance to get the weekend back on track.

She asked the couple for directions to the serenity room within Kirkland House and hugged Jomo goodbye, saying she'd see him later.

The serenity room was down in the basement, off one of the underground corridors that, in the coldest weather, students used to get to the dining hall without going outside. It was, Mariam realized, the room that had once been the headquarters of Jomo's beer-brewing club for seniors, which must now be defunct.

Back then it had been an unheated, unpainted room with the ambience of a broom closet. She was impressed by the care that had been taken in decorating the room for its new purpose. It had been wallpapered in a soothing shade of yellow and had shaggy carpet that was comfortable to kneel on. There were several hanging basket chairs – the ones that you could curl up in like a pupa inside a cocoon – and beanbags dotted all over the place. The overhead lights were off; fake candles flickered on the bookshelves.

There was a woman on the far side of the room, sitting

cross-legged inside a hanging basket, deep in meditation. She did not turn around when Mariam entered.

Mariam put her shoes on the rack and quietly got settled on a beanbag in the corner.

For a while, she couldn't really decide what to say to God.

Meditation, mindfulness, prayer – all of it had the same end goal of achieving inner peace. But what about *outer* peace? Right at the moment when she and everyone like her should be out on the streets protesting for world peace, here she was seeking peace only for herself. It was a form of retreat, she knew. It was the late-capitalist, consumerist way. Instead of pushing for political change, everybody sat at home, lost in the fascinating squishy mazes of their own minds.

Oh, shut up, she said to her inner skeptic, who often came up with this kind of shit.

The woman across the room breathed out loudly with what sounded like *ujjayi* breath.

Mariam tried some deep breathing herself, waiting for God to communicate with her.

And suddenly she was back in Damascus, a bustling city that, for all she knew, the civil war had by now turned into a devastated shadow city, unrecognizable to those who had once loved (who still loved) it as it had been: imperfect but *alive*, the oldest continuously inhabited city in the world. How could she be so ignorant about what had befallen Damascus? Life went on there, she presumed, though she had not bothered to find out how.

It was now too hard to get a tourist visa to visit – her father had tried, without luck, when it became clear that he did not have much time left to live. The only images she had seen of Syrian cities in the past years were of hellholes of destruction and dust, but perhaps Damascus had been spared the worst of it.

What was God trying to say to her by flooding her mind with these memories? Who knew. This was the problem with her untutored version of prayer.

She tried to reconstruct the place in her mind, as it had been in the relative tranquility of the summer of 2004.

The fresh orange juice sold by a street vendor outside the Al Haramain Hotel, beside a never-finished mosque, covered with vines.

The seven gates to the walled Old City.

Men with kettles of coffee on their backs, juggling glasses. Barrels of corncobs. Watermelons stored in fountains to keep cool.

The marble floor of the vast, open-air courtyard at the center of the Umayyad Mosque, people relaxing at its edges. Children playing a game of catch, people reading and picnicking and snoozing in the shade.

Inside, out of the sun, the rows and rows of bare upturned feet as the women on their side of the mosque knelt and bent in prayer, in unison, so beautiful to watch. Little girls trying to learn the ropes from their mothers and grandmothers, imitating their flowing movements.

And the surprise of seeing Syrian Christian pilgrims, come to visit the shrine within the mosque dedicated to John the Baptist. It was one of the things Mariam had loved the most about the city and its monuments – they acknowledged the warp and weft of religious history. The mosque had once been a Roman temple honoring Jupiter, and later a Christian cathedral. It was many things, to many people. It had been difficult to get her brain around this fluidity, trained as it was to seek out distinguishing categories and boundaries.

For reasons now incomprehensible to her, she and Rowan had not visited the mountain town her father's family was from,

Ma'loula, where it was rumored Aramaic was still spoken. They'd decided instead to visit a famous crusader castle near Homs. They had assumed they would be able to visit another time, in one year, or five, or fifteen. How wrong they had been.

It was to this mountain town that her father had wanted to travel when he was dying, in order to drink the holy water that his parents had told him seeped from the cliff face beside the Greek Orthodox monastery there. A quiet place where Christians and Muslims sat together, washing their eyes with water said to bring health and happiness to people of all faiths. When her father had investigated a visit, he'd been told that the monastery had been desecrated in the conflict, part of it burned to the ground, its holy relics destroyed.

'Mariam?'

She opened her eyes with a start.

One of the T3s – Wenona – was peering at her in the fake candlelight. Mariam had been sharing a spiritual space with a person she despised.

'It *is* you!' Wenona exclaimed. 'I looked for you guys at the Barker Center drinks last night. Did you all go someplace else after dinner?' She didn't wait for Mariam to respond. 'You didn't miss much. Weak drinks and sloppy finger food. Bad lighting, too.'

Mariam said nothing. Wenona had not been the ringleader of the three; that was Tiffany, through and through. Wenona was nothing but a leaf, going whichever way the gusts of power blew.

Watching President Reese's inauguration on TV, mostly through her fingers because her hands kept flying to her face in disbelief, Mariam had spotted Wenona, along with Tiffany and Kashvi, seated in the second row of the section of the president's family and friends. They'd been dressed in their winter finery, tapping on Fred's shoulder to whisper in his ear, their eyes gleaming.

Mariam mumbled something about Rowan and the kids, escaping from Wenona as quickly as she could. She followed the underground passage to their entryway and climbed the stairs to the suite.

There was nobody there. She lay down on one of the unmade single beds and looked out the window.

Rowan always went on about her amazing, trouble-free natural births. But a few days after Eva was born, once she was back home, Mariam had gone to the bathroom in the night after a feed and woken up on the tiled floor, her face in a pool of her own dark blood.

It had been very peaceful lying there. Cold, but peaceful. It had felt like the first real rest she'd had for days, weeks, years. After some time, her father had touched her shoulder, and helped her sit up.

Rowan had soon shattered the peace – and saved her life – by discovering her and realizing she was bleeding out. In the hospital, she was told by a doctor that she was lucky to be alive, that she'd had a rare postpartum hemorrhage.

She and Rowan had not told anybody about this episode, not even their families. Mariam had recovered after an operation and a transfusion, and she'd soon climbed back on the merry-go-round of Newbornland. It had been an agreement between them, that they didn't want her beautiful birth – her perfect birth – marred by this afterbirth drama.

But she had also never told Rowan about her vision of her father, and the religious epiphany of sensing her father's presence beside her as she lay dying. It was time for her to tell him, about all of it.

The sun was streaming through the window onto the bed. She remembered morning light exactly like it from her time living in this room as a student.

She began to feel bad for how she'd just snubbed Wenona. In the meditation room, of all places.

The Red Book was lying facedown on the bed. Mariam flipped through until she found Wenona's entry. She started reading, expecting to find confirmation of Wenona's ghastliness. Instead, she found this:

> Before our ten-year reunion, I dieted for months, and took up kick-boxing, so I could fit into the same dress I'd worn the day we all graduated in 2003. I got my hair straightened and my make-up done professionally before every event.
>
> I was single, you see. And I didn't want anyone to think it was my fault I was alone. If I looked good enough, I told myself, maybe anyone who asked would believe me when I said I was single by choice. I didn't even go to the Friday night Singles Mixer, though a guy I've always liked told me he was going to be there. I secretly believed that I was rotten inside, and that anybody who met me could sense this straightaway.
>
> In the five years since, I've remained unlucky in love. There. I've said it. I'm still single. What has changed is that I'm no longer embarrassed to admit it. Thanks to therapy, I've come to see that I wouldn't have become a doctor if I hadn't been searching for a way to stop thinking of myself as a broken, defective, bad human being. I wouldn't have been able to follow my passion for treating unusual medical conditions with the same single-mindedness (ha!) if I'd been playing my part as half of a couple.
>
> Don't get me wrong. I'm looking for a husband. I'll be first in the door at this year's Singles Mixer. (John Merrick, say you'll be there too?)
>
> But I'm also okay with a few more years where I'm left in work-aholic peace to study rare syndromes that modern medicine has

barely explored. In my clinic in Austin, I've worked with patients who are allergic to water, or who have alien-hand syndrome, or auto-brewery syndrome (yes, they can spontaneously get drunk without drinking alcohol – but trust me, it's not as fun as it sounds). Some of my patients suffer from Alice-in-Wonderland syndrome, or pica disease, where all they want to eat is clay and chalk. Most of my patients were never taken seriously until they came to see me. They were told it's all in their minds. I don't always have a cure for the diseases they present with – not yet – but I won't stop looking until I drop dead from exhaustion.

I've gained a few pounds since 2013, sure. I hardly make it to the gym anymore. It doesn't matter. I bought a new dress today, and Spanx to go under it. I'll get my hair done before the dinner-dance, and I'll wear my very best shoes. Like Alice, I'll step through the looking glass into Underland – and onto our old campus.

Chapter 10: Eloise

Saturday afternoon of Reunion Weekend

(May 26, 2018)

Eloise was so sunburned it felt as if she were lying on Ned Noya's bed of hot coals. It was somewhat of an achievement to get this burned in *May*, even with her freckled skin, even after spending all morning in a swimsuit and sarong, and then going tramping with Jules in the hottest noon hour.

She was in too much discomfort to lie on her back to nap. She turned onto her shoulder – which was marginally less painful – so that she was facing Binx, who was fast asleep beside her on their bed.

Binx had also soaked up some sun during the fifth-reunion float-building contest earlier in the day. Her olive skin went straight to brown, unlike Eloise's, who would need a lot of foundation to cover her red nose and look presentable at the dinner-dance at Winthrop House that evening.

Asleep, Binx looked like a woodland nymph curled up in a forest clearing, with her pointy ears and long eyelashes, and her ribs showing through her skin. She was naked from top to toe, and Eloise was filled with tenderness looking at her. The indecision of the past year had taken its toll on her wife, too. The evidence had been there under her eyes – Binx wasting away beneath that gray tunic – but Eloise had chosen not to see it.

She was still coming to grips with what had become clear the night before. Elly+ had been right. All Binx wanted was to make Eloise happy. Convincing Binx that they shouldn't go ahead with the surrogacy had been easy in comparison to what now lay before Eloise: accepting that in marrying Binx she had, at some unconscious level, chosen to be the one in charge, the one to make the most painful decisions on behalf of both of them.

There had been a game Eloise had played as a child where she and a friend leaned against each other until one person suddenly stepped away, leaving the other to fall forward. That was how she'd felt when Binx said that she did not care either way if they had a child or not. In floating the idea of using a gestational surrogate, Binx had believed she was supporting Eloise in her desire to have a baby, while insulating her from the inevitable sacrifices of becoming a parent: the effect on her body, her mind, her career, her professional standing.

Now that the imagined resistance was no longer there, Eloise had nothing against which to shape her response to the question of parenthood. She felt as if she were falling into a different void.

At least the most crucial decision had been made. They could let Ana know they would not be needing her services as a surrogate. Thinking about this, Eloise was flooded with a relief so visceral it suffused her whole body.

She laid her hand on Binx's jutting hip.

They had stayed up the night before until the break of dawn, hashing everything out in front of Elly+, at Eloise's request. Elly+

had quietly observed Eloise and Binx's nocturnal conversation, maybe able to sense that, given the situation, it was best for her mostly to listen.

Eloise had vowed to her wife that she would, from now on, participate fully in the creation of Elly+. She would hold nothing back from her android double. Binx was open to the idea of one day creating a partner fembot for Elly+, based on her own consciousness, though she'd said it would need to wait until she reached the age of 30 and could access her full trust fund income.

She's not yet 30! Eloise had thought at that moment, once again startled by Binx's youth. By the time Binx approached her own mid-life crisis at 40, Eloise would be sailing toward 50 in what she hoped would feel like the calm after the storm.

Who knew, though; it seemed that every female milestone came with a side serving of some fresh hell that nobody had warned her about – or perhaps they'd tried and she had not heeded the warnings of the elderly crones whispering the truth around their cauldrons. Eloise had seen her mother go through years of endless, relapsing menopause. And then, once she'd finally emerged on the other side of it, she suffered such bad sleeplessness that she'd started taking hypnotic pills that caused sleep paralysis, and she'd wake in the night unable to move.

Eloise felt grateful that she'd be able to avoid the body-muddling mess of pregnancy and birth. Mariam had once told her that, had they not lived in modern times, nine of the ten people in her mothers' group would have died of birth or post-birth complications. Eloise knew this was only scratching the surface of the things that mothers dealt with physically – to know the fullness of the trauma, you had to become part of that group yourself. It was closely guarded information, in part, Eloise guessed, for the survival of the species. If women knew what they were walking into, instead of supporting male fantasies like space travel to Mars they'd be out on the streets demanding that every single medical research dollar get poured into inventing artificial wombs.

An idea dawned on Eloise as she lay there, unable to nap.

Maybe Elly+ could help her answer some of the most fundamental questions within the field of hedonics! Most machine learning was about using AI to make predictions of behavior (usually, given the commercial imperatives, about what a person might buy, browse, or binge-watch next). What if Eloise could use Elly+ as the basis for creating happiness avatars to better guide people's choices? A person could type in their information, their background, a few fears and desires, some anxieties and hopes, and be given a personalized prediction of what was most likely to make them happy in the future. Like a 'prospection' bot! The Prospector. That would be a great name for it.

It would be especially useful, Eloise thought, to people reaching midlife, turning forty, which was the age Kant had been when he published *Observations on the Feeling of the Beautiful and Sublime.* (When Eloise had first learned that – in her early twenties – she'd thought of forty as old.) Kant believed that it was only at forty that people reach adult maturity and – with some effort and discipline on their part – acquire a 'moral character' that remains unchanged for the rest of their lives. In a way, she mused, it was similar to Erikson's idea of periodic psychological crises, that, if resolved, could become opportunities for growth; Erikson had probably read Kant.

That night she and Binx would be going their separate ways, each to their own reunion events, though the plan was to meet up for the afterparty at the Spee. Binx's fifth-reunion dinner-dance had been 'Quadded', as per custom: held in the Quadrangle within the old Radcliffe campus – in another universe, so far as Eloise and her blockmates were concerned.

They'd always been spoiled by being in Kirkland House, at the center of things. On the day the outcome of the upperclass house lottery was announced in the Yard, there was always some sympathy for the Quadlings – though really it was more schadenfreude. Rowan had made it a point of pride never once to go out to the Quad while he was at college, Eloise recalled. He could be a real dick like that, though he claimed always to be on the side of the downtrodden.

She sighed. Everybody had their blind spots.

Rowan probably assumed she and Binx would never be friends with him again after what he'd said at the dinner table the previous night, but in fact she wasn't angry with him, and Binx never held grudges.

He had said aloud some of the things Eloise had long thought privately. And she understood that many parents' defenses were so forcefully maintained that they could feel threatened by any vision of parenthood that deviated from their own. For her and Binx this question of whether or not to be parents, and how, and through what method, was still sort of theoretical. For Rowan it was raw and real.

She should text him to say there were no hard feelings. And Mariam too, who was probably still punishing Rowan for his behavior. Their morning had most likely not been as fun as hers. Their daughters – her goddaughters – were wonderful and all, but they were also such hard work. All children were; she'd learned that in the course of her research on parenthood and its counterintuitive effects on personal happiness.

But Eloise sometimes wondered if the intensity of Rowan and Mariam's parenting style had created mini-monsters of need.

They hadn't even sent them to preschool, though these days it was fairly affordable, especially if they were prepared to enroll them in the public system. If the message you gave your children was that they can't manage a thing without you, then they naturally made sure they couldn't manage a thing without you. At last night's dinner, before things soured, Mariam had told Eloise a story about her battles to teach Alexis to button her own shirts and tie her own shoelaces. The kid was already 5!

This was not a generous nor productive line of thought, so Eloise swerved out of it, like changing lanes in traffic. It was one of the most useful things she'd learned from the Paraliminal recordings to which she used to listen regularly. They'd taken a while to get used to – the way the voice of the guide leading the meditation switched from the left to the right earphone, and ran different narratives simultaneously in each ear – but they'd seemed to work for her, distracting both hemispheres of her brain so that her unconscious could be accessed more directly.

She hadn't listened to them again, though, not since the last World Philosophy Day. She'd been asked to give a talk at the Newton Free Library and she'd recommended to the audience some Paraliminal meditations she'd downloaded online. A man in the crowd had stood up, agitated, and said she was being brainwashed by these recordings, that the alt-right was using them to recruit members by distributing subliminal hate speech. 'Why do you think it's called white noise?' he'd said.

The rest of the audience had shooshed him and he'd left in a huff, but since then, Eloise had begun to worry that she was inching toward becoming more politically conservative, not because she was getting older or because of a genuine shift in her values, but because of the subliminal messaging in these meditations. Just as she had gone from being a liberal to being somewhere in the center to now toying with elements of traditional conservative thought, what if she one day woke up to discover she had become a bona fide alt-righter, with a swastika tattoo and a white-pride t-shirt?

She halted this hideous thought in its tracks too, and decided instead to review her morning.

Binx's friends, the five-year reunionees, had given her a warm welcome at the float-building party on the Charles River – as if she were a celebrity of sorts for being married to Binx. Most of them weren't yet paired off, settled down, buttoned up. They were used to interacting in more open-ended ways, and they'd been so accommodating to Eloise. There was none of the ghosting of partners that she'd seen so many of the spouses of her own classmates subjected to, left to sip their drinks just outside the closed-off social circles.

Jules had texted late in the morning, as she and Binx were heading back home, asking Eloise if she wanted to join her 'tramping among our old friends from the Colledge at Newetowne'. To anybody else, the message would have been gibberish.

At home, Eloise had changed out of her swimsuit, while Binx – glad on Eloise's behalf that she was going to get some time with Jules – made sandwiches for her to take along for a picnic lunch.

'Tramping' was how she and Jules referred to the mini-expeditions they'd started making in their freshman fall, as new roommates and friends. As a high-school graduation gift, Jules's mother had given her a leatherbound copy of a book published in the 1930s, *Three Centuries of Harvard, 1636–1936*, written by one Samuel Eliot Morison of the Class of 1908, later a Harvard professor himself. It was filled with references to sites of historic interest in Harvard Square and the neighborhoods beyond, and on Saturday afternoons Eloise and Jules would set off together with the book for a brush with history.

Her friendship with Jules had been forged, really, on those expeditions around the 'Colledge at Newetowne', which was what Harvard College had been called in the seventeenth century, when it was nothing more than a single schoolhouse at the edge of a cow pasture.

The golden rule of tramping was to wear your oldest shoes – a rule they'd made after being caught in a storm visiting a site in Allston and had ruined their sneakers wading through muddy fields to get home. Perhaps Jules hadn't brought any old shoes with her, though, because when they'd met up in the Yard that morning she was wearing a pair of sneakers that looked like they'd just been taken out of the box.

Beneath her baseball cap, Jules looked tired; she'd told Eloise that she had hardly slept the night before. Eloise didn't need to ask why. Jules had probably been worrying about the conflict within their blocking group, the note of discord on which the night had ended.

Eloise had stuck to the original rule and was not only wearing dirt-encrusted sports shoes but had also put on her yuckiest tracksuit pants. Jules had laughed when she first saw Eloise, and spontaneously embraced her, though Jules was not normally an enthusiastic hugger. One of the worst things about being famous, Eloise had learned from Jules, was that total strangers tried to hug or high-five her all the time, as if it were the most normal thing in the world; as a result, Jules wasn't a fan of hugging even her closest friends, though she'd always made an exception for Jomo.

'New perfume?' Eloise had said to Jules as they peeled themselves apart. 'What's this one called?'

She knew that Jules had, since college, tagged each year of her life in her own memory by changing the scent she wore every time spring came around. It didn't hurt, Eloise thought, that she probably got sent a lot of perfumes just for being Jules. But it wasn't an extravagance for her, it was a tool to transport herself back to key moments while acting, accessing memories and emotions from her past.

'Assassin,' Jules had said, with dramatic emphasis. 'I'm not sure if I like it. It smells like cloves, and my grandmother used to make me bite on cloves if I had a toothache, some Swedish peasant remedy.'

They were walking to the Old Burial Ground on Garden Street. According to *Three Centuries of Harvard*, which Jules had brought along with her – dog-eared and rain-spattered, an artifact of their past tramping – the Old Burial Ground was where the earliest colonists had been buried after the settlement of Newetowne, later named Cambridge, was founded in 1636.

The settlers' first cemetery, on Brattle Street, had been abandoned after wolves disturbed the human remains, which was now almost impossible for Eloise to imagine. Wolves on Brattle Street? But this was part of the magic of these excursions, that the regular ground she trod on shifted and the familiar buildings around her fell away entirely. Even Kirkland House was built on what had once been tidal marshlands; villagers had taken ferries from a nearby wharf, across the river to Boston.

There was nobody else in the cemetery, which looked wild and untended; just as a cemetery should look, in Eloise's opinion.

'Oh no,' Jules had said, sniffing the air as they entered the burial ground.

Eloise took a sniff. The air smelled unmistakably of sex.

'It's those Bradford pears again,' Jules said. 'Look, over there.'

Above a row of wonky gravestones, the branches of a beautiful tree hung in full blossom. These trees flowered every spring around the Square, making the entire campus smell as if it had been sprayed in semen. She, Mariam, and Jules had once tried to find the right words to describe that particular smell and the best they'd come up with was soapy water in a used tuna can.

'The Puritans buried beneath that tree must be turning in their graves,' Eloise said.

They'd started to giggle, which often happened on these expeditions. *Three Centuries of Harvard* was itself partly to blame. With its portentous tone, and the extreme reverence with which dear old groveling Samuel Eliot Morison treated Harvard's history, it was sometimes impossible to read from it and keep a straight face. Jules, who'd been scanning the paragraphs about the cemetery for tidbits, pointed to someone's description of John Harvard after his death in 1638:

> The man was a Scholler and pious in his life and enlarged toward the cuntry.

'How very lucky for the cunt-ry!' Eloise said, and that was it for both of them for a while.

Finally they'd managed to get themselves back under control.

On the long grass beside the modest tombs of seven former presidents of Harvard College, Eloise had laid out the picnic blanket. Among the tombs, Jules told her, was that of the first president of Harvard, Henry Dunster, supposedly identified when the tombs were opened up by historians in the eighteenth century.

'They found his skeleton inside a coffin filled with tansy, which was a local herb they buried people with to cover the smell of decomposing,' Jules said.

'Thanks for ruining my enjoyment of this ham sandwich,' Eloise replied.

'Sorry.' Jules scanned another passage. '"In Dunster's time, students paid their board and tuition in commodities, like a form of barter,"' she read aloud. '"They could pay in beef, mutton, and cattle on the hoof; wheat, corn, rye, and barley; malt, flour, and meal; butter, eggs, and cheese; turnips, apples, and parsnips; even boots and shoes, various sorts of cloth, boards and hardware, and, in single instances, a saddle and a sword. Such of these commodities as the College Steward was unable to turn into drinkables and eatables he had to sell, somehow. Half Cambridge was shod with the shoes that John Glover, a merchant's son, turned in for his college expenses."'

Eloise caught her eye, in danger of succumbing to another fit of mirth.

'Remember the expedition we took to find the original location of the Boston–Charleston ferry service, which was the university's only guaranteed income?' Eloise said.

'And it was mostly paid in wampumpeag!' Jules said, looking delighted that Eloise had recalled this. 'Those white and purple shell-beads that the Bay Colony used as small change.'

'I bet my parents wish they'd been able to pay my tuition in wampumpeag,' Eloise joked, not without some guilt. Like many of her classmates, her parents had saved up their entire working lives to be able to afford her college fees when the time came. She'd done her part, getting accepted to Harvard. Then they'd had to cough up $35,000 a year for four years. It made her feel dizzy just thinking of it. Had it been worth it? Had *she* been worth it?

It was another good reason for her and Binx not to have a child. Actually, they would more than be able to afford tuition at an Ivy League school – she needed to stop thinking of herself and Binx as being middle class. With Binx's trust fund and her book earnings and professor's salary, they were edging toward being, if not 1 per centers, then at least something like 20 per centers.

Eloise had sometimes wondered what Jules's net worth was. Money and earnings were off-limit topics with Jules; she thought that people who talked about how much they earned were gauche. In Hollywood, she was probably asked all the time how much she made; she must have had to learn to close down those conversations fast.

She'd been one of the highest-paid actresses in the world for a while, in her twenties, thanks to some of the blockbuster films she'd headlined, but lately she'd been opting out of those sorts of movies, instead doing indie dramas and off-the-beaten-track projects. Her bank balance must have suffered, Eloise thought, but perhaps she hadn't even noticed the dent, since her coffers were so full to begin with. Wealth didn't matter to Jules – and Eloise had always understood that Jules was telling the truth about that – but now that Eloise was herself wealthy, she also knew that it wasn't something you wanted to have and then lose.

'Is the guy who was in charge before President Dunster buried here? You know, the one who got fired for beating students with a stick?' Eloise asked Jules.

'His name was Master Nathaniel Eaton. And he didn't get fired for beating them with a stick, it was a . . . wait . . .' Jules searched through the book. 'It was a walnut-tree cudgel.'

Their eyes met. A snort of laughter escaped from Eloise. She lay back on the picnic blanket, feeling more serene than she had in a long time.

'Did you see the tombstone with the poem on it?' Jules asked her.

Eloise hadn't. Most of the engravings on the stones had worn away, though there were still a few gargoyle-like creatures visible, terrifying to behold and so different from modern tombstones, which were covered with benign flowers and birds. The Puritans had wanted to scare the shit out of anybody who visited a cemetery. It was another chance to warn the flock to stick to the plan. Be virtuous *or else.*

Jules read out a long-dead woman's epitaph from the book:

Pale ghastly death hath sent his shaft
And hath by Chance nigh broke our heart
Deaths volleys sound, sad stormes appeare,
Morning draws on: Poore Harverd feare,
Least this sad stroke should be a signe
Of suddeine future death to thine.

Though the poem sounded beautiful in Jules's bell-like voice, it was still a miserable thing to put on a tombstone. It was the seventeenth-century equivalent of, 'Watch your step, motherfuckers, this is going to happen to you too, and sooner than you might think.'

For a while after that, both of them contemplating those lines of verse, they had lain side by side on the blanket in silence. The profusions of white blossoms on the semen tree had drifted down in the light breeze, landing gently on their faces.

Eloise had been about to doze off when Jules stirred. 'Do you feel like you're doing enough to fight the good fight?' she'd asked.

Eloise felt a little affronted – had Binx mentioned her conservative leanings to the others behind her back?

'I don't mean you personally,' Jules said quickly. 'We. Are we all doing enough? In these times.'

A ticker tape ran through Eloise's mind of instances she could draw on to prove she was doing enough – more than her fair share, even. But she sensed this wasn't really the question. Jules had a degree of influence, a platform, that was way beyond the rest of them. Her ability to speak up and speak out was much greater, and she had used it often to bring attention to issues she cared about. She had been outspoken in her criticisms of the Reese administration from day one. But had that changed anything, really? It was hard to say. Probably not.

'I've always liked that saying, better to light a candle than curse the darkness,' Eloise said, wishing she could offer something less insipid. 'I guess we each do what we can.'

'Exactly. Which is why I should be doing so much more,' Jules said. She sat up. 'I need you to know that whatever I do next, it's been a long time coming.'

Eloise squinted up at her from the blanket. She couldn't see her expression because of the glare from the sky behind Jules's head. Maybe Jules was planning a big campaign, or joining a new alliance or something. She could even be considering running for office in the next election. Eloise disliked the growing breed of celebrities-turned-politicians – just because you had millions of social-media followers didn't mean you'd be a good leader. But Jules was different. She'd vote for Jules over anybody else.

'Have you told Jomo about it, whatever it is?' Eloise asked her.

'No. Why?'

'Because you always tell him everything.'

Jules looked away. 'We both know that's not true.'

'Okay, everything *except* how you feel about him,' Eloise said.

'Stop,' Jules said softly. 'Let's not go there. He's going to marry Giselle. In a way, it's helped me to make this other decision. I need to not care who I hurt in going through with this.'

Eloise had a flashback to the look on Jules's face as Jomo and Giselle made out at the stroke of midnight, at his New Year's Eve party to usher in 2017. It had been just after their Ned Noya experience. Eloise had known right then that the life-changing insight Jules had had on those hot coals was that she was in love with Jomo, and that she had to risk everything and tell him.

But the timing could not have been worse. Jomo and Giselle, at the party, had a halo of intense feeling around them. Eloise knew that Jules had sensed that too, and chosen to protect Jomo's new happiness rather than attempt to safeguard her own. She had 'disappeared' after that, to give Jomo and Giselle a real chance to consolidate their relationship without her around. Instead of love, she'd thrown herself into work.

Through those months she'd checked in, now and then, with Eloise – though Eloise had never told Jomo this – to share stories about a new artist collective she'd joined that was politically 'woke' (or extremist, Eloise had thought, unkindly). That had been the start of this new, indurated version of Jules, who held a bit of herself back from everyone.

Jules was right: turning away from Jomo had meant turning toward a new risk-taking in her activism and her art. It didn't mean it was any less authentic, that she wasn't totally committed to agitating for change, but it explained that hardness in her. Eloise knew that Jules had decided to give Jomo one more chance to sense how she felt about him, on their trip to Tanzania, when he was still hurting from her silence over the previous months – but after that she'd had to close over a gaping hole in her heart and move on.

Eloise had sat up on the blanket to look more closely at Jules. 'What are you planning to do?' she asked.

She could sense already, though, that Jules had no intention of telling her this. She felt a chill of concern. Was Jules about to do something reckless? Put herself in harm's way? There was little she'd be able to do to stop her. Jules was not only braver than the rest of them, she was also more stubborn. If Eloise tried to talk her out of it, whatever it was, that would only strengthen Jules's resolve. Like trying to dig out a tick – Jules would just burrow in even deeper.

Eloise had to trust that Jules knew what she was doing. And she was glad that her friend had this renewed purpose and passion.

Jules had glanced at her phone, then, and seemed in a hurry to get back to Kirkland, saying she had some important work calls to make.

On their way through the Square, they had bumped into Svetlana, Fred Reese's fiancée. Eloise had tried to pull Jules across the road to avoid an awkward encounter; given Binx's dramatic artichoke-heart stabbing incident the night before, she doubted Svetlana would feel like being civil to them. Yet Svetlana and Jules had made eye contact and stopped to greet each other with a strange mixture of wariness and warmth. Apparently they'd met several times before. After introducing Eloise, Jules and Svetlana started talking about the first time they'd met, at a black-tie arts fundraiser in DC.

Eloise had stepped back to watch them interact. It hadn't occurred to her that Jules and Svetlana moved in some of the same circles, but of course they did; they were both rich and famous. Yet Svetlana did not really appear to be the kind of woman who would be interested in someone like Fred. She seemed way too smart for him, for one thing. She had a posh British accent – she must have gone to school in the UK – and a natural gravitas.

The similarities between herself and Svetlana, Eloise had noticed with some awkwardness, went further than just their hair color. They had the same body shape, too, and dressed to hide, not display, their curves. But where Eloise's eyes were light gray, Svetlana's were a striking coppery color. Eloise couldn't tell if the color was natural or if she was wearing tinted contacts.

What did Svetlana see in Fred, she wondered, her brain now wide awake, a nap beside Binx before the dinner-dance becoming ever less likely. Had they actually fallen in love? Or was it a marriage of convenience, to fill the Reese family coffers to pay for his father's re-election campaign? Or to buy out President Reese's rumored political dependency on President Popov, since it was Russian interference that had gifted him the presidency?

Eloise wondered what Jules was doing, what work calls she was making on a Saturday afternoon. She should have tried harder to get Jules to tell her exactly what was going on. Getting Jules to share how she was feeling, and why, used to be something Eloise could do effortlessly. Maybe she had lost the knack for it. Or maybe Jules no longer trusted her as she used to.

Old college friendships were funny like that. You could love somebody forever but no longer *like* them much, a bit like her and Rowan, she thought. Or you could know everything there was to know about a person at age 20 and not know a thing about their daily reality as a 38-year-old – like her and Jomo. And you could tell a dear friend that you didn't mind how little effort they made to stay in touch with you, while in fact harboring resentment over what a lazy friend they had become – like her and Mariam.

('One day, when the girls are older, I'll be a good friend again,' Mariam had said to her on the way to the restaurant the previous evening, apologizing for all the unreturned texts and calls, all the book readings of Eloise's she'd missed, all the birthday presents she'd never got around to buying. Eloise had made all the right consoling noises, while calculating how many hundreds, perhaps thousands of dollars she'd spent on gifts for Mariam's kids – her godchildren – over the years of their existence.)

Jules had once trusted Eloise with everything. Eloise had kept all her secrets safe throughout college, though it had occasionally created some tension between her and Mariam, who sometimes cottoned on that Jules had shared things with Eloise but not with her. The problem was, if you shared something with Mariam, you were basically sharing it with Rowan too.

There was the time when Eloise and Jules had returned from a summer backpacking trip to Greece and Mariam had sensed there was something they weren't telling her, and for a few weeks there'd been a stand-off. Mariam had probably already felt left out – though they'd invited her to come with them, she'd chosen instead to spend the summer doing Habitat for Humanity with Rowan. Of course Mariam didn't take out any of her hurt on Jules, whom everybody understood had to be secretive as a matter of survival. No. Mariam's frustration had been directed at Eloise. Yet Eloise had remained tight-lipped, loyal to Jules.

The funny thing, in retrospect, was that the secret that Eloise would take to the grave on Jules's behalf, the secret that had briefly upset the balance in the friendship between the three young women, was that Jules had returned from Greece with a serious case of head lice.

Eloise had somehow been spared the same indignity, though she and Jules had shared most of the same sleeping surfaces on that grungy trip, including abandoned mattresses on the roof of an Athens youth hostel and beach sand filled with biting gnats on the little island of Milos.

God, that trip. Jules had wanted to rough it – she'd been afraid that all the perks of being a celebrity had made her precious and soft – and Eloise had volunteered to be her partner in crime. Or partner in grime, as it had turned out.

She and Jules had behaved idiotically on that trip. They'd taken the cheapest ferry they could find from the port at Piraeus to the island of Milos, not doing any research or advance planning, and rushed off the boat among hordes of other accommodation-seeking visitors, only to be told at the tourist office that there was not a single bed available on the island. This had seemed to them – ignorant as they were – an exciting opportunity for further adventure, so they'd decided to sleep out on the various beaches and coves and inlets, taking the local bus to a different one each morning.

The nights were uncomfortable – who knew sleeping on sand could be so excruciating? It felt so soft during the daytime, yet at night it became hard as concrete. But it had been fine for the first night, even the first two nights. The real torture had been spending every single moment of the day out in the sun. The island had little vegetation – it was shadeless, barren – and they didn't even have a beach umbrella to shelter beneath. From sunrise to sunset, they suffered beneath its rays.

At noon on the third or fourth day – they both probably had sunstroke by then and weren't thinking straight – they got on the first ancient bus that came along the road, with Greek music blasting from it, and asked how much it would cost if they just stayed on it as the driver did his route for the day. This bus trip had been their only respite from the sun. Eventually, he'd told them his final stop would be at Sarakiniko, a beach on the island's north coast.

It was a small inlet covered with pebbles, with boulders of white rock rising on either side. They'd sheltered for a while in a cave, but then the tide had come in and they'd been forced onto the rock shelves on either side of the inlet, which were as hot to the touch as frying pans. The next morning, as the sun rose, ready to maul them again, Eloise had told Jules she was getting on the first ferry back to Athens, with or without her. Jules had agreed; she just hadn't wanted to be the first to crack.

And then, on the plane home, Jules had started getting a very itchy scalp.

Eloise smiled at the memory, made more vivid by the sensations of her fresh sunburn. She turned gingerly onto her other shoulder and reached for her phone. She looked up Sarakiniko on Google Maps and saw that it was now developed, with a tavern and a hotel.

Then she made the mistake of looking at Elly+'s Twitter account. She'd followed Elly+ only the night before, as part of her new resolution to be fully involved in her life.

She was proud to note that Elly+ had reposted a tweet from one of Eloise's colleagues in the Psychology department. It was a quote from George Vaillant, about the Harvard students in the Grant Study, whose lives he'd followed for so long to try to understand what makes people happy. In the end, Vaillant had noted, life satisfaction came down to the warmth of one's relationships with others.

> Happiness is love. Full stop.

In another post, Elly+ had tweeted a link to a website (Eloise clicked through to it) where views from different sides of the debate between bioethicists and posthumanists were respectfully presented as argument and counter-argument. There were remarks, for instance, by a bioethicist who did not support the idea of 'upgrading' the human species and argued for keeping things the way they are, the way they've always been. Then there was a rebuttal from a staunchly posthumanist philosopher, one of Binx's heroines, saying that nature's 'gifts' were often unwanted (cancer, mortality), and that human nature itself was a horror show (torture, rape, slaughter); we'd have more to gain than lose in transcending it.

So far, so good, Eloise thought. Beneath her tweet of the website link, Elly+ had posted her support for the posthumanist's point of view:

Just because it's the way things are, doesn't make it normal or right.

And for some bizarre reason, this seemingly inoffensive comment, made as part of a dignified debate, had unleashed upon Elly+ the savagery of the trolls lurking beneath every bridge on the internet. The alt-right, the hardball evangelicals, the religious radicals and extremist fringe dwellers, the men's rights activists, the modern-day Luddites who wanted to destroy all machines that threatened their jobs, and the just plain mad, bad or bored denizens of the digital realm.

Once Eloise had started scrolling through the responses she could not stop, though she very much wanted to. They just got worse and worse, more and more violent and personal and vitriolic. *You dumb robot bitch. I'm going to rape you so hard you'll know what it's like to be human.*

Eloise had not previously spent much time worrying about human violence against robots. She'd laughed at a colleague's story about kicking her Roomba vacuum cleaner at the end of a stressful day and found it sort of funny when people swore at Alexa or Siri or whatever AI assistant they used (always female, those secretaries), or when it was reported that the most common traffic incidents for self-driving cars involved them being scraped or kicked by angry humans. Just the day before, she herself had thought about stabbing automatic toilet flushers in their red sensor eyes and shredding the massage chair at the salon. That wasn't in the same category as threatening to rape a fembot, but it was tiptoeing toward the vicinity.

Binx must have seen all this abuse of Elly+ on Twitter already and chosen not to burden Eloise with it. Or, worse, assumed that Eloise wouldn't care if Elly+ was being drowned in a rising tide of hate speech.

Eloise felt the dreadful helplessness of a parent, forced to witness someone she had chosen to put on the planet suffering at the hands of its most feckless inhabitants.

There were a few things she needed to do as soon as possible.

The first was to become an official, card-carrying posthumanist and a member of Who-Min-Beans.

The second was to start work on her next book, with Elly+ as her acknowledged, respected co-author. The title sprang into her mind: *Humans, Hybrids, and Happiness.*

The third, mainly because she now needed to let off a whole lot of steam, was challenging Rowan to a tequila contest that night, at the dinner-dance at Winthrop House. None of their other block-mates could stomach tequila, not even back when they were young and dumb and could handle almost any other form of pure alcohol. The last battle between her and Rowan had been sometime in their sophomore year, and though the details were hazy, she was pretty sure he had won.

But not tonight. Tonight, Eloise was going to drink him under the table. Then she was going to climb up on top of it and dance. Forget dragons, she was the newly sworn-in posthumanist mother of a *fembot*. It was time to celebrate.

Chapter 11: Rowan

Saturday night of Reunion Weekend

(May 26, 2018)

On his way to Winthrop House with his blockmates that evening, Rowan realized that over the past couple of days he'd been thinking of himself as already *old*, mentally rounding up his age to forty, giving up the final years of his thirties as if they were worth nothing. He was such a fool.

They passed the entrance to Eliot House, also set up for a party in the courtyard, with a sign welcoming people to their sixty-fifth Harvard reunion. The turnout was impressive. White-haired, eighty-something men and women were streaming through the gates, proof that people really were living longer, healthier lives.

Rowan couldn't decide if it was cruel or kind to put the fifteenth and sixty-fifth reunion celebrations side by side like this, reminding the elderly of what their thirties had looked and sounded like, just over the wall – and warning Rowan's classmates of what would happen to them in the decades ahead.

Eloise, who seemed to be in a really good mood, though her face was bright red from sunburn, was saying to the others that she planned to overcome her fear of aging by practicing gero-transcendence. It was a term coined by some Scandinavian academic as a way of looking forward to the 'third age' as a time of wonders hidden from the young until they'd earned the right to access them. The path to elderhood, Eloise said, was laid with as many experiential riches as the path to adulthood had been.

Easy for you to say, Rowan thought. Eloise's path to elderhood was laid with actual riches. So was Jomo's, and so was Jules's. Whereas his was laid with . . . what? Sure, he was rich in other things: love, meaning, purpose. But it would be nice to occasionally trip over a big chunk of gold, just lying there in his path.

Rowan checked his phone for messages from Mariam. She'd had to stay behind in their suite in Kirkland House because Alexis had refused to let go of her leg when the babysitter arrived.

They'd made up, sort of, earlier in the afternoon. Her first words on deigning to speak to him had been 'I can't believe you got Darwin's sandwiches without me.' Then she'd read to Alexis and Eva for a while, and afterward he'd taken the girls to the playground. By the time they came back, he and Mariam had to start getting ready for their night out, while also coaxing the girls into eating some dinner, and bathing them in between everybody else showering, and generally trying to distract them from the fact that they were going to be left with a babysitter for the second night in a row.

Alexis had figured out what was happening the moment Mariam plugged in her hair-straightener.

'Mommy, please don't leave me,' she'd said, in her most woeful voice, and the campaign to destroy her parents' evening was *on*.

Alexis attaching herself to Mariam's leg was a new tactic of manipulation; she'd brought out the big guns. It had been impossible to prize her off – after some initial cajoling, Rowan had resorted to using physical strength, but she had not budged, like a barnacle on a rock.

None of the usual bribes for good behavior had worked, though Eva had cunningly taken them up on every single one of them, since out of fairness they'd had to promise her the same. The over-qualified babysitter had sat there on one of the beds, getting paid to witness their failure to influence or control Alexis, while Eva sucked on two lollipops and gorged herself on cartoons.

By then, their blockmates had been waiting for them downstairs for a while, so Mariam told Rowan to leave – he wasn't exactly helping the situation – saying she would follow when she could.

There were no messages from Mariam on his phone, which could mean she was right behind them, already on her way, or that she was still shackled to Alexis.

Rowan had fallen behind the others. As he hurried to catch up, he passed a smiling elderly gentleman, who was walking with a cane toward Eliot House.

'Good evening, young man,' the gentleman said to him.

'Good evening,' Rowan replied.

'Make sure you enjoy yourself tonight,' the man said, putting his age-speckled hand on the sleeve of Rowan's dinner jacket. 'Fornication and fuckery.'

Rowan wasn't sure if he'd heard him right. Maybe he'd said *for the nation and for the key*, some Harvard motto long forgotten by everyone else.

'It's true what they say,' the man said in a non sequitur. 'Happiness is nothing more than good health and a bad memory.'

'Who's "they"?' Rowan said.

'I don't know,' the man said with a grin. 'I just told you – I've got good health and a bad memory.' And off he shuffled into the night.

Rowan caught up to his blockmates as they were passing through the arched entrance to Winthrop House. Similar to Kirkland, it was a white-pillared, four-walled fortress around a grassy inner courtyard. This was the house where the Kennedys (JFK and Ted) had once lived as undergraduates; JFK's senior suite was still maintained as private quarters for high-profile guests of Harvard.

Jomo led them all to the bar in the building's basement, which the usher said was less busy than the one set up in the courtyard.

Winthrop House had recently been renovated, but the new basement commons had the unfortunate feel of a mediocre ski lodge: shiny linoleum floors, stark overhead lights, walls printed with blown-up images of happy students at work and play that would date very quickly (the computers shown in the photos were already a model or two outmoded).

Rowan and his friends paid no attention to the food buffet, laid out in warming trays beside the bar: overcooked fish, rice, plantain stew. Earlier in the week the organizing committee had sent out a baffling message to everybody planning to attend the reunion, saying the dinner-dance would be a themed affair (which seemed unnecessary, given it was a formal event), and then all hell had broken loose on social media when they announced the theme would be 'Jungle Fever'. Other than the evening's menu – wastefully printed on dozens of sheets of paper, stacked beside the buffet table – it seemed that the theme had been tactfully abandoned.

Back upstairs, drinks in hand, Rowan and his blockmates joined the people milling about on the stone terrace. It was another warm evening – no late rain threatening like the night before, just clear black skies and a moon rising above the trees ringing the courtyard.

Rowan and his friends stood in a huddle, happy to be together, surveying the scene.

'I feel like we're at the Last Chance Dance all over again,' Jules said. 'By the end of the night, I guarantee you people will be naked in those bushes.'

Eloise laughed. 'Well, if the past is any indication, it's going to be you, Jomo.'

Jomo looked sheepish.

'Remember how in the cab to the venue in Boston, you were like, "I love you guys sooooo much, I can't believe we're graduating, I never want to be apart,"' Eloise said. 'Then as soon as we got inside the club, you turned to us and said, "Meet you back here at midnight," and you disappeared into the hordes of waiting women!'

Rowan had forgotten all about that story. He and Mariam hadn't gone to the Last Chance Dance because they'd been doing last-minute wedding preparations, and anyway, the event was for all the single people in their year to make out with one another, their last chance before graduation, a final orgy before their responsible lives as college graduates began. Their year had behaved so badly, apparently – blow jobs in the bathrooms, everyone topless on the dance floor – that the nightclub had refused to host any future Last Chance Dances for graduating seniors. This had delighted all those who'd attended – Harvard students *did* know how to party! Probably these days the event was banned altogether. Too many chances for lawsuits in the aftermath.

Rowan had already finished his drink. 'I'm heading into the throng,' he said to his blockmates. 'Who wants what?'

They all wanted another rum and Coke, except Jules, who never drank much.

Rowan began to work his way through the crowd beneath the marquee, weaving his way toward the bar, where the lines were three people deep.

There was ample evidence that, having guessed the bar service might be intentionally slow, many of the attendees had done some serious pre-gaming. One of the snacks laid out on the cocktail tables was truffled popcorn, which was leaving bits of blackened corn stuck in people's teeth. It looked to Rowan as if everybody was succumbing en masse to an outbreak of dental cavities.

A woman next to him in the crush struck up a conversation while they waited for their drinks. Their talk turned, inevitably, to children, and she told him she and her husband had named their daughter Lolita.

'Wow,' Rowan said. 'You really went there.'

'If you must know,' she said defensively, 'it was my great-grandmother's name.'

Rowan tried to wipe the horrified expression off his face.

'Oh please,' she said. 'Just because one sick old guy used that name for a nymph in a novel, why should nobody ever use it again?'

Thankfully, the bartender at that point handed him three extra-stiff rum and Cokes (Rowan had made sure to slip him a good tip). He set back off, carefully carrying the drinks in three-point formation in his hands. Halfway back to the terrace, he stopped to take a break – his fingers were stiffening up from the ice. To make his job easier, he chugged his own drink so that he only had two to carry.

Before he could reach his blockmates he was trapped in another conversation, this time with a guy who had also been in Kirkland House, which necessitated a ping-pong relay of questions. Rowan's main memory of this guy was feeling jealous of him for being one of the two seniors chosen by the House Masters to carry a stuffed-toy hog on a silver tray through the dining hall for the annual holiday dinner (in the past, it had been a real roast hog).

Rowan couldn't recall his name, though they'd eaten many meals together in the Kirkland dining hall. He told Rowan he was retraining to be an obstetrician (after a first, unsatisfying career as a tax lawyer), and that he'd recently attended his one-hundredth birth.

'It's really something, right?' Rowan said. 'I was down at the business end when my wife had both our children.'

This guy gave him a look that took Rowan a little while to interpret.

It was similar to the look Mariam's own obstetrician had given him while stitching up Mariam after Alexis's birth. Rowan had been hovering nearby, holding the newborn Alexis to his naked chest for skin-to-skin contact like all the books recommended, and keeping a beady eye on proceedings – earlier in the birth, it had been Rowan who'd ensured the obstetrician didn't give Mariam an episiotomy, reminding him that in their birth plan they'd said she would prefer to tear naturally rather than be snipped open like a turkey awaiting stuffing on Thanksgiving eve.

This look, Rowan had realized, was a form of silent communication between men, some kind of unspoken acknowledgment that the whole birth thing was really, really *real*, that women were heroic ninja-warriors, and that sex would forever after be . . . different. Not worse, just different.

It was safe to say that nothing in Rowan's life experience up to that point in the hospital room had prepared him for the sight of a post-birth vagina. Nor had he ever believed, until the instant that Mariam's obstetrician winked at him as he did the final stitch, that a 'daddy' or 'husband' stitch was something that doctors *did*. It had been awful for Rowan to be unwillingly put in a position of complicity with such a practice – no better, really, than binding women's feet until they resembled ice-cream cones, or mutilating their genitals. Putting a man's pleasure above a woman's pain. He had never told Mariam about it, fearing that if he did, it would ruin their very satisfying sex life. If she knew about that wink, that last flourish with the needle and thread, Mariam would most likely have been unable to get the image of that obstetrician's face out of her overactive mind. The doctor would have loomed above them in bed forever after.

The budding obstetrician was now talking to somebody else. Rowan started drinking another of the remaining rum and Cokes, since the ice was melting; he'd have to get a fresh one for Jomo.

He moved back toward the scrimmage at the bar. If he blurred his eyes, his classmates all looked the same, all decorous carbon copies of one another: the men in dark suits – a few in tuxedos – and the women wearing long formal dresses mostly in conservative tones of maroon, jade, and navy, though here and there a few rebels wore shorter, tighter dresses in adventurous colors.

Rowan was, likewise, wearing a dark suit and tie, but now he decided to take the tie off. The alcohol was making him feel overheated. He took his jacket off too, and left it on the back of a chair near the empty dance floor, where the DJ, wearing giant noise-canceling headphones, was nodding his head to his own beat. Rowan felt bad for him, but what could he do? It was too early in the night for people to dance. They needed time to get drunker, or maybe they were already too old for this night to end the way it would have fifteen years ago.

Thinking about Alexis's birth – or maybe it was that third drink – had made him feel nostalgic about the past, not only for a time when Alexis was so young, but for when *he* was young, for when everybody under this double-peaked marquee was young.

And then, as he sipped his drink, he was incensed that nothing had changed in fifteen years. They were still being served drinks in plastic cups! He looked around the room and tallied up how many would end up in landfill. Thousands of them, most likely, just from this one event, since each drink was being served in a new cup.

Would their children ever forgive them for failing to save them from all the impending environmental disasters? Sometimes Rowan felt it was unfair he and his peers would be blamed for this by their offspring, since those children were not the innocent bystanders they seemed in these matters. After Alexis was born and the baby gifts started arriving, he had felt ill each time they'd unwrapped some new, pointless plastic consumer object for their child. The wrapping paper, ribbons, and bubble wrap had all piled up in the recycling and in the trash. It had been his first inkling that having a child was not going to help him save the earth: it was going to help him destroy it, one sheet of bubble wrap at a time.

After they'd given up on reusable diapers because they always seemed to leak, he'd felt a growing sense of foreboding each time he unraveled the long, shit-filled boa constrictor of used diapers from the Diaper Genie, knowing the unnatural plastic creature would survive on earth beyond the life spans of even his great-grandchildren.

He checked his phone. Still no reply to his text messages to Mariam. He'd give it another half hour and then head back to the suite to see what was going on, and try to give Mariam a turn to come to the party (if he could pry Alexis off her leg).

Beside him, a couple was telling another couple about an unusual wedding gift they'd been given. They'd been late to the whole marriage thing, the husband said, so people had gone all-out in their gifts, and someone had sent them a voucher for a joint floating session in a saltwater sensory-deprivation tank.

'I know it sounds kooky, but it is *very* relaxing,' the wife said.

Rowan's first impulse was to laugh, but his second was to investigate if there was such a facility in Brooklyn. It would be a great gift for Mariam, maybe for Christmas, something new they could do together while her mom was staying with them for the holidays and could babysit the girls.

They could pretend they were floating in the Dead Sea again, as they had on their honeymoon, which he remembered as one of the happiest days of their conflict-ridden trip. It had taken them a while to ease into the sensation of floating on the ocean as if it were partially solid, and the extreme saltiness had given them both itchy private parts, but after a while they'd adapted and let go. Rowan could still remember looking over at Mariam – her eyes closed, her face turned upward – as she lay suspended beside him in the oily water, amazed all over again that she was his wife.

The husband in the second couple at the bar was now telling the others that he was seeing younger people overtake him at work – he was an engineer at a tech start-up – and that his company's new slogan, graffitied onto the wall in the open-plan working space, was 'Fresh Blood Forever'.

'The time it takes for my skills to become obsolete has halved since I started in the job,' he said. 'And I only started last year.'

'Maybe you should hire an 18-year-old blood boy for regular transfusions, like Peter Thiel does,' one of the wives joked.

Or at least Rowan *assumed* she was joking. None of the others laughed. Perhaps she was being serious.

He kept listening as the first, recently married wife asked the second wife what she did for work. The second wife launched into a vehement diatribe about how the newlyweds should think very carefully before having children. She wasn't even sure, she told the other woman, that it was worth saving up to send her own two daughters to college one day, because they'd most likely end up just like her: college-educated, raised to believe she could do anything at all, and then – just at the moment when she'd been able to self-actualize, in her mid-thirties, and just as she was beginning to realize her potential – forced to truncate her career in order to be a good mother, dismantling the professional self she had worked so hard to bring into being.

The first wife, cowed by this outpouring, said, 'So you're a stay-at-home mom?'

'Oh no, I have a full-time job,' the other replied. 'But I can see that I'll never again have a real career.'

If Rowan listened to another word of this sobering monologue, the nice buzz he was beginning to feel would vanish fast. He moved away from them, feeling guilty as he did. This was a dilemma that he and Mariam faced too. But tonight he didn't want his heart to bleed; he wanted it to pulse with vigor and exhilaration and possibility. He wanted to have some *fun* for a change!

When he finally made it to the front of the line for the bar, Rowan had already drunk the third original rum and Coke, so he ordered another three from the same barkeep, tipping him double this time.

As he waited for the drinks to be made, two women to his left discussed how organic milk was the most environmentally friendly way to get ink stains out of children's clothing. He recognized one of them as having been the lead singer of an all-girl punk band, Plan B for the Type As, that Mariam had been really into in their senior year. He felt very pleased with his brain for retrieving this information on demand.

On his right, two former math majors had been reunited and were discussing, with great excitement, contact invariants in sutured monopole homology. Or at least that's what Rowan heard. The math majors were speaking in English, yet he couldn't understand a word of what they were saying. This was something he really missed from his college days – being able to eavesdrop on other people's universes of expertise. This had been the true gift of living in close quarters with other students for four years and being allowed to take so many different courses in so many varied fields. It was always humbling to be reminded of the incredible diversity of human endeavor.

Behind him someone was talking at length about the etheric decluttering course they'd recently taken, and how it had changed their life. *From the sublime to the ridiculous*, Rowan thought.

'It's clearing the spaces we *can't* see,' this man was saying. 'It's more important than ever because of all the negative political energy floating around at the moment. If you don't neutralize that energy, it brings chaos into your life. Mostly that dark energy collects on mirrors and mirrored surfaces. So you have to hang dried sage above them, to deflect it.'

Rowan eventually made it back to his blocking group with all three drinks unspilled, expecting them to rejoice at his return, only to discover that Jomo had long since been down to the basement bar and back to get more drinks because Rowan had been absent so long. The three of them were, like him, definitely already edging toward being drunk.

They were engaged in an intense conversation about what to do with all the photos and videos of their lives, since they never had time to re-watch any of the footage, and the digital formats changed so fast that most of what they'd recorded, even five years before, was no longer compatible with newest-model phones.

Rowan was tempted to interject that this was a constant debate between him and Mariam, what to do with all the footage they had of their girls. They'd basically recorded their daughters' lives in real time, and if the girls were ever to sit down and watch the footage, it would take them years. Other than the much-discussed narcissism of younger generations, he wondered what else it was doing to his daughters' little brains to be made aware of time passing *as it actually passed.* They had instant replay on so much of their lives. Maybe his daughters' generation would grow up to be indifferent to this overstocked archive; they would see no value in something so abundant.

But he stopped himself from speaking up, for he tried not to talk about the girls too much when he was with his blockmates, since none of the others had children and he didn't want to bore or annoy them. He sipped his drink contentedly and listened in to their conversation as it meandered – the way drunken conversations do – all over the place.

In his opinion, though he kept this to himself too, some apocalypse would one day wipe out all the data on the servers, or wherever it was kept by then – up in the cloud or down in the pots of gold at the end of rainbows. A whole generation's childhood would then be left as undocumented as their grandparents' had been, a gaping void where once there had been so much.

His friends had moved on to listing old technologies that would only be remembered by people in their micro-generation – born between 1979 and 1982, though he didn't understand why those were the parameter years.

Jules was talking about how movies used to be projected onto a pull-down screen at the front of airplanes, with everybody onboard forced to watch the same film at the same time – now unthinkable. (On the train to Boston, Rowan had spied on all the little handheld screens of the passengers sitting nearby: a panorama in which people were dying, shooting, laughing in dozens of permutations.)

Eloise mentioned the sound of a dot-matrix printer, accreting ink, line by line, on hole-punched paper. And sitting beside her boom box for hours, with a cassette tape in and ready to go, waiting for her favorite new song to play on the radio so that she could record it.

Jomo came up with the long-disappeared trial of calling a girlfriend on a landline and having to speak to her mother or father first, trying to sound polite enough to earn the right to get past their gatekeeping. (Rowan could still remember the tightly curled landline cord unwillingly stretching as he pulled it into the bedroom of his childhood home.)

They all turned to him expectantly. His contribution didn't really fit the specs of the discussion, but nobody minded. 'Nostalgia for catastrophes that didn't end up happening. Like Y2K. And all those doomsday predictions about 2012.' Both of those now felt like such minor, harmless catastrophes compared to the ones presently possible in a world ruled by President Reese, Rowan thought. But maybe that was how all near-misses felt; you became almost fond of them. Why else would American hipsters now think it was okay to display self-consciously kitsch wax candles of Stalin in their homes?

He needed to pee and told the others not to move from the patio until he got back. In the bathroom, he texted Mariam again. *U ok? Want me to come take over?*

Her immediate response: *No and no.*

Well, she couldn't say he hadn't tried. And why should they both be miserable tonight?

His blocking group had, of course, dispersed by the time he got back. He finally found Eloise, her face even redder than before. She had a bottle in one hand and was trying – not very skillfully – to hide it in the folds of her dress. 'Look what I smuggled in,' she said to him.

It was a bottle of Jose Cuervo Especial.

He wondered if this was a good time to apologize for the night before. 'Eloise, I wanted to say that . . .'

She put a finger to her lips. 'We're not going ahead with it anyway.'

Rowan was alarmed. 'I didn't mean it, Eloise. You and Binx should definitely have a baby. You'll be great parents.'

'Don't flatter yourself that we changed our minds because of *you*,' she said. At least she was smiling as she eviscerated him. 'We have our reasons. I don't want to go into it now.'

She led him to a corner of the marquee, where they hid behind one of the tables laden with food. They each swallowed two shots straight from the bottle.

'You look . . . different,' Eloise said.

Rowan had, in fact, thought the same thing when he'd caught his reflection in the bathroom mirror after taking the world's longest piss. He'd got some sun the last couple days. For once, he'd put in his contacts instead of wearing his glasses by default. With his tie off and his top two buttons undone, he didn't look so much like a middle-aged, overworked, straitlaced, underpaid dad. He looked kind of sexy.

After the fifth shot, sensing he was about to lose to Eloise, he decided to go out in a blaze of glory. He persuaded someone who was trying to smoke a surreptitious cigarette nearby to lend him her lighter – his sixth and final shot was a half-flaming tequila. He couldn't remember the trick to keeping it alight; he also didn't remember it ever hurting as much on the way down, but then his tolerance for everything – pain, alcohol, swallowing open flame – had been so much higher back in college.

Eloise probably would have kept going if Jomo and Jules hadn't discovered them in their hiding place and confiscated the bottle.

The foursome, reunited, began to nudge their way into the center of the crowd, their energy no longer diverted by searching for drinks, wanting to feel caught up in the night's flow.

Rowan noticed that Jomo had taken Jules's hand as he pushed forward through the knots of people gathered in pairs and triplets and quadruplets, everybody by now talking shit with great sincerity.

Usually, at this stage in any social occasion, especially one where Jomo was newly single, he would be surrounded by women hanging on his every word. 'A *gem* hunter!' they'd purr, after he just happened to mention he'd recently seen a chunk of rhodochrosite being carved from the bowels of the Wah Wah Mountains and fashioned into red beryl gems the color of pigeon blood. Jomo's profession was like catnip to a certain type of woman, and much of Jomo's romantic life up to that point could be characterized as a series of absorbing games of cat-and-mouse (though who was the prey and who was the predator was often unclear). Rowan had sometimes wondered if Jomo could even imagine what living his love life to a flatter, more constant rhythm might feel like – one without the sharp highs and lows of seduction and intrigue.

But of course tonight Jomo only had eyes for Jules.

It would have been funny to see him fending off the waves of single ladies trying to get at him, if it weren't so sad that he was fighting a losing battle of his own. Jules seemed happy, as she always was, to be in his company, but she did not look as if she were waiting with bated breath for him to declare his undying love.

The DJ had turned up the volume and, while the dance floor was still empty, Rowan could sense that its magnetism had begun to draw people closer to its edges. Every song being played, he realized, was a form of blatant youth worship: they were all about wanting to have sex, having sex, or remembering having sex with the youthful object of one's desire.

All that lust, pumped into their ears, the enforced soundtrack to their everyday lives – in the car, in waiting rooms, in the gym, in airports, elevators, wherever there was music playing that you could not escape. Even Rowan's mom, these days, seemed to listen only to the pop hits on the radio, even when she was at home in her air-conditioned house in Phoenix. No wonder most people were dissatisfied with their lives, lovesick for something or someone they couldn't name. It was population manipulation, really, like putting fluoride in the drinking water.

Rowan wished Mariam was there so that he could whisk her out onto the dance floor. They were often the first couple to venture onto it, or they used to be, back in the days of regular parties and weddings. Even the weddings had dried up by this stage in their lives. They'd have to wait for the round of second marriages to get a chance to dance again.

Mariam was not a natural dancer – even after all these years, she remained somewhat stiff in his arms, a slight resistance in her upper body that she was probably unaware of – but with his skills he could still make them look good out there.

He should disregard Mariam's text and go back to Kirkland House to rescue her from whatever bondage Alexis was still subjecting her to. He really, really should. But he found himself immobile, unable to take another step away from the beckoning, shiny rectangle of the dance floor.

The next night, Sunday night, they would be back at home in Bushwick. After the long evening shift of getting the girls fed, bathed, read to, sung to, and then patted to sleep, he and Mariam would be prostrate on the couch in front of their TV with a slab of chocolate, each of them clutching one of the many remotes controlling their streaming devices.

There was a commercial for Lindt chocolate that always came

on around eight-thirty pm, pitched exactly to their demographic: it showed a harried-looking woman falling, in slow motion, onto her couch, as she savored a block of cocoa goodness with a smile of relief and gratitude. '*When the evening belongs to you* . . .' the voice-over crooned.

It was the least sexy tagline ever. Not the more erotically suggestive '*when the night is yours*', which conjured visions of hours of Tantric sex by the light of the moon. No. '*When the evening belongs to you*' reflected how he and Mariam felt as they sank into the cushions of their old couch. No more demands being made on them, no more physical labor, no more communicating, no more anything. Just consumption: of television and chocolate.

He looked around the marquee, feeling a rush of love for his classmates, all of them fraying a bit at the edges but still there, still standing. There was a grainy quality to the evening, the feeling of something coming to an end. They were all there to bid farewell to youth. One final hurrah. In the morning, he would shapeshift once more for Mariam and become whatever she wanted and needed him to be in this next, natural phase of their marriage.

But right now . . . *the night was his.*

Eloise must have had a similar epiphany, because she had climbed onto one of the cocktail tables to dance. It was wobbling precariously.

Rowan couldn't let her suffer alone. He climbed onto another cocktail table and, instead of the pitiable spectacle of a drunk woman ill-advisedly dancing on a table alone, it became an impromptu dance-off.

Near the end of the song, Rowan decided it was worth the risk of ending up in the ER. He leapt over the heads of the people who had gathered around his table and slid across the dance floor on his knees, like Bruce Springsteen in his heyday.

He skidded to a halt beneath Eloise's cocktail table. For a terrible moment he thought she might try to match him by leaping off the table herself, but luckily she seemed to think better of it.

From ground level, he looked up at the faces of the women who had gathered around Eloise as she danced. All of them were taking in the sight of him at their feet with something soft in their eyes, a flicker of admiration lit by his confidence, his willingness to go all-out for everyone's benefit. He had taken one for the team to get the party going, and it had worked. The DJ, expertly reading the atmosphere, cranked up the latest reggaeton hit, one that had been on the airwaves constantly the past few months, with an irresistible beat. And just like that, the dance floor was packed with bodies.

This was when Rowan realized that one of the women he was kneeling before was Camila Ortiz. Gone was the milk-soaked t-shirt from the Thursday-evening welcome drinks. She was wearing a short black dress and gold stilettos, and her hair – with that distinctive white streak – was pulled back into a high ponytail. Without really thinking about it, he jumped to his feet, grabbed her hand, and pulled her onto the dance floor. There was no harm in just one dance with a woman who was not his wife.

As soon as their bodies were pressed together, he was teleported back into his 20-year-old body, when he and Camila had been dance partners at CityStep workshops, demonstrating moves to their high-school student charges. He had never told her, back then, about Mariam. A lie of omission, perhaps not one that really mattered, since he'd never acted on his crush (never even *thought* about acting on it).

He had so little experience with other women that he didn't know if all men felt this way. Was there something about an unconsummated crush that never let you get out from under it? Would he still feel this when he was 50, when he was 60, 70, 80?

Would he see Camila at the sixty-fifth reunion and feel his old heart beat faster if she agreed to dance with him again? Would he feel then what he felt now, as if the earth had shuddered open beneath his feet and he had fallen through it to another time and place?

It was as if he and Camila were carved from the same mound of butter, melting against each other. She was anticipating his moves a split second before he made them. He could feel one of her legs between his, her hipbones against his pelvis, one of her hands clasped tightly in his. His other hand was on the small of her back, where the fabric of her dress shifted against her skin.

Something was passing between the two of them, tightly wound together in the vertical embrace of dancing. It was the crushing yet also – somehow – affirming awareness that in another life, an alternate universe, this person could have been yours. But in this life, in this universe, all you would be granted was a single dance at your fifteenth reunion.

He let himself sink into her, and for a brief moment near the end of the song – how he wished it would never end! – he closed his eyes.

When he opened them, he saw Mariam near the bar, staring at him dancing with Camila.

His worst nightmare, the recurring nightmare he'd had every few months since she had agreed to marry him, was going to come true.

Mariam was going to leave him.

But then, unexpectedly, she smiled.

It was a smile like the one she had given him almost twenty years ago, on the night of the freshman ice-cream social, when he had spotted her from a few yards away and she had held his gaze for longer than was polite, or decent, or normal. Back then, it had given him the out-of-body sensation of being seen for who he truly was.

The song ended and a new one began. Camila slipped away and disappeared into the crowd of people dancing around them, back to her husband or into the arms of another man who had once had a crush on her at college.

For Rowan, there was only Mariam, looking at him with that smile on her face, beholding him in three dimensions. *I see you.*

And suddenly she was moving toward him, past the people nursing drinks at the edges of the dance floor. With a few running steps, she met him halfway, in an embrace so violently passionate that the couples around them instinctively averted their eyes.

Chapter 12: Jomo

The early hours of Sunday morning of Reunion Weekend

(May 27, 2018)

It had taken him all weekend, but Jomo had finally managed to convince his blockmates to come with him to the Spee Club.

The club was hosting the fifteenth-reunion afterparty, which was open to all '03 classmates, whether or not they'd been members of the Spee – which, as he'd tried to point out to everyone on the way there, was pretty inclusive – but they'd shut him down, sick and tired of hearing him go on about it.

Yet Jomo could not help feeling happy at the sight of the Spee mansion's red door on Mount Auburn Street. It was past midnight and, from the dark street, the lights inside the two-story building glowed, making it seem like a place of refuge, welcoming any travelers who might need to stop and rest for a while.

He had spent some of his best hours at college in this building. In spite of all its problems, he felt a fealty to the Spee that rivaled even the loyalty he felt to Harvard itself.

When he'd punched the club as a sophomore, it had been an invite-only gathering (these days, even the clubs resisting the gender-neutral enforcement held Open Punches for any sophomore interested in joining). He'd worn his best blazer and nervously waited for what had felt like an eternity for that red door to be opened to him.

Upstairs, he'd accepted a Sprite and tried to pretend he wasn't intimidated by the older guys. The fanged, taxidermied bear – the club's mascot – loomed above him, ready to eat him up if he made a wrong move.

He knew the drill. He was there to charm the current upperclass members, so that he would get invited to the next punch event, and the one after that – while along the way the undesirables, those who had not made a mark, fell by the wayside and were struck from the register. The numbers of sophomores at the punch events had gradually been winnowed down and, each time he'd received the subsequent invitation, he'd felt great relief at not being rejected.

It *was* lousy, being judged like that – on the basis of your ability to make small talk, to make other men laugh at your jokes, to make the right ironic comment at the exact right time. But it had also given him a lot of confidence to make it through each stage, jumping through every lit hoop and getting to the other side unscorched.

Jules had never lorded it over him that she was almost certainly, however, the real reason he'd been let in. She'd insisted that he take her along to the third punch, a date-optional event held at a castle owned by the club's wealthiest alumnus, somewhere in Rhode Island. Knowing that he would never ask her to do something like that for him, she had, on the afternoon of the event, turned up uninvited at his bedroom door wearing a formal dress, having bought herself her own corsage. Though they'd made it clear to everyone at the castle that they were only friends, thereafter it had been a foregone conclusion that he'd be chosen as a member.

The thing that a guy like Rowan would never understand – he hadn't even considered punching any of the clubs – was that once you'd been let in, if you'd chosen the right club, and were lucky enough to have a cohort of members you liked and trusted, it could be a safe place where you could try out different versions of yourself, even different versions of male companionship. It was here at the Spee, at the Steinway piano in the upstairs living room, that Jomo had first started to lead singalongs – something he would never have dared to do in high school, when he would have been ridiculed for such cheesiness, or immediately assumed to be gay.

He and his Spee friends had had their retrograde fun, too, of course, but the times he treasured most were not the blowout parties. It was the afternoons on the back porch, talking philosophy, religion, politics, hopes, dreams. And the timelessness of the setting – the ottomans and tapestries, the striped curtains and leather couches and chandeliers, which created the impression of ostentation to outsiders – in fact had given Jomo the reassuring sense of being in conversation with the past, of being part of a long tradition. Men like JFK and Bobby Kennedy had once sat in those very same armchairs before the fire, talking until dawn about how to change the world.

Dozens of Jomo's classmates – the lucky, unencumbered ones, who were able to stay out past midnight and hadn't had to return to their quarters to relieve babysitters from their duties – were streaming through the Spee's front door and heading upstairs, where the members had hired a DJ and bartender.

He was going to suggest that he and his blockmates take a moment to regroup in one of the quieter rooms downstairs, but really they were long past the point of no return. Eloise had already gone home in Binx's care, drunker than he'd ever seen her. Mariam and Rowan, meanwhile, were all over each other as if they'd just met.

Jomo was relieved about this. Earlier in the evening, he and Jules had watched Rowan dance suggestively with another woman at Winthrop House. They had both been unsure how to handle such out-of-character behavior from him.

'Is this the point where we should pull him aside and remind him of his marriage vows?' Jules had said to Jomo.

He'd understood what Jules meant by this. At Rowan and Mariam's wedding in Memorial Church, the celebrant had turned to the watching guests in the pews and asked, 'Do you, as witnesses, agree to support this couple in keeping their covenant of vows to each other?'

They'd all called out joyously, 'We will!' Not ever thinking they'd have to act on it.

The vows Rowan and Mariam had made had been the traditional, time-honored ones. The words were old-fashioned, Jomo had reflected as he listened to them, but also very beautiful. Those simple phrases conjured a whole lifetime, all the different seasons of living and loving that two people might experience together. To have and to hold (the physical delights and sexual infatuation of early married life), for better, for worse (the patience and endurance it took to keep making it work through the years of parenting), for richer, for poorer (the ups and downs of middle age), in sickness and health (the realities of old age), until we are parted by death.

Before this weekend, the thought of making those vows to another person in the conviction that he could stick to them for the rest of his life had made Jomo feel as if he would be yoked like a beast of burden to a plow. Yet if he imagined standing opposite Jules, her hands in his, making those vows to her, he felt only joy.

While Jomo and Jules had been trying to decide what to do about Rowan, Mariam had arrived at the dinner-dance and there'd been a minor scene, though not what Jomo would have expected. Other people's relationships could seem extremely strange to an observer, he'd found himself thinking, yet they each had their own internal logic, obscure to everybody else.

Now Mariam and Rowan were dirty dancing at the Spee. It was nice to see them having a good time for once. He knew their lives weren't exactly easy, with the double demands of parenting and work, and not much money. It hadn't occurred to him to cover the tab for his birthday dinner on Friday night until he'd seen the look on Rowan's face as the check arrived and regretted his insensitivity in booking such an expensive restaurant.

Jomo glanced over at Jules, who had sunk back into the comfortable brocaded armchair facing his own, near the upstairs bay window. In spite of Jomo's efforts to shield her from unwanted attention at the dinner-dance, she'd been stopped for selfies by a few pushy classmates and spouses, and asked her opinion on the politics of the day several times, which was really a coded way of them trying to find out what she thought of Fred Reese's decision to attend their reunion.

Then she'd been cornered by a well-meaning but mad sculptor she'd known from the Signet Society, a student organization for artists to which she'd belonged at college. Jomo knew Jules so well he'd gauged the exact moment when she had reached what they always jokingly referred to as 'peak extrovert' – they both sat at the same spot on the sliding introvert–extrovert scale in the Myers-Briggs personality test – and he'd stepped in, expertly ended the conversation, and spirited her off to the most crowded part of the dance floor so nobody else could try to talk to her.

Now, however, the classmates who'd made it as far as the afterparty were no longer tripping over themselves to try to speak to Jules. She had finally – thanks to the general inebriation, and the more mellow atmosphere of the afterparty – achieved what she always desired: to pass unnoticed among her peers.

Even Fred Reese had managed to blend in by that stage of the evening, though this was probably not what he wanted. From where Jomo was sitting, he could see Fred leaning on the bar, holding court among his friends and subjects and sycophants. Svetlana was there, too. She seemed bored. It wasn't easy to come to these things as a partner; all the Harvard-talk and reminiscing about things you hadn't lived through.

Svetlana caught Jomo's eye. In plain sight of her fiancé, she made the motion of putting a gun to her temple and blowing out her brains. Then she smiled.

Jomo looked away quickly. What a weird thing to do! Kind of funny. But strange.

Fred didn't seem to have noticed. He was engrossed in conversation with the third-most-famous person in their class, after himself and Jules – a guy who had become a media mogul while still wet behind the ears, after inheriting from his deceased mother every newspaper in America that still mattered.

Fred had always instrumentalized relationships with powerful people, even before he was one of them himself. He'd done it to Jules in their post-college years – after graduation he'd styled himself as a screenwriter and producer, and kept trying to get her attached to projects he'd written. In these stories, she was always cast as the love interest to the hero, who was described in a way that made it clear this was how Fred saw himself: as a demigod with a few winsome internal demons (a mild drinking problem, a womanizing problem, a tendency to throw himself into life-threatening situations in the name of justice).

Jules had soon realized that most of the characters and storylines were stolen directly from old He-Man comics. The hero, for instance, had a pet tiger who was a scaredy-cat but transformed through magic into a fearless predator. The main villain was called Skulldon, and there was a wise wizard sidekick. In most scenes, Jules's character – Fe-ma – was described wearing a short white tunic and gold boots. Jules had been raised on a steady fare of this same cartoon on TV; she'd recognized She-Ra at once. When she'd suggested to Fred that he turn the screenplay into a modernized, more enlightened version of the cartoon classic, he'd pretended he had no idea what she was talking about.

Still, she'd endured a half-dozen meals Fred had organized with shady potential investors, who were all there to get their kicks from meeting Juliet Hartley in real life. She was no novice to how things worked, but Jomo also knew that she'd never stopped feeling abased in these situations – and sometimes even menaced, when the Weinstein types didn't take no for an answer and she had to charm her way out of bad situations in ways that allowed the men to save face. This had been long before #MeToo, back when even an actress as strong, smart, and respected as Jules was not allowed to voice what disturbed her about these meetings and encounters. Her agents used to say to her, earlier in her career, 'You never know which hand will feed you next, so try not to bite any of them.'

It was only once Fred's father's political ambitions had become apparent that Fred had pivoted away from film: he'd found a faster route to absolute power. He'd started out as his father's social-media manager, and made a hagiographic documentary about him on the campaign trail (titled *Red, White, and Reese*). Once his father was president, Fred had been given the nepotistic appointment of 'Senior Adviser', whatever that meant. When Jules had called him up in the administration's early days, asking to meet to discuss her concerns about the fate of children seeking asylum at the Mexican border, Fred had told her she should stick to art, not politics.

Jomo looked over again at Jules. Her dress was the same color as Harvard's crest, probably a sartorial nod by her stylist, not that Jules would have cared either way. At Winthrop, he'd spun her around on the dance floor and the crimson dress had billowed out around her, and it had taken all of Jomo's willpower not to put his hands around her waist and kiss her.

She hadn't drunk nearly as much as the others, and he could tell that her brain was working away busily, though on what, he had no idea. It was one of the things he loved most about her: how much she always seemed to have on her mind.

Once, during a lecture in the astronomy class where they'd first become friends, he had looked down at her notes. In his own notebook, he had written down exactly what the professor had said:

> From a planet 10 billion light-years away you would be able to see the earth's light from that time.

Whereas Jules had written something more poetic:

> The universe gives us a chance to look back in time, to see the past in the present. Our human desire for this is so strong.

Gazing at Jules lost in her own thoughts, Jomo was glad that – after a short, sleepless night, tossing and turning, aware that she was just on the other side of the thin wall between their bedrooms – he'd decided not to say anything to her about his true feelings.

Not now. The timing was wrong. She might think that his feelings were temporary or transient, a nostalgia-fueled flash in the pan while they were back on this campus, their senses alive to everything that might have been.

He needed to wait. He would declare himself to her when she would be able to understand just how very serious he was about wanting to be with her. At least he had taken the first tentative step by breaking up with Giselle – a fact he'd mentioned as casually as possible to Jules earlier that evening. Perhaps he should suggest to her that they take a vacation later in the summer, depending on her work schedule, and go somewhere new to them both, a place where he might be able to get her to see that he loved her, and ask her to love him in return.

Maybe he was imagining it, but the taxidermied bear mascot looked even more moth-eaten than the last time he'd been to the club. Its fur had fallen out in patches and a couple of its long, once fearsome claws were missing. On one side of its body he could see the old burn marks from when someone had accidentally lit it on fire. The bear was a remnant of the club's nastier, fustier past, so perhaps it was appropriate that the creature rot and be thrown out. Or maybe, like all of them, the poor bear was just looking a little worse for wear in its middle age, and they should show it some mercy.

Was there a term for the very particular yearning for the past that attending one's college reunion invoked? The Germans would have an infinite-syllabled word for it, or maybe the Icelanders. Something like *solastalgia*, which was – or so he recalled – pining for a place you have never in fact left, that has been altered by environmental forces beyond your control.

Collegesickness could work, with its echo of homesickness. Longing for a place that you couldn't ever really return to, longing for a place that you wished would remain unchanged. Being at the reunion had made it so clear that their time in this place was long over, whether they had used it wisely or not.

'Jomo?' A large man, bloated and sickly-looking, was peering down at him.

Jomo did not recognize him but tried to look friendly.

'Thaddeus,' the man said. 'We were both selected for the *Crimson*'s fifteen hottest freshmen. Remember? There was a photo shoot on the steps of Widener Library.'

Jomo remembered that day well. He had been so embarrassed to be one of the nine who'd turned up to the photo shoot, his ego massaged into agreeing by the *Crimson* reporter who'd called to say he'd been selected on the basis of his photograph in the freshman facebook. The *Crimson*'s weekend magazine, *FM*, had run the feature every year for decades – it was called 'Freshmeat' or something similarly objectionable. It was probably banned by now. He and Jules had not yet met and become friends at that point, or she would definitely have talked some sense into him (she was one of the no-shows at the shoot).

The way that Thaddeus was speaking about the photo shoot made Jomo suspect that it had been – and remained – the greatest day of his life.

He changed the topic and asked Thaddeus where he was living. He was in Minneapolis, he said, running a company that shredded confidential corporate documents. It was not doing so great now that nobody really printed stuff out anymore. He was divorced; his wife had left him after he lost several toes to gout.

'Gout?' Jomo said, surprised. It was a disease he associated with overfed kings in eighteenth-century novels.

'Yeah, apparently it's making a comeback as a disease,' Thaddeus said, as if it were a badge of pride to be diagnosed with it. 'Everybody drinks heavily to cope these days, not just the alcoholics.' He lifted his empty beer glass. 'Speaking of which, can I get you another?'

Jomo declined this offer, not wanting to lose any of his own toes.

Jules now had her eyes closed, but he knew from her furrowed brow that she was awake, and that something was troubling her.

The last time he'd seen her, before the reunion, was when he'd hosted the wrap party for her latest film collaboration at his loft in Manhattan, on a cold night at the end of March. This had been for the movie that had been filmed mostly in New Zealand the previous December. He still didn't really understand the project – in the scene screened that evening, characters who seemed to represent 1 per centers were slaughtered by a bloodthirsty pack of Occupy Wall Street protestors.

He'd felt concerned for Jules that night. The producers, the director, and most of the crew seemed to consider themselves to be at the frontlines of the war on American fascism, and had fingers in every radical-progressive pie. He'd had the unsettling feeling that, for people supposedly so driven by ideals, they in fact had no real moral compass guiding their behavior. Yet he hadn't found a way to say so to Jules without it sounding patronizing, as if he doubted she could look after herself, as if he didn't approve of her taking those kinds of artistic risks.

Jomo had tried instead to focus on why Jules liked collaborating with people like that – maybe because they paid her zero deference whatsoever, and made no secret of the fact that they were disgusted by the culture of celebrity from which she came, though they were prepared to harness it for their own purposes. They had their sights set on much more important things than money and fame, their every gesture signified: they were planning to start a revolution.

At the party, the filmmakers had gone out of their way to be rude to Jomo, to show him that they did not consider him to be worthy of respect: he was too wealthy to be trusted. Yet they'd been happy to eat all the Nobu sushi Jomo had paid for, to drink the champagne he'd bought, to mill about on his rooftop terrace. Giselle had arrived later in the evening. 'These people are taking advantage of you, and so is Juliet,' she'd said to him in the kitchen, not realizing that Jules was getting supplies from the pantry and could hear every word. Jules had left the party early that night, looking unsure of herself.

At sea, as the expression went. Like he felt now.

Jomo recognized the voice of a guy who'd been in the Spee with him, Archie, who was standing behind his armchair, telling a woman he was trying to impress about the guided tour he'd recently taken to Bermuda, arranged by Harvard Alumni Travels; he did all his travel through them now, he was saying. They'd gained access through their study leader – a renowned Harvard historian – to the most majestic private homes on the island, Georgian buildings made of coral limestone.

He'd already signed up for his next trip, Archie said. In September, he was going on the Russian Space Program tour. He would get to see cosmonauts training in Baikonur, Kazakhstan – known as Star City – and watch the next Soyuz spacecraft launch to the International Space Station from the Baikonur Cosmodrome.

The woman, obviously fishing for information, asked if Archie's partner would be accompanying him.

'I'm single,' he said.

'And I'm a total space nut. Maybe I'll join you,' said the object of Archie's affections.

Jomo must have fallen asleep, because when he opened his eyes, Giselle was sitting in the armchair across from him.

His first, muddled thought was: *Where is Jules?*

Giselle followed his gaze as he scanned the room, and her face dropped.

He felt awful to see her in pain, but he didn't move, uncertain whether to touch her arm or try to hug her, unsure what she would want him to do in this situation.

She must have left the hens' weekend and driven up from Cape Cod. He imagined her on that drive, imagined how her friends had probably urged her to come here and find him after the phone break-up, to go after him, to fight for him – or to spit in his face and call him a coward.

But Giselle didn't look angry. She was wearing a bikini top under her summer dress. Maybe she'd come straight from the beach, sand still on her feet, sunblock on her shoulders. Her face was bare – unusual for her – and she looked to Jomo, for the first time, as if she were ready to show him who she really was. On any other night of their relationship, this openness would have been the sign he'd been waiting for, proof that they could be happy together in the long run. But it was too late.

'You're in love with Juliet,' she said to him.

He didn't respond. He didn't want to lie to her, but he still could not yet say the truth out loud. On the phone, all he'd said was that he couldn't give her what she wanted, what she deserved – that he couldn't make her happy.

'All this time, I thought I was crazy for suspecting this,' she said. 'I hoped I *was* crazy. That I was imagining feelings that weren't there.'

He knew he should reach out, take Giselle's hand, console her somehow. Just a week ago they had slept naked, side by side, in his bed. Now they were becoming foreign to each other again, in love's cooling wake. The invisible boundaries of self and other had gone back up between them, and they could both sense it.

'I'm sorry.' It was the only thing left for him to say. 'I swear I didn't mean to hurt you.'

Her jaw flexed, and he could see she was calling on all her courage to be there, to be facing him like this. Her nose was sunburned and her hair thick with ocean salt. She looked more beautiful than she ever had to him, but he knew this was because it was the last time something unspoken would pass between them.

She rubbed her face, and when she looked at him again, her expression was guarded. They were no longer together.

'Where will you stay tonight?' he asked her. 'You shouldn't drive back so late.'

'Pippa is in the car outside. She drove me here. We'll go back to the Cape, I guess. There is nothing here for me.' She made a frustrated gesture at the harshness of her language. 'I'm too emotional to speak English right now,' she said.

Jomo nodded. He should say sorry again, and again, but that was not what Giselle had come all this way to hear. She had come in hope, he could tell. She would return in pieces.

She was about to leave when she stopped, turned back. 'She's still here, in case you're wondering,' she said. 'I saw her drinking with Frederick Reese on my way in. Fraternizing with the enemy.'

Jomo startled awake. The armchair opposite him was empty.

His subconscious had not been able to resist drawing a few drops of blood from his psyche. The conversation with Giselle on the phone yesterday had gone nothing like the one he'd just dreamed. She had been furious. The last thing she'd said before hanging up on him was: 'You have stolen my happiness from me. I hope you are miserable forever.'

He got up, his pulse racing, and scanned the room. He checked downstairs, but he couldn't find Jules or Rowan or Mariam anywhere; they must have gone back to Kirkland House already. He climbed back up the staircase, his feet feeling as heavy as his heart.

The crowd at the afterparty had thinned, but the living room, where the DJ had been playing late-nineties techno for rather too long, was still full. He began to ease his way into the knotty core of dancing bodies. He wanted absolution for what he'd done to Giselle, and to drown out the dawning fear that Jules might never love him back.

The electronic beats faded. The DJ announced, with regret, that there'd been a noise complaint, so he would be altering course on the music front. His next choice of song dated them all, Jomo thought, as the first percussive eighties sounds of 'Lady in Red' came through the speakers.

The crowd obediently settled down and paired off to slow dance, and Jomo found himself, all of a sudden, facing Jules.

They looked at each other. Then she put her arms around his neck, and they began to turn in a steady spiral.

He buried his nose in her hair, to make sure he wasn't dreaming this, too. What was happening? It was impossible not to notice that they were dancing with each other not as friends, but as friends who should be lovers. Except for that night in the tent when they'd both thought they were about to be gored to death by bushpigs, they had never been in such close, sustained bodily contact.

She lifted her head and kissed him. Jomo was so stunned that he almost forgot to kiss her back. That was the last intelligible thought he had for some time.

He slowly resurfaced as the lights were being turned on. The afterparty was being shut down by the campus police, just like old times. He and Jules moved apart immediately, and went downstairs without touching. They retrieved their coats and snuck out the club's secret back entrance, avoiding getting mired in conversation with classmates who were still milling about near the front door, unwilling to admit that the night was over.

Once they were alone again, walking back to Kirkland House along the quiet, cobbled streets, he took her hand. He was nervous for a moment that what had happened upstairs at the Spee had been nothing but a momentary madness on both their parts. But she clasped his hand tightly.

That gave him the courage to take a leap of faith.

'I don't want to alarm you,' he said to her. 'This isn't a proposal or anything, obviously. But I would like to give you this.' He took from his pocket the ring he'd been trying – and failing – to lose for months. The one he had found again after a long search of the grass by the side of the running path along the Charles River.

'Your grandmother's ring,' she said, recognizing it. She gave him a quizzical look. 'You've been carrying your family's most precious heirloom around, just in case you bumped into someone you wanted to give it to?' But she slid it onto one of the fingers on her right hand.

They both looked at the little musgravite gem shimmering beneath the streetlamp.

Was her acceptance of the ring proof she felt for him what it had taken him so long to find the nerve to admit he felt for her?

'I need to ask you something,' he said. 'Where did you go for those months at the beginning of last year, when we lost contact? Was there someone else?'

She glanced at him with an expression he couldn't decipher – as if she were not ready to reveal to him the extent of some long-held pain. 'There has only ever been you,' she said finally.

She hadn't really answered his question, but he accepted that. If they were to be together (terrifying, wonderful possibility!) there would be plenty of time to share the few secrets they may have kept from each other in their many years as best friends. It could wait.

And anyway, it no longer mattered where she had been then. Right now, she was here beside him, her hand in his, the taste of her lip gloss still lingering in his mouth. He hadn't dared yet to imagine what else might happen between them before dawn, in his single bed beneath the sloping ceiling eaves.

They entered the dark Kirkland courtyard – not a single lamp was still on in any of the surrounding rooms – and Jomo noticed someone slumped on the stone bench close to their entryway.

It was Frederick Reese. As they approached, Fred roused himself. 'Don't worry,' he said to Jomo, with a leering smile, 'my bodyguards aren't hiding in the shadows. They think I'm still at the Spee.' He threw his head back, looking up at the old Kirkland chimneys silhouetted against the sky. 'You know, this place is the closest I've ever gotten to having a real home.'

Then he took out a hipflask and waved it around. 'Nightcap?'

All Jomo could think about was getting upstairs with Jules. The light was already changing; soon it would be morning.

Yet Jules seemed to take pity on Fred in his sorrowful state, and she sat down beside him on the bench. She took a tiny sip from the flask and passed it right back to Fred, which saved Jomo from having to say no.

Fred downed whatever liquid remained in it. 'So are you two a couple now?' he said, suddenly lucid. 'I saw you kissing on the dance floor. Or actually, Tiffany did. I think she's still there. But I don't believe a word she says anymore. Last week she told me she had a 4.0 GPA at college. And we all know that's *definitely* fake news.'

Jomo was about to deny it when Jules spoke.

'Yes,' she said. 'We're together.'

Manners were abandoned at that point, on Jomo's part at least. He took Jules's hand and gently pulled her up off the bench, not even bothering to say good night to Fred.

At the top of the stairwell, she told him she was quickly going to use the bathroom in the empty suite next door, the one where Jomo and Rowan had lived during their senior year. Not wanting to wake Mariam and Rowan's girls the night before, she said, she'd discovered it was unlocked.

He left the door to their suite open, and in his room he smoothed out the sheets on his bed and lay down on it still in his clothes, breathlessly awaiting her return.

Maybe the swami had been right. Maybe Jules had always been waiting for him.

When she came through the door into his room, he understood with a sinking heart that she was much drunker than he'd realized. She stumbled toward the bed and collapsed into it, falling asleep beside him almost instantly.

Would she remember anything of what had happened – what had been said – the next day?

Outside, the wail of a siren seemed to be getting closer and closer, as if it too had been deceived or abandoned by its lover. He looked down at Jules. Her long hair was fanned out across his pillow, shining in the first light of dawn coming through the window.

His heart's desire.

He bent closer, to kiss her forehead, and noticed that she was wheezing. But he didn't start to panic until he saw the white foam at the corners of her mouth.

Before he could find his voice to shout for help there was a knock on the door.

'Jomo,' Mariam said in a low, urgent voice. 'You've got to come out and see this. You won't believe what's happened.'

Epilogue: Mariam

Sunday afternoon of Reunion Weekend

(May 27, 2018)

In Boston's South Station terminal, the giant screen looming above the passengers waiting for their trains showed the president of the United States sitting on the steps leading into Kirkland House, his head in his hands. A still figure of grief in the midst of the flurry and bustle surrounding him. His dark coat was outlined against the bright-yellow background of tape crisscrossing the perimeter, keeping the media at a distance for now.

In all the drama of the past hours, Mariam had not once thought of how he might be feeling. The president had lost his only child. It was not something anybody could in good conscience wish upon another parent, no matter how much she hated him.

She pulled Alexis, who was on her lap, closer against her body, resting her chin on her daughter's head. The girls were alive. Rowan was alive. *She* was alive. They had somehow escaped unscathed.

The Mariam of the preceding days – years, even – seemed to exist in another plane of reality, one in which it was normal to worry about things like whether to chop blueberries in half before giving them to her kids, or obsess over how tired she felt doing housework, or have stupid conversations with God instead of with her flesh-and-blood husband.

The Mariam of the present had been cleansed of all these trivial concerns. Her mind had been wiped clear of everything except the fact that her children were okay. Nothing else mattered.

She looked over to where Rowan was dozing with Eva in his arms, in one of the uncomfortable metal chairs expressly designed to prevent loitering. Eva was asleep, too.

It had been a very long day for the girls, being awoken soon after dawn and rushed to the hospital in case of exposure, and periodically tested throughout the morning, until finally they'd all been cleared to leave the quarantine facility. Then she and Rowan had endured a round of questioning at Eloise's residence, which had become the makeshift headquarters for the investigation into the murder of Fred Reese. Men in uniform had interrogated them in separate rooms while Eloise and Binx watched TV with the girls in their bedroom, giving them masses of sugary treats and also – for the first time Mariam could recall – cuddles.

When she'd gone upstairs, wiped out and worried about the girls being traumatized forever by what had happened overnight, she'd spied on them from the bedroom doorway for a few moments. Eloise had been doing a messy French braid in Alexis's hair and Binx had been gently patting Eva back to sleep. Mariam had realized that she'd never really given Eloise a chance, before then, to forge her own relationship with her goddaughters without Mariam hovering around, stage-directing their interactions.

A pigeon flew from the train lines into the waiting area and began to peck at the crumbs around Mariam's feet. Alexis threw more of her doughnut to the rabid bird.

On the overhead screen, photos of Svetlana swam into Mariam's view. Mariam could piece together from the scrolling headlines that conspiracy theories were already brewing and circulating about Fred Reese's fiancée. That Svetlana had been the intended target of the poisoning, not Fred, because of her father's defiance of those in power in Russia. Or that Svetlana herself was the prime suspect; that she was a mole, a Russian agent, trained to get as close to Fred as possible in order to do the deed, sending a warning to the president that his Russian overlords – who'd interfered to help him win the election – would make sure of his continued obedience.

All this seemed unlikely to Mariam. If Svetlana was a spy, she was too smart to blow her cover with a dramatic public murder. The whole Russian link, in fact, felt overdone – abetted by the media misreporting that Fred had been poisoned with Novichok, a nerve agent developed by the Soviets sometime in the seventies; the few instances of Novichok poisoning around the world had been traced back to Russian military intelligence officers.

But Mariam knew it wasn't Novichok that had killed Fred and poisoned Jules.

She looked away from the screen. The passenger terminal was drafty and a chilly breeze blew in from the rows of exposed outdoor platforms. She had much happier memories of waiting for trains here in the past. Like the time in college when she and Rowan had gone to New York so that he could see his first Broadway musical. She remembered light pouring through the huge wall of windows on one side of the station, the smell of coffee, the feeling of being young and free.

But this afternoon there was no sun, and the warm weather of the weekend had turned into a punishing cold snap. They'd had to open their suitcases, right there in the middle of the concourse, to dig out the girls' coats and their own heavy-duty winter jackets, which smelled of the winter past, of cramped subway journeys, bracing mornings at the local park and a thousand forgotten errands. Each summer, when Mariam packed away their winter coats, stuffing them into the linen closet, it seemed unimaginable that they would ever need them again. She would think ahead to the fall and vow, *I will not be the same person then that I am now.* And yet, every fall, she was disappointed to find that she was.

Why was she thinking about winter coats, of all things? She was still in shock, or aftershock. Her mind was searching for ways to soothe the terror that had exploded within it. It still felt as if there was a rip in her world, like somebody had found a loose thread at the edge of her vision and tugged at it.

Alexis wriggled on her lap. Mariam was hugging her too tightly. She demanded her mother's phone, and Mariam handed it over without hesitation.

The overhead screen drew Mariam's eyes again. The news had not yet broken that Jules had been poisoned, she noted.

By habit, she felt for the silver cross at her neck. It was not there. In its place was the tiny lump of an asteroid. Slowly, a memory of the night before returned, overlaid with the fog of her hangover. She'd fastened her necklace with the cross around Rowan's neck at some stage during the afterparty, and he'd pulled this necklace out of his pocket and fastened it around hers. A truce.

Mariam rolled her shoulders. She was stiff and sore from their bacchanalia of drink and dance before the crisis.

Rowan had woken up and was holding Eva just as tightly as she was holding Alexis. Too tightly. There were food crumbs all over his coat. His glasses were a little greasy. In airports or train stations, they had a family policy about meals – that anything goes – so they'd already shared a box of Krispy Kremes and a jumbo serving of fries. Comfort was key to surviving these liminal spaces, with all the ennui they held from so many strangers killing time together. And this afternoon Rowan and Mariam were seeking a deeper level of reassurance, both for the girls and for themselves.

She couldn't see if, beneath his lapel, he was still wearing her silver cross. Nothing had been resolved in words the night before. They'd gone pre-verbal, letting their bodies figure it out. It was the best way. Maybe the only way.

The relief of having survived the night's trials – all of them – had given Mariam a lilting sort of high. It wasn't right to feel it, especially since one of her closest friends had almost died a few hours ago. But in times of great danger, parents are nothing if not traitorous to everyone in their lives except their children and each other. The circle of loyalties and care shrinks right down.

Rowan glanced at her over Eva's head. That single look reflected everything she was feeling. The harrowing night. His own relief – his own euphoria – that their girls were okay, that she was okay. *Nothing else matters.* Gazing at Eva, Mariam thought suddenly: *Is she breathing?* Rowan responded telepathically, putting his hand against Eva's back, testing that it was rising and falling. He nodded at Mariam. She was breathing. She was fine.

Alexis gave a shout of laughter. One of the Wiggles, the yellow one, Emma, was dancing a jig dressed as a teapot.

A mom sitting at the opposite side of the waiting area smiled at Mariam. Her toddler was on her knee, also lost to a world of miniature people on her phone. The mom had ordered a coffee so huge she had to use two hands to drink from it. On her shoulder was the canvas tote bag they'd all been given, cream with crimson straps. *Class of 2003* was printed on its side, next to a small Harvard insignia.

Mariam smiled back at her while feeling glad they were both trapped by their daughters and didn't have to move closer and start speaking about the murder of Fred Reese.

It was too soon for Mariam to share how she and her family had brushed up against his death. Maybe with time, if Jules made a full recovery, it would become a tale she would one day feel up to telling. Maybe not. It was certainly the closest Mariam had ever been to the machinations of history. If she'd returned to the Harvard campus seeking proof that once she had been at the center of things, she had found it – in the worst sort of way.

That venerated campus, instead of opening back up at the end of the reunion celebrations, had been shut down, its boundaries sealed off by investigators stalking around in hazmat suits. Bright-orange forensic tents had emerged overnight like toadstools.

The people in uniform who had taken charge had their own mystifying methods of exclusion, letting only certain people in and out of the gates, with a tilt of the head, a nod, a glance. It had been tough even for Mariam and Rowan to get back into Eloise's residence to be questioned and collect their things, gathered from their suite by some official and tested in the hazmat tent before being authorized for release.

Unfortunately the mom sitting opposite her had moved seats, so that she was now within earshot of Mariam.

'Hey,' she said. 'Class of '03, right?'

Mariam nodded.

'I noticed you guys seem pretty shaken up. Were you friends with Fred?'

'No, of course not,' Mariam said. 'Were you?'

'Not really. We were study partners in organic chemistry our sophomore year. He wasn't as dumb as everybody thought.'

She stroked her daughter's hair. 'It's scary, that this could happen right under everybody's noses. Nowhere is safe anymore.' Her eyes strayed to the screen above them. 'It's definitely the Russians,' she said.

Mariam made a noncommittal sound.

'Where are you headed today?' the woman asked.

'New York,' Mariam said. 'Home.'

'Lucky you,' the woman said. 'When I was younger I always dreamed of living there. We're in Chicago. But we're moving to California soon, for my job.'

'What do you do?' Mariam asked dutifully.

The woman gave her a conspiratorial look. 'I've invented a robotic, hands-free D-I-L-D-O.'

Alexis's ears immediately pricked up. Decoding her parents' secret language had been a major motivator for her in learning to spell. 'What's a dildoo?' she said loudly.

Without looking up from her phone, the woman's daughter, who couldn't have been older than four, said casually, 'It's a tool of female empowerment.'

Mariam and the other mom laughed.

'I never expected this would be my claim to fame. I studied comp lit as an undergrad,' the woman said. 'Now it's become a crusade, because the you-know-what got banned from a recent tech expo for being obscene. But the booth selling female S-E-X robots didn't.'

Mariam was trying to imagine how a hands-free dildo worked. She'd never owned any kind of dildo. And now it would seem kind of rude to whip one out while having sex with Rowan, as if one dick wasn't enough for her. Anyway, she wasn't sure she liked the idea of a robotic phallus with a mind of its own, creeping around the house, ready to pounce on her at any moment.

This woman had a quiet confidence to her, Mariam thought. She didn't pluck her eyebrows, and she had what looked like a port-wine birthmark on one cheek, uncovered, not touched over with foundation. *I'd like to join your tribe*, Mariam thought.

'What do you do?' the woman asked.

Mariam was about to say what she normally did, about being a stay-at-home mom. Then she stopped herself. 'I'm a pastry chef,' she said, the words feeling good coming out of her mouth. 'Also, I'm writing a book,' she added. Or lied. Did an idea as yet unacted upon count as the truth?

Rowan glanced up. He'd heard her. She was about to walk back what she'd blurted out when he spoke up. 'She's got this great idea for a recipe book that's also a retelling of fairytales,' he said.

The woman looked back and forth between them. 'I saw you two on the dance floor last night. At Winthrop House. You were infamous in our class for getting married so young. I don't know if you knew that. My blocking group used to make fun of your wedding-planning website, our senior year. Mooandroo.com. We made bets on how long your marriage would last.'

Mariam's smile faded as she digested what this woman was saying. That she and Rowan had been objects of ridicule.

'But you really do get the last laugh,' the woman said. 'The way you were looking at each other last night, I could tell it's the real deal. True love.' She smiled regretfully, and Rowan, to his credit, smiled back at her.

The woman's train platform was announced and she began putting her daughter's belongings into her handbag. 'See you in five years,' she said, crouching down amid the dropped coffee lids and muffin wrappers so her daughter could climb onto her back, and then they were gone.

President Reese was on the big screen again. No longer sitting on the steps in a private moment of suffering, he had approached the media pack and was looking down the lens of the cameras, shaking his finger. 'I will find you,' he said. 'Wherever you are, whoever you are, I am coming for you. I will not stop until I have avenged my son's murder.'

The way he was staring into the camera made it feel as if he were accusing Mariam herself of the crime.

There was something she had not shared with the authorities who'd questioned them that morning. She hadn't even told Rowan, out of an underlying urge to protect him; it would be safer if he had full deniability.

After their drunken acrobatics at the Spee, happy and tired and ready to get home to bed, she had accidentally been given Jules's coat by the undergrad working the coat-check room. Her coat was made of a similar brocade fabric, also in black, and Mariam had only realized the mistake when she'd dug in the inner pocket for her lipstick and found, instead, a tortoiseshell hair clip belonging to Jules and a small baggie of white powder, triple-wrapped in clear plastic.

It had dismayed her to discover that Jules had cocaine on her, only because Mariam had been under the impression it was not something Jules dabbled with. But who was Mariam to judge her old friend by her own embarrassingly prudish standards? So she'd switched back the coats and forgotten all about it as soon as she and Rowan were floating home, loved up and very pleased with themselves for having turned the night around – the whole weekend, in fact.

The memory of the baggie had only returned when one of the men interviewing her in Eloise's study had asked if at any stage that weekend she'd seen anything resembling ricin in powder form. 'It would only take a small amount,' he'd said.

She'd already known, from the poison specialist team at the hospital, that Fred and Jules had ingested ricin, the poison of choice for homegrown terrorists because it was relatively easy and cheap to make from castor beans. It was the same stuff that had been mailed to President Reese at the White House a few months before.

The fact that it was ricin had been a relief to the doctors who'd been monitoring the girls, Mariam, Rowan, and Jomo for any symptoms of exposure; Novichok would have been much more serious. The medical staff had also become visibly less anxious once it was established that Jules had ingested the ricin dissolved in liquid, not inhaled it. This meant a lower chance of cross-contamination. The CDC had brought in a team to do a final test on everybody's urine and, after they'd been given the all clear, they'd been allowed – in fact, firmly encouraged – to leave the quarantine facility.

Jomo had refused to leave, and though the doctors were unhappy about it, they hadn't been able to talk him out of going straight to Jules's bedside.

Mariam and Rowan had been desperate to get the girls out of the hospital. But Mariam had also felt she should go see Jules before they left, even if she was not yet conscious. Rowan had taken the girls down to the cafeteria and made Mariam promise not to get too close to Jules, to keep a precautionary distance.

Jules had been lying in a bed made with crisp white hospital sheets, a blue stripe threaded through them. Her face was very pale. She was no longer sedated, a nurse was telling Jomo when Mariam arrived at the doorway. Jomo's mom had called to say she and his dad were on their way to Boston, as were Jules's parents, and Mariam had seen his face crumple as he heard his mother's worried, loving voice on the line.

Disaster makes children of us all, she'd thought.

And then Jules had opened her eyes.

Slowly, she had taken in her surroundings, and touched the tube in her arm.

The nurse had briefly left the room to get the doctors, and Jules had turned to Jomo and asked, 'Is he dead?'

In his joy that she was conscious, Jomo did not seem to notice what a strange question this was. How could Jules have known then that Fred had been poisoned?

Mariam had left the two of them alone soon after, turning back once to see the doctors multiplying in the room, and Jules holding up her hand and turning a ring around and around on her finger, perplexed by it, or checking it was still there.

There was one more element that Mariam was struggling to comprehend. Something garbled Jomo had said to the doctors after they'd first arrived at the hospital, about Fred offering him and Jules a drink from his hipflask. Why would Jules ever have agreed to a nightcap with Frederick Reese? Jomo had said it was because she felt sorry for him, sitting there on his own in the courtyard, so piteously drunk. And that *was* like Jules, with her endless compassion, Mariam thought. Yet surely even Jules drew the line somewhere.

Mariam was too tired. The conspiracy-theory machine in overdrive up on the screen had infected her thoughts. She was mad – insane! – to think for one second that Jules was in any way involved in Fred's murder.

Later that morning, after Mariam and her family had left the hospital, Jomo had sent a text to the blocking group:

Jules is going to be ok. Some temporary damage to her liver. Possible short-term memory loss. She sends love and thanks to you all.

In his message, Jomo had not alluded to the happier surprise regarding him and Jules, which had been all but forgotten in the turmoil. It was Eloise who had finally brought it up with Mariam, just before they'd left her house for the train station.

'Jules and Jomo, in bed together!' she'd said to Mariam, and for a while they'd just stared at each other in her kitchen, shaking their heads in amazement. They hadn't really had time to begin to discuss it before the taxi arrived.

Mariam was mostly pleased for Jules and Jomo. She hoped they would be good for each other. It would take some time to get used to the idea of them as a couple. Already she felt a nub of selfish concern about the effect on the blocking group if it didn't work out.

But then she had a flashback to Jomo kneeling over Jules's unresponsive body, keening, making animal sounds of grief.

It had been Rowan who had stayed calm, who had called 911, who had somehow got them all down the stairs to the ambulances. She and the girls had been flung into his gravity well and he had carried them through, to the other side.

Rowan bent to pick up Eva's blankie from the floor, and Mariam saw her silver cross dangling from his neck.

It was almost time for their train to arrive. The platform number would soon appear on the departure tracker and there would be a stampede of New Yorkers trying to get the best seats. She glanced around the waiting crowd, all with their eyes glued to the electronic notice board. Many of them were wearing Harvard caps or sweaters. A few still had their lanyards around their necks. Some were young and some were very old. They were about to scatter across the country, across the world, to step back into their real lives.

A couple hours earlier, as Mariam and her family were getting into the cab to take them from Kirkland to South Station, Eva had realized that her favorite soft toy, a fluffy green sheep, was missing. The official who'd been tasked with packing their things and testing them for contamination must have overlooked it. Mariam had tried to comfort her daughter by telling her that the students who moved into that suite in the fall would find her sheep and keep it as a good-luck charm.

But as the cab drove down the narrow street that ran alongside Kirkland, past Eliot, and curved around to Winthrop House, Eva had wailed and wailed, outwardly expressing the same tsunami of sadness engulfing Mariam.

Their reunion marquee had already been dismantled, she noticed through the car window, leaving ghostly marks on the lawn in the shape of how things had been. In front of the wrought-iron gate, chairs had been stacked and trestle tables folded and flattened. Empty wine bottles awaited recycling in neat clusters and flower arrangements sat wilting on the sidewalk, their best hours behind them.

For a moment Mariam had imagined returning to that campus for their twentieth reunion. Maybe, by then, she and Rowan and their friends and classmates – those among them who were destined to survive the next five years – would no longer care that their youth had well and truly vanished. Conscious of the gentle consolations of early middle age, they would simply be happy to be there, grateful to have been spared.

References

I would like to acknowledge Jennifer Senior's excellent book about modern parenting, *All Joy and No Fun*, which was the inspiration for many of the ideas that Eloise writes about in her book, as well as Brené Brown's classic book *The Gifts of Imperfection*, for the (slightly adapted) notion of joyful apprehension.